CRUSHED

Gina Robinson

Gina Robinson
SEATTLE, WASHINGTON

Book Layout ©2014 BookDesignTemplates.com
Photography: Kelsey Keeton of K Keeton Designs
Model: Nathan Weller and Tessi Conquest

Crushed/ Gina Robinson. — 1st ed.
ISBN 978-0692305973

For Jeff

CHAPTER ONE

Morgan
Alcohol is a big, fat liar. It seduces you with its charm
and then whispers sweet lies, like, *You look really hot
doing a keg stand in a skirt that shows off your butt
cheeks and new pink thong.* Totally forgetting that you
have the flattest butt on the planet. And it's impossible
to back arch in that position to accentuate your butt's
very few positives.

Or, *Yeah, scooping jam directly from the jar with
your bare hands and slathering it on your face in an
attempt to find your mouth is really going to impress
the house guy you've been in love with forever. He's
totally going to fall in love with you now.*

Or, *It's a great idea to sleep with the house guy's
best friend out of revenge. That will show Zach. He'll*

notice you now. And, *Telling Dakota all your hurts and deepest private thoughts is perfectly reasonable. He's a sympathetic guy, right? His lips are sealed.* Never mind that he's Zach's best friend from high school and the president of the top frat on campus. And could ruin you without giving it a second thought.

Or my personal favorite, *Go ahead. Lie down in the alley behind the frat and Dakota's car. You should totally sleep there. It's comfy and safe.*

Liar. Liar. *Liar!*

I took a deep breath and clasped my hands in front of me as I waited to be called before my sorority's standards board. We Delta Delta Psis were notorious partiers and rule benders, always skirting both university and Greek rules and regulations. In the past, the board had been known for its leniency. But I had a sick feeling this time would be different.

The meeting was secret, as all standards board disciplinary meetings were. Just between me, the chairman, and the four general committee members. They were all under gag orders not to even mention the meeting had taken place, let alone what had gone on in it or who had been involved. It wasn't like I was going to talk about being disciplined. But secrets had a way of finding the light here in the Delta Delta Psi house. Like knowledge, gossip was power.

Besides, me being disciplined was inevitable, and every girl in the house knew it. I mean, the campus cops had rushed me to emergency for treatment for alcohol poisoning and charged me with a minor in possession/minor in consumption. They didn't even have to have me blow a Breathalyzer. I'd been passed out in an alley behind a frat. Though, to be fair, it would have been hard for the cops to distinguish the beer on my breath from the scent of beer flowing out of the frat house and down Greek Row. Even so, there was no doubt I was in some kind of trouble. I had my fingers crossed it was of the hand-slapping variety.

What more could the sorority do to me, really? Thanks to my dad's lawyer, less than two weeks after the incident, I'd gotten off the MIP/MIC charge with a continuance with a dismissal. Which meant the court deferred charging me. If I didn't get any more violations in the next year, the charges would be dismissed and my record would be squeaky clean. Ha! No criminal convictions.

As part of the terms of the deal, I lost my driver's license until my twenty-first birthday, which was in January. Just a few months away. I could deal with that. Oh yeah, I had to pay a small fine. A couple hundred. And pay to attend a session of Alcohol and Drug Information School. ADIS, as they called it.

Dad was footing the bill. Crap, he was a bit pissed at me. Fine, he had to do his dadly righteous anger thing. Like his drinking never got out of hand. Still, I got it. Do as I say, blah, blah, blah.

Much as it sucked, I could have done worse. Like jail time or been fined up to $5000 for a gross misdemeanor. And gotten a record. Dad had given me the speech about getting a record and how it could ruin my entire future.

Maybe I shouldn't have been so nervous. But my hands were actually trembling. I had one of those ominous feelings you can't explain. Like logic said my sorority twin Victoria was head of the standards board. She and I were, and always had been, tight. We'd had each other's backs since we pledged. So what was the biggie? The worried, irrational side of me wished my smooth-talking lawyer could have come with me to the standards board and pled my case.

Victoria and I were twins, meaning we shared the same big sister in the house. Vicki been elected to the position of head enforcer by a nearly unanimous vote last spring before school got out for summer. Mostly because she was a total boozehound who'd been in the kind of trouble that typically got you called before the board. Because of her tendencies, she understood over imbibing and wasn't judgmental. She prided herself on being more like a friend than a tyrant. Better yet, the power of the position had not gone to her head. Not that I had seen.

She was a business major with a head for house politics. Which made her extremely popular. And dangerous when she chose to be.

She'd bragged to me about putting together a balanced board. "It's key, Morgs, absolutely key to keeping things running smoothly around here." She'd given me that intense look of hers. "Join me. Take a seat on the board. You won't be sorry."

"Vics, me? Seriously? I don't want to play cop. I already have a reputation for being a bitch. The last thing I need is another hit to my rep."

I was suddenly regretting my decision to pass on her offer.

The board consisted of Victoria's little, her best friend in the house, and the house brainiac, who was even-keeled and mellow, logical. And the obligatory harsh member who was short on mercy, asked by Victoria to join the board to give it a feeling of real justice.

And so I stood in front of the door to Victoria's office on a Wednesday evening, waiting for the board to mete out justice.

You're not supposed to be the villain in your own life. But right now, even I had to admit I was. Grandma always said I was my own worst enemy. Yeah, so okay. She was right. Worse than that, I was the house villain because of what I'd done to Zach.

The door to Victoria's office opened. She waved me in. She wasn't smiling. My mouth went dry.

I closed the door behind me. Victoria took a seat behind her desk. The rest of the committee stood behind her like a firing squad.

Victoria scowled at me. "Damn it, Morgs!" She looked pained, like this was the last place she wanted to be, too. "You're making my job difficult."

The rest of the board stood silently behind her, not wanting to look me in the eye. Not even the morally uptight Brenda could make eye contact.

Victoria sighed. "Have a seat."

"No thanks. I'd rather stand." I lifted my chin like I was unafraid and unashamed. People often mistook this posture for being stuck up. But I was just bucking myself up and hoping that looking confident would chase my insecurities away.

"Have it your way." Victoria nodded like she approved. "There's no question of your guilt. Crap, Morgan. What have I told you a bazillion times? Drink all you want, but be smart about it. Don't post pictures with a drink in your hand. Don't walk around campus with an open container. Especially until you're of age.

"Getting drunk. Passing out behind a parked car in a dark alley behind a frat—"

"I wasn't passed out, exactly. I was more like resting." I should have kept my snarky mouth shut. My humor fell flat.

Victoria sighed. "Getting that drunk is dangerous. You could have died." Her eyes narrowed, like she was angry I'd given her a scare. "If you weren't out cold, why didn't you move when Dakota started his car?"

"Impaired reflexes?" I tried to sound jokey.

Victoria was having none of it. "What am I supposed to do with you? The cops hauled you off to the hospital. They had to administer meds in an IV and keep you overnight. It's kind of hard to look the other way. Especially with the Office of Student Affairs breathing down our necks.

"They've been looking for a way to impose sanctions on us for over a year. It's an open secret our illustrious university president, Dr. Lawrence, would love to shut down the Greek system. My hands are tied. We have to take appropriate action."

I met their eyes. "I'm sorry." All I could do was throw myself on their mercy. And I *was* sorry. Things had spiraled out of control before I'd blacked out. I didn't remember half of it.

I wasn't sure why people couldn't understand that I was drunk when I'd called for Zach's head. That I wasn't in control of myself. I regretted it almost immediately after I sobered up. But by then it was too late. Since then I'd been living with the guilt of getting Zach fired and all the hateful glares from my sorority sisters who were on his side.

No one would believe me, but I was on his side, too. He'd saved my life.

"Really?" Brenda stared me down. Her sudden, staccato word startled me. "Were you sorry or just wasted when you screamed at Kelly to kick Zach out and fire him? If you'd kept your mouth shut and not squealed on Zach and Alexis, we could have ignored their romance and looked the other way. Snitches are any standards board's worst enemy." She crossed her arms.

"Sisters don't rat out other sisters. Not when what they're doing isn't hurting anyone. That kind of crap forces those of us on the standards board to act. Contrary to popular belief, we're all here out of a sense of duty to the house. Not because we like dealing with this crap and are on some kind of power trip."

I wasn't surprised Brenda was defending Zach. He was Brenda's favorite live-in houseboy. He was almost everyone's fave. Including mine. He treated us like little sisters, coming to our rescue, listening to our problems, and ignoring our faults when we were at our worst. Maybe that was why I'd loved him.

Zach had always understood me in a way that very few people did. And then, even after I'd treated him horribly and gotten him fired, he saved my life by pulling me out of the way of Dakota's car. Even though I'd been passed out and didn't remember it, I owed him forever for that.

I blinked, trying not to show weakness, hoping no one noticed I was on the verge of tears.

Dad's words came back to me. *Never let them see you sweat. Hang tough, Morgs. All the time.*

People thought I was tough. And mean. I wasn't. I wasn't intrinsically mean. I'd just learned from my dad to go after what I wanted with everything I had. When I'd wanted Zach, I pursued him and used every trick I knew. Was that so wrong? Was I wrong to try to convince him of how right we were for each other? I might even have succeeded if Alexis hadn't pledged the house and stolen him away.

So I'd been a fool for love. And done some crappy stuff. But I wasn't a villain. Just dogged and determined. And now, defeated. Crushing on Zach had ruined me.

"I'm sorry," I said again. It was feeble, but what else could I do?

"You nearly got him killed." Brenda had never liked me. Being sorority sisters didn't magically make our personalities mesh. She wasn't going to let up.

But what she said was true. Dakota had backed over Zach instead of me. And put him in the hospital with brain trauma so severe that he had to take a break from school and go home to recover. So, yeah, I was the wicked witch here. But I hadn't meant for that to happen. Although it sounded like I was making excuses, I was more like Elphaba in *Wicked* than the portrayal of the wicked witch in *The Wizard of Oz*. Misunderstood. Taken out of context. And though no one would believe me, I would take it all back if I could.

"Dakota's in deep shit now, too, because of you." Brenda's eyes glittered with anger. So that was why she couldn't look at me. She wasn't sympathetic. She was furious. Besides being buddies with Zach, it was an open secret she had a thing for Dakota.

I hung my head. I was sorry. Honestly sorry for being such a green-eyed bitch. I saw that now that it was too late. But it's not easy to kill a crush. Emotions don't just die on command or when it's convenient.

Victoria cut her off. "Ease up on her."

The other three board members were stiffly quiet. I could almost feel how much they wanted to be anywhere but here.

Brenda shut up, but the death glares from her continued.

"I'm sorry. We have to discipline you, Morgan." Victoria sighed. "Discipline is not meant as punishment. Discipline is meant to instruct and correct. And build our house to be a better place because each member is her fullest, best self."

Crap. A speech. My heart pounded. This sounded canned, not like Victoria at all. I'd been hoping they'd fine me and I would go on my way. But now...

"The five of us have discussed the situation and reached a unanimous decision, which is for your own good. Morgan Peterson, you are now on social probation through the end of the semester. Effective immediately."

My heart nearly stopped. "But—"

"This means you will not be allowed to participate in any house parties, mixers, dances, or functions, other than philanthropy events, until you have successfully completed both your court-ordered Alcohol and Drug Information School and the entire semester without incurring more infractions or being brought before the board again."

I stood perfectly still, stunned.

Victoria got out of her chair and came around to give me a hug. "Come on, Morgs. You'll be all right. Your drinking has gotten out of hand. This is your chance to get it back under control and get a little perspective."

She took a breath, like there was more bad news coming. "There's one more stipulation—you need to learn to get along with Alexis. She's your little. You owe it to her to mentor her properly and shape her into a vital member of our house."

I stared at my twin, stunned, even though I shouldn't have been surprised. Alexis was the villain here, the girl who'd stepped in my territory and not backed off when I'd warned her to. For her and Zach's sake as much as my own self-interest. I'd known from the first time Alexis had seen Zach that she was going to mean trouble for him. I'd tried to stop her. And this was how I was repaid.

I kept my chin high. "Exactly how am I supposed to get along with her?"

Victoria shrugged. "The usual way—take her out to lunch. Buy her a coffee. Sit down and chat. Maybe even study together. You took History of Rock and Roll, didn't you? She's taking that class now." Victoria smiled, looking relieved the interview was almost over. "You'll figure something out. You have a lot of wisdom and experience to offer her. You just have to find it in yourself."

CHAPTER TWO

Dakota

I met with the prosecutor behind closed doors at his office less than two weeks after I ran over—and nearly killed—Zach, my best friend from high school. Tom Lesser, my dad's law partner, represented me. I'd known Tom since I was a baby. "Lesser" was really a misnomer. He was a big, affable man, all charm and smiles and good-old-boy networks. Until you faced him across a courtroom. Then he went for your jugular.

Justice moved exceedingly slowly in the big, bad real world. This tiny college town had not learned that slow was the cool way to do things. Here, justice—regarding alcohol violations at least—moved at lightning speed. Probably to keep the courts from being totally clogged. Alcohol violations were as common as beer was on campus. But few involved vehicular assault, or whatever they were calling it.

Tom had warned me beforehand to keep my mouth shut and let him do all the talking. Speak only when spoken to, like I was a kid. And even then, wait for him to give me permission to answer any questions. Despite his common, tired middle-aged man appearance, Dan Green, the prosecutor, laid a mean trap with the stealth of a ninja. You would never see it coming. That was what Tom told me. And he should know.

I sat next to Tom. I was clean-shaven, hair freshly cut, dressed in a dress shirt and slacks, looking like the fair-haired boy next door. Like the kind of guy Dan would trust with his daughter. A guy who couldn't possibly get into any trouble.

Smiles, handshakes, greetings, and story swapping were over. Tom and Dan were old buddies, apparently. Tom was buddies with everyone. But suddenly, things were all business. And the two men were no longer old friends, but adversaries on the opposite side of the gray area of justice.

Across his big mahogany desk, Dan, a wiry man who looked bored and was almost begging for something that would surprise him, stared seriously at me. Meting out justice was serious shit. I was his fifth Homecoming Week case of the day.

"You're asking for a continuance with a dismissal?" Dan adjusted his glasses. "This isn't a simple minor in possession/minor in consumption. Your client was driving while intoxicated. He hit and nearly killed another student."

I stared into my lap and swallowed hard, thinking of Zach and the crazy-grateful way he'd reacted to the whole thing. Like me hitting him had let him atone for his past sins and save the life of a sister of sorts as repayment for taking one. Zach and the mysterious way his mind worked attracted girls like a magnet. And had always driven me crazy. He was impossible to understand.

"Technically, my client was still on private property. Not on the public roads, where the campus police have jurisdiction. He was simply backing his car in what amounts to a private driveway." Tom smiled. "Look, Dan. I know you've read the case notes. There were extenuating circumstances. By his own admission, the victim, Zachary Harris, admits he jumped out behind Mr. Bradley without warning, giving him no time to react and stop."

Dan looked neither amused nor moved. "To save a young woman Mr. Bradley was about to run over with his car." He glanced at me.

I sat like a stone, unmovable, trying to be unreadable, about to be stepped on by justice. Grateful as hell to Zach that he'd saved me from killing Morgan. Or even merely maiming her. Furious with her for putting me in this position. Why the hell did she lie down in that alley? Why hadn't I walked her home?

Morgan had always seemed so tough. But she'd been an emotional basket case that night. We both were. I shouldn't have taken advantage of her. We shouldn't have taken advantage of each other.

Tom looked completely unfazed by the accusation. "It remains to be seen whether my client would have *actually* hit Miss Peterson. His car is equipped with a backing camera and object detection. Just a few inches more and his car would have warned him of the young lady's presence. He may very well have stopped in time. We'll never know for sure now." Tom's tone was as smooth as a lake on a calm summer morning.

Dan looked like he wanted to throw both of us into that lake. Like Tom's story was a bunch of bullshit.

"You've read the statement I submitted from Mr. Harris. The victim has asked the courts for mercy for my client, saying he doesn't blame Mr. Bradley for his injuries. And maintaining that if it were up to him, Mr. Harris wouldn't press charges. In these extreme circumstances, I think it's worth taking his wishes into consideration.

"Zachary Harris accidentally ran over and killed his baby sister when he was a toddler. He feels that one accident nearly ruined the rest of his life. Being a true friend, he wants to spare Mr. Bradley the same fate. Let's not lay more guilt at Zachary Harris' feet.

"My client was doing what almost every student on campus was doing that Friday night of Homecoming Week—partying. Spirits ran high after his team won the powder puff football tournament. He wasn't taking as much care to pay attention to his surroundings as he should have. And yes, he was drinking.

"But he's just months away from his twenty-first birthday. This is his first offense. He has a clean record—not even a speeding ticket. His father has made recompense to the victim for injuries incurred. And Mr. Bradley has abstained from alcohol since the incident. He has apologized to the victim. And been forgiven.

"We're not asking for mercy. We're asking for reason. There's no need to take punitive action for what is an unfortunate accident and temporary lapse of judgment. One that my client has owned up to and learned from. He's an ideal candidate for a continuance. Don't ruin his future with a criminal record over a stupid college mistake."

Dan stared at us, studying me. My mouth went dry.

"You make a good case, Tom." It was hard to tell whether he believed his own words. "I'll grant your continuance. If Mr. Bradley agrees to my terms. He will surrender his driver's license until his twenty-first birthday. Attend the first available session of Alcohol and Drug Information School at his own expense, and pay a two-thousand-dollar fine. If he doesn't get into any more trouble within the year, the charges will be dismissed."

I released a breath I'd hardly been aware of holding.

Beside me, Tom tensed. Two thousand dollars was extreme. The maximum was five thousand, but most people got off with paying a few hundred.

"And he will attend a victims' panel," Dan said before Tom could speak and argue for better terms.

It was clear he was making a power play. The longer we considered his offer, the steeper the terms became. And everything was non-negotiable.

"Thank you, Dan. On behalf of my client, we accept." Tom stood and extended his hand to shake Dan's.

"Good. The next session of ADIS begins this Friday night. Make sure he's in it."

Outside the courtroom, Tom hugged me.

"Thank you, man," I said, slapping him on the back. "It was touch and go there for a minute."

We stepped into the frigid sunshine of an early November day.

"The bastard. Two thousand dollars! Your dad's going to chew me out for not trying to get away with less." Tom winked at me and pulled his keys out of his pocket. "I gotta run. I have a flight out in less than an hour. Stay out of trouble. I'll see you at Thanksgiving."

He glanced both ways and crossed the street to his parked rental car. He'd flown in from Seattle last night. Tom was always in motion, one of Seattle's top criminal defense attorneys. He had pressing cases that needed attention at home. If he hadn't been Dad's partner, he wouldn't have stooped to take my puny case.

I pulled out my cell phone and called Zach like I'd promised him. "Hey, you saved my ass, man. That statement of yours was genius. I got a continuance."

"What? They're not throwing your butt in jail?" Zach laughed.

It felt good to hear him recovering. He sounded more and more like himself every time I talked to him.

"Sorry to disappoint." I walked toward the corner, heading back to campus and the frat. "No, they're just fining my ass. Two thousand bucks. Dad's going to go apeshit."

"Two thousand. That's a bunch of bullshit," Zach said.

"It's peanuts compared to what I could have gotten." I changed the subject. "You sound good. How are you feeling?"

"Still have the headaches, but I'm getting there," he said.

I swallowed my guilt over being the cause of them. Zach had been so young, he couldn't remember running over his baby sister. I had been so drunk, the details of hitting him were fuzzy. We were even that way. "I still don't get how you're grateful to me."

"I told you—now I know how it felt when I hit my baby sis. It was quick. There was no pain. Until I woke up."

"That's supposed to be comforting? You're making me feel like shit. How much pain have I put you through?" I turned the corner and headed up the steep hill toward Greek Row.

Zach laughed. "It is to me. You're on your own, bud. Don't worry. I'm not going to sue you for pain and suffering. Though living with Mom was giving me second thoughts. Eighteen years of ignoring me, and suddenly she's suffocating me with her motherly attention. Staying with Dad is a welcome respite."

"Still at your dad's? They haven't started playing ping-pong with you yet?"

Since the accident when he was three and ran over his little sister, neither parent had wanted him. Since the night I nearly killed Zach, they were falling all over him, having a contest to show who was sorrier and who could spoil him the most.

"Nope. I'm still at Dad's. And still feeling like I woke up in an alternate universe. Who the hell are these attentive parents? I didn't realize how good I had it being the invisible child. This makes me sound like an ingrate, but I'm getting sick of all the fawning and attention."

"Cheer up," I said. "It's just a matter of time before they bounce back to their old bitchy selves."

He laughed. "Yeah, you're probably right." Zach paused. "I had a visit from Jordan yesterday."

I took a deep breath of the cold air. When I let it out, I watched it curl skyward, like it was portending doom. "Yeah?" I said as casually as I could, pushing back the guilt. "That was nice of her."

Jordan was my girlfriend back home. We'd been off and on again since high school. My parents didn't like her. BFD. I kept her a secret from them. Jordan thought it was bullshit, which caused a ton of stress in our relationship. We were teetering on the edge of off. She didn't like my friendship with Zach's girlfriend Alexis. If she found out about Morgan...

"She didn't tell you?" Zach's question was pointed.

I tensed. "No. Why? Should she?"

"Chill, Dak," Zach said. "I'm worried about you two. Jordan acts like she thinks you're freezing her out. After all we went through..."

"Are you talking to Jordan behind my back?"

"I just told you about it, didn't I? Is there someone else?"

I cursed beneath my breath. "She put you up to that." I crossed another street and picked up my pace. "Jordan's always been the jealous type. She's imagining things. We're fine."

"Whatever you say," Zach said. "How are you handling the fallout from your fake relationship with Alexis and her, and me betraying you?" Zach laughed.

It was a long story. Alexis and I had pretended to be a couple to take the heat off her and Zach and me and Jordan. In retrospect, it had been a dumbass plan. At the time, I thought maybe I had a shot with Alexis. Yeah, I know. That makes me look like a douchebag.

"I'm bearing up. Getting ribbed a lot. But since you saved Morgan's life and mine, they're coming to terms with our friendship."

"Alexis insists she has to keep up the pretense of betraying you," Zach said.

"Yeah, she refuses to rat me out. I told her it's okay with me. But she refuses to step out of the fire and save herself." I paused. "You got a good one, Zach. My parents are giving me shit for, quote, 'losing her.'"

Zach laughed. "Nothing new there. Your parents give you crap over who you date all the time." He paused. "You should come clean with them and admit you're back with Jordan."

Like hell, I thought. My old man would shit bullets. Right now, I couldn't afford to be in deeper shit with him.

CHAPTER THREE

Morgan

A little before five Friday afternoon, the sorority house pulsed with music and laughter. We weren't the most prestigious house on campus for no reason. Delta Delta Psis knew how to party. Knew how to dress. Knew how to look. We were famous party girls and flirts.

The happiest day of my life was the day they offered me a bid. Me, tagalong baby sister of my family, had arrived. Me, the child who never belonged, who didn't know the family stories, who'd never known my oldest brother, who had no shared history with my much older siblings, finally had an outrageously fun group of sisters.

It had been touch and go for me during rush. I was sure another house was going to offer me a bid. At our university, you're only allowed a bid from one house. You either take it or leave it. If more than one house wanted you, they decided among themselves who got the honor of offering.

I knew I had to take extreme measures to have a prayer of getting in. So I suicide bid the Double Deltsies. Suicide bidding is the riskiest move you can make during rush. If the house you suicide bid doesn't want you, you end up without a bid at all. I was scared I would end recruitment week without a bid and have to wait to try again during informal rush the following semester. Be a semester off and miss all the fun fall events.

To my absolute amazement, my strategy worked. I never looked back and never regretted a thing. Until now. Most of the girls blamed me for the accident that put our favorite live-in houseboy Zach in the hospital and on medical leave from school. They blamed me for getting him kicked out of the house when I caught him in bed with my little.

They didn't understand—I loved the house. And I had loved Zach. Loved them both so much that I wanted the rules respected and things to stay the same. Zach unobtainable and living in. Our sorority strong and vital.

They didn't understand how I'd lived my life striving for the unobtainable. It was something I was only realizing about myself—I was afraid to commit to reality. Afraid of really putting myself out there for a guy who was free to fall in love with me and be available. Afraid I was unworthy and unlovable.

I know—that's some serious crap, right? It's not like I sat around self-evaluating all the time. But since the accident, I'd had a lot of time to think. And a couple of alcohol abuse evaluations with a psychiatrist in the student counseling services.

She said my drinking was a way of self-medicating and numbing my pain. Dousing my fears.

Pain? I didn't think I had any more than the usual. Yeah, my siblings, who are all much older, treated me like I was their niece, not their sister. One even called me that, like she was embarrassed by me and the fact that our parents had sex after forty.

And my grandma, my steady force and biggest fan, had been having heart problems. Like, serious heart crap. In and out of the hospital, verge-of-death stuff. I hadn't told anyone in the house. I didn't need a pity party.

Others might argue that I had pushed Zach to break the rules with me. Live-in houseboys were forbidden from having romantic relationships with the girls. Violating the rule would cost them their job. I had tried to seduce him in defiance of those same rules, but only when I was drunk and or when my defenses were down. But was that really any different than all the other stupid crap people do when they're drunk?

Now I was on the outside, a social pariah, banned from the fun, as my sisters discussed their Friday night plans. As I walked through the living room, Katie, one of our first semester pledges, stopped me.

"What are you up to tonight, Morgan?" Her gaze flitted over me.

I was wearing yoga pants and a T-shirt, no makeup, my hair up in a high ponytail. The best parties never started until after ten. It wasn't like not being ready was a giveaway of my social probation status.

Katie's innocuous little question was loaded. The pledge was probably fishing. On the one hand, I always knew where the best parties were. Giving her the benefit of the doubt, she simply wanted the party scene scoop. On the other hand, she was one of Alexis' best friends. It was highly likely she was trying to trick me into confessing that I'd been put on probation.

I shrugged, noncommittal and full of false bravado. "I haven't decided."

What a cool liar I was. I was going to Alcohol and Drug Information School at six. Taking the bus because the prosecutor had confiscated my driver's license. My adorable blue Prius was parked in the sorority house parking lot out back, collecting dust until my birthday. I had already decided I was going on the best, most comprehensive birthday run ever next January. After I took my car for a spin.

I walked past Katie into the kitchen, thinking that I'd gone two full days avoiding Alexis rather than making nice with her. Call me rebellious.

Seth, Zach's former roommate, was hard at work in the kitchen, helping our cook Betty with dinner prep.

I smiled sweetly at him. "It smells delicious in here. I'm starving. Can I snag something to eat before I head out?"

Dinner was at six, precisely when I would be in school. I could have gotten something to eat out, but why bother when I could flirt with Seth and get something now?

When Seth saw me, he raised an eyebrow, clutched his chest, and fell back like he was having a heart attack.

"Shut up!" I gave him a gentle shove.

"Come on, Morgs. Don't give me a heart attack while I'm holding a knife." He sliced the air with it. "Is the infamous queen of partying and drinking on an empty stomach actually going to *eat* something before she goes out?" He made a show of glancing out the window. "Hell can't be frozen over. It's not even freezing here."

I rolled my eyes. "Stop teasing."

Betty glanced at us from the corner of her eye, and smiled. "Give her something, Seth. I don't need her death on my conscience."

It was the wrong thing to say, given how close I'd come to being road kill. Betty was usually kind, but her statement was clearly barbed beneath her lighthearted tone.

Seth sighed, defeated, and plopped a large spoonful of Betty's homemade mac and cheese, gooey with butter and cheese, on a plate for me.

"What? No bread?" I said. "To absorb the alcohol?"

"That's an urban myth. Protein and fat work better. Enjoy." He handed me a fork.

He watched as I took a bite and rolled my eyes upward in appreciation, punctuating it with a sigh. "Delicious! Betty, are you trying to make us all gain the freshman fifteen?"

She laughed and returned her focus to finishing dinner.

After the incident, I'd had a heart-to-heart with Seth. He understood me now, I hoped. Zach had been his roommate and they'd been tight. I knew he missed Zach, and blamed me—originally, anyway.

I leaned in and whispered in his ear, "I don't need protein and fat. I'm not drinking tonight. I'm doing the opposite—going to ADIS."

"Shit, Morgs." His look softened.

"Keep it to yourself, okay?" I took a deep breath. "Everyone knows I have to do it. But I haven't told anyone else I'm going tonight. I couldn't stand their pity or their judgment.

"Oh, and just so you know, I'm on social probation for the semester. Don't spread that around, either. Only the standards board knows for sure."

"Why are you telling me?" He looked puzzled.

"I need a friend." I was sincere.

"And I'm it?" He stared at me like he was debating whether I was telling the truth or pulling his leg. "Fraternizing with the help. You must be desperate." He grinned that roguish grin of his, the one that made his dimple crease. "Are you sure you can trust me?"

I shrugged and smiled at him, but my heart was pounding out of control. He was teasing and pulling my leg. Seth was the king of teasing. But his words held a lot of truth—I was desperate for a true friend I could confide in. And I had just handed him the power to blackmail me and lend truth to the rumors that were already flying.

"Just trying to even the balance of power," I said, as evenly as I could.

His eyes lit up, like he knew I was still trying to make amends. He pulled me into a hug. "Selfish, babe. You want cover for when you pretend you're partying." He rested his chin on the top of my head and whispered, "If you need a ride, call me."

Seth was a good guy. I returned his hug and blinked back tears.

Dakota

I got to school early, registered, paid my fee, and took a seat in the back of the class. My dad had chewed my ass off when I told him about the fine. He lectured me for half an hour on my stupidity. It had cost him real money. Dad hated paying for shit that could have been avoided.

My buddies at the frat were preparing for a night of first-class partying. Most of them hoping to get laid. And I was in school to learn all about the dangers of drinking. It was a joke. Until *she* walked in.

My pulse raced. My palms sweated. My dick went involuntarily hard. An absolutely stunning girl stood silhouetted in the doorway—blond, slim but with the kind of figure I found sexy as hell. Fresh-faced, no makeup. Her cheeks pink from the cold. Her eyes warm and bright with exercise and expectation. Her hair curled into the faux fur that rimmed the hood of her coat. She wore flat Ugg boots and yoga pants that left just enough to my imagination.

She hesitated at the door, like she was uncertain and nervous. My hero instincts kicked in. I liked her sweet vulnerability. Just as I was about to get out of my chair and play gentleman, introduce myself and see where things led, I stopped cold, recognizing her with a start.

Morgan Peterson? Without makeup. *Shit.*

You'd think my dick would have gone soft at the sight of her. The damn thing didn't. My pulse involuntarily sped up. What was it about Morgan Peterson that turned me on even when I was furious with her?

Morgan

He was here. Oh, crap, crap, and triple crapola!

Why? Why, why, why me? Of all the Alcohol and Drug Information School sessions in the world, why did he have to be sitting in *mine?* If I had had a cloak of invisibility, you can bet I would have used it.

My heart took a nosedive for my stomach and hit with a splash. On a scale of one to ten, it would have gotten a ten for style and the way it somersaulted and made my stomach turn over.

I hesitated in the doorway, looking over my classmates and fellow law-breaking, hard-drinking minors. My hopes of finding an anonymous, sympathetic crowd were dashed. I mean, if anyplace, this was the place for compassion and support, right? We'd all screwed up one way or another. And been dumb enough to get caught. But I didn't imagine any of the rest of them had almost been run over by one of our fellow classmates.

His eyes went round and wide. For half a second he looked like he had when he'd been perched over me, making love to me. His expression had been so sweet then. And passionate.

My breath caught involuntarily. Just like it did every time that stupid recollection sneaked up on me. If I could erase that particular memory, I would have. Of all the things I couldn't remember from that night, that was the one thing I couldn't forget.

He leaned forward in his chair, like he was about to rise out of it to greet me.

A spark of recognition crossed his face. He froze and fell back into his seat.

Screw you, Dakota Bradley.

I abandoned my plan to slip in almost invisibly and scoop up the least prominent spot to sit. I uncrossed my fingers. Stupid finger crossing had failed me. Crappy superstitions.

Nobody dissed me and got away with it. I was a lot of things, but I wasn't a coward. Dad had taught me not to cower before an enemy. Face them head-on.

I unzipped my coat, shook my hair, and walked straight toward Dakota until I stood directly over him. "Fancy meeting you here." I slid into the seat next to him with the full intent of making him uncomfortable. Damn him. He deserved it.

"Morgan." His voice was hard. "I almost didn't recognize you. Not wearing your war paint? What happened? Lose your makeup trowel?"

I laughed to put him in his place. "You silver-tongued devil!" I paused for effect. "Or are you just the devil? Sometimes it's hard to tell." I laughed again, drawing attention from a couple of guys sitting around us. "Following me around?"

"I was ordered by the prosecutor to attend this particular session." The look in his eyes was positively glowering. "You must be following me."

"In your dreams, Tau Psi. Wasn't your meeting with him just this week?" I stared Dakota down and kept my chin high. "I signed up last week." I tilted my head and studied him. "Did they order you to go to a victims' panel, too?"

He paled.

Yeah, I was a witch for bringing it up. But then, I had a reputation to maintain.

"Yeah." His voice was soft and almost sounded guilty. "I'm sure you knew that."

I shrugged. "No. Just a lucky guess." I smiled sweetly at him and made a point to look like I was thinking hard on something. "When did you say it is? I wonder if there's still time for me to apply to be one of the victims."

He paled. "Shit. Can't you let that go? I didn't hit you. Okay? I didn't even see you."

I took a deep breath. "Yeah, too bad for you. Close only counts in horseshoes and hand grenades, right?"

"Morgan—"

The instructor walked in just then, along with a bunch of last-minute stragglers.

"Class! Everyone take a seat. We're on a tight schedule. I'm Dr. Smith. But you can call me Larry."

He was pale, stale, and middle-aged. I thought, *Oh boy, this is going to be fun.*

Every one of the twenty or so seats was full. Great, a full crowd. Of mostly guys. There were only two other girls. Mercifully, I didn't recognize anyone but Dakota.

Larry shut the door. "Nothing I like better than having a bully pulpit before a full house!" He grinned devilishly.

It was dead silent.

"Lighten up, people! This isn't torture. This is more like mildly boring punishment. It's irritating having to miss a night of drinking and partying, isn't it?" He reached into the bag he carried, pulled out a sheaf of papers, and handed the stack to the guy next to him. "Take one. Pass them around. Confidentiality agreements. Non-disclosures. Signing them is optional."

That wicked grin of Larry's deepened. "Participating in class without signing one is strictly prohibited. You're all ordered by courts to be here. Most of you are in college. You figure out what that means." He laughed.

"'In order to build the trust necessary to be honest about personal behaviors and experiences, participants must honor the confidentiality of all in attendance.'

"That's right out of the instructor's handbook. And absolutely true and essential. What goes on here stays here. If I, or the courts, get wind that any of you has violated the trust of another participant, any agreement you made for leniency and continuance will be voided. And you'll be at the mercy of the prosecutor and the courts.

"The university may seem large, but the community is actually very small. Don't push your luck." He handed around a box of cheap pens. Then he passed out workbooks like we were elementary school kids.

I signed the stupid confidentiality form with a flourish, realizing that it could be my salvation. If I was brave enough to take it. Or got the right opportunity.

Larry collected the signed forms and stuffed them in his bag. "'The mission of the Alcohol and Drug Information School, ADIS, is to promote public safety by reducing the number of injuries and fatalities due to driving under the influence of alcohol and other drugs.' That's a quote from the website.

"I'm here to teach you effective decision-making skills, with the goal of reducing recidivism. My job is to provide you with accurate information about alcohol and other drugs to assist you in making changes to your high-risk substance use behavior." Larry paused. "So much for the official part of my speech. Now for a pretest. You have ten minutes to complete it. Log in on your laptop or phone with the password you were issued when you registered..."

A stupid pretest. Just what I needed. As I logged in and began taking it, it met my meager expectations. Lame. I glanced over at Dakota, wondering how he was answering the questions.

He was deep in thought. But when he caught me looking at him, he turned his back on me and covered his phone like I was trying to cheat off him. *As if.*

Question number one—have you ever blacked out after drinking too much?

No. I only went to sleep in an alley. Not the same thing.

Too bad it was only a yes-or-no question. No elaborating. This wasn't an essay test. I rocked at those.

Dakota

Morgan was trying to see my answers. The snoopy bitch. I turned my back on her. Morgan didn't have a hard-earned rep as the bitchiest of the Double Deltsies for nothing. She had a heart as hard as diamonds. Yeah, according to the scintillating materials science class I'd taken, diamonds were still the hardest substance on earth. The rock hounds hadn't met Morgan. She put diamonds to shame.

But nothing shamed her.

Somewhere beneath that hard exterior she put on was a complicated, sensitive, passionate girl. That beautiful girl rarely came out. Only when Morgan was hurting and dropped her prickly crustaceous shell. And that was usually because of Zach. The only times she opened up to me were when he'd hurt her. Each time was like a sucker punch to my gut. I didn't know why the shit I was the guy who had to pick her up and put her back together. I didn't know why I put up with it.

Morgan and I had our own sorry past. If you can call it that. Is a one-sided love affair and a few hookups a past? Or is it just fucking stupidity in every sense?

The simple truth is, I fell hard for her our freshman year. Against all reason and common sense. Before I realized she was into Zach.

Shit, even at a university with over twenty thousand students, the one girl I'd wanted had already fallen for my ex-best friend. Zach and I had had a major falling out the summer before, just after we graduated from high school. That was before our recent patching up of all the shit between us.

Zach had just gotten a job as a houseboy at her sorority. Without it, he would have been SOL as far as paying for college. His parents didn't give a crap about him and refused to help pay for anything. The most popular guy from my high school class was now the Double Deltsies' servant. And I didn't give a damn.

On the other hand, through a stroke of luck, and a lot of schmoozing, I'd pledged the best frat on campus. My absolute top choice. This was a group of guys I would have connections to for life. Guys with connections. Guys going places. Guys who knew how to have fun. My future looked rosy, as my grandma would say. While Zach was struggling.

Even with Zach and my statuses reversed from high school, where I was always playing second to him, and roughly ten thousand girls to choose from, Zach had gotten Morgan's attention. And didn't want her.

The vision of Morgan the first time I saw her was forever written in my memory. Do you believe in love at first sight? I sure as hell didn't. But the moment the Double Deltsies walked into the first party my frat threw for them that fall, I fell for her like I'd never fallen before. Free fall with no parachute.

If you're an adrenaline junkie, you know the feeling. Like you can't breathe and all the colors of the world are more vibrant than they've ever been. Like your heart won't stop pounding and each beat is full of thrill and fear. Like you should back out of whatever danger-ous dumbass thing you're doing. But you know you won't. Because you know you love the rush too much. But was it sustainable?

Nearly all the Deltsies were blonds of one shade or another, real or bleached. In early September, the heat was stifling during the day. In the evening, the air grew crisp. The Deltsies arrived right on time at sun-set, a crowd of blonds with hair haloed by the setting sun. Short skirts. Crop tops. Flip-flops. Bodies that gave a guy a hard-on just thinking about them.

In that crowd, I don't know how Morgan stood out. Must have been that damn aura of charm and seduction that surrounded her. Or maybe it was her bright smile. Or her tinkling laugh that made her eyes sparkle. Or her naïve vulnerability. She wasn't jaded and desperate back then, like she was now. Just a fresh-faced fresh-man looking for a party and a good time.

I still remembered the way the setting sun lit her hair. The look of wonder on her face, like she couldn't believe her good luck to be a Deltsie partying with us. I can describe the skirt she wore in great detail, as if I were a fashion merchandising major or some shit.

I'd screwed up my courage and brought her a beer. "You look thirsty." It was a cheesy line.

She looked up at me from beneath impossibly long lashes. As she took the plastic cup from me, our fingers brushed. It was innocent and a turn-on at the same time.

She lifted the beer to her lips and took a great chug, leaving a white mustache of foam on her upper lip. I had to restrain myself from leaning over and licking it off. Instead, I watched with rapt attention while she slowly and deliberately licked it off herself.

"You're right. I was thirsty." She set the cup down, grabbed my hand, and pulled me to the dance floor.

Our first dance was a slow dance. I couldn't keep my hands from straying to her completely grab-able ass. She didn't push my hands away. I figured she liked it.

After the dance, she took my hand and pulled me out to the front lawn so we could watch the fading brilliance of the sunset. We talked and talked. The way she hung on everything I said, I thought she was really into me. She wanted to hear about my high school football career. I told her stories about me and Zach. Much later I realized she wasn't interested in me. She was pumping me for info about Zach.

It was a fucking shame, too. At the time, I was dating Jordan. I had every intention of being faithful to her. Until I got to school and saw all the hot babes. Even then, I remained true. Until Morgan led me on.

I broke up with Jordan for Morgan. I couldn't stand the guilt of leading Jordan on when I was falling for someone else.

Morgan and I even hooked up a couple of times. Right now, sitting in ADIS, I didn't dare think about the mind-blowing sex we'd had.

Like a young, stupid freshman, I'd thought we had a thing going. Until I realized Morgan was using me to learn about Zach and make him jealous. She'd used me again. But this time, we'd used each other. I felt totally shitty about it. Somehow Zach had still come out the hero. Being hero was his gig, not mine.

I'd slept with Morgan that night, thinking I could get her out of my system. Half amazed she was still in it. I'd taken advantage of her weakness and vulnerability. And she'd taken advantage of me. We were even. But somehow, we weren't.

I caught a whiff of her perfume and flashed back to holding her in my arms as she cried over my best friend, just as Larry called time.

"That's it for the pretest. It's mostly for the state's information. They use it to see how effective these classes are. You'll take a posttest last thing tomorrow before you leave." Larry grabbed the chair behind the podium upfront and pulled it to the front of the room. "Now that the formalities are over, let's all get to know each other before we start the meat of the class. Grab your chairs and make a circle around me."

If I thought I could escape Morgan, I was wrong. She and her chair stuck with me. When I set mine down, she put hers indecently close to mine. Like she was trying to get a rise out of me. And she sure as hell was.

"Let's start by introducing yourselves and telling us how you ended up here. And anything else you care to share. Who wants to start? Raise your hand."

When no one volunteered, Larry homed in on Morgan. Of course he did. She was the hottest chick in the session. And she looked so damned deceptively vulnerable and sweet. Like a lost puppy who'd been accidentally rounded up with the wolves. And the wolves were literally circling.

"You." Larry pointed at her. "Morgan, isn't it?"

She nodded, looking at him like he was a mind reader. "How did you know?"

"I had a one in three chance of guessing right." Larry was a real trip. "I heard him say your name." He pointed at me. "There's a story here," he said. "Why don't you tell it? How did you get here?"

I froze as the rest of the class stared at Morgan.

When she chose to use it, Morgan had a smile that could melt a guy's heart. She flashed it at Larry, using all her Double Deltsie charisma. "I drank too much."

"Go figure," Larry said.

The class laughed.

"Why don't you elaborate? We're listening." Larry rested his elbow on his knee, and his head in his hand, like he was all attentive ears.

Morgan rolled her eyes. That got a laugh. She followed it by licking her lips and gnawing them like she was nervous. "Everything here is completely confidential?"

I froze. Damn her. She better not—

"Absolutely, Morgan." Larry leaned forward in his chair like he was completely attuned to her. "Anything you share is safe here. It won't leave this room."

She nodded and glanced sideways at me.

Ah, shit. I felt the crap about to hit the fan, and there was no way to stop it.

"It was the Friday night of Homecoming Weekend. My sorority and Mr. University's frat—" She pointed at me.

I was supremely embarrassed about being a beauty king, and Morgan knew it. It was a joke, not an honor. That was the way the guys saw it. I'd taken my share of ribbing over it.

"—had just won the powder puff football competition," she said. "And with it, the Greek Homecoming competition. The Tau Psis threw a victory party." She looked directly at me. Her eyes misted over and her lips trembled.

I looked like the biggest douchebag in the world. I'd only competed for Mr. University because Morgan's sorority insisted. Our team got points for every guy who entered the competition. The win was a surprise and a joke. The judges had picked me as a way of thumbing their noses at the university. I'd just been picked up for driving under the influence the night before.

"I got bombed. We got bombed." She paused, and my heart stopped. "And hooked up." She made it sound like in her right mind that would never have happened.

I sat frozen, dreading the worst and unable to stop it.

She took a deep breath and stared in her lap, wringing the crowd for sympathy. "When I left the party, Dakota got in his car and tried to run me over."

CHAPTER FOUR

Morgan

I felt Dakota stiffen beside me. I'd gotten him good, and he knew it. The whole class was glaring at him while I played the victim.

"Shit, Morgan." Dakota scowled at me and looked around helplessly at everyone else. "It's not what it sounds like." He turned his attention back on me. "If you'd let me walk you home—"

"I don't remember you offering. In fact, I don't remember much at all." I made it sound like an indictment of his lovemaking.

Our "lovers' spat" had the class enraptured. Which was exactly what I wanted.

Dakota's eyes were hard and his jaw was set as he stared at me like he really did want to commit vehicular homicide on my person now.

Come on, Dak! I wanted to say. *Lighten up and play along. This meeting is going to kill us with boredom if we don't have some fun with it.* I winked at him so only he could see, hoping he caught my conspiratorial meaning and played along.

"If you hadn't laid down behind my car—"

"I think we have a pretty good picture of why both Dakota and Morgan are here," Larry said. "Alcohol impairs good judgment. Am I right, Morgan? Dakota?"

I had a hard time holding down my smile as I nodded. "Totally." I shot Dak a sideways glance.

"Sure," he said. "It impaired my judgment *much* earlier than when I got in my car."

One of the guys sniggered.

Larry clipped Dakota's introduction, only allowing him to give his name and crime. I didn't pay much attention to the rest of the introductions. None of them compared to ours, and I think everyone knew it. After introductions, class lapsed into a dry lecture about the effects of alcohol and other drugs.

Finally, nine rolled around and Larry dismissed class for the evening. "See you all bright and early at eight tomorrow morning. No hangovers. If I so much as suspect one, you've violated the terms of your agreement with the prosecutor and courts."

"On that cheery note," I said as I slid my coat on and gathered up my purse and workbook. I dashed out of the room, eager to breathe in the bracing night air and be done for the night with the tension of the stupid class. Done with dealing with Dakota Bradley.

I raced down the hall toward the exit, walking as quickly as I could, hellbent on escape.

"Morgan!" Dakota called to me. "Hey! Wait up."

I ignored him.

I wasn't fast enough. He caught me at the door as I stepped outside. "How are you getting home?"

"Walking." I looked up the hill toward campus, thinking I would take the shortcut through the Hillside Apartments and past the science and engineering buildings to Greek Row.

Dakota read my mind. "Seriously, Morgan? Shit. You're going to walk right through rape alley?"

"You're exaggerating."

"It isn't safe."

I held my keychain pepper spray up. "I'm prepared. What are you going to do? Offer to drive me home?" I laughed.

"You're a cruel bitch, Morgs." He actually smiled, which caught me off guard. He took my arm. "I'm not letting you make a fool or a murderer out of me again. I'm walking you home."

I could have shaken his arm off. But I didn't. His firm grip felt good and protective. I didn't know why I suddenly felt I needed protecting. And I didn't know why I was reacting to Dakota when we'd never really been more than fuck buddies in times of great need.

"You got me good in there with your gag order." His breath made puffs of white in the clear night air.

"So you caught that, did you?" I was glad he was smart enough to recognize my stealth move. "You haven't bragged about it already, have you?"

He looked straight ahead, unreadable. "No. You?"

"Why would I admit to it?" I looked straight ahead, too, fighting the wounded feelings I didn't understand. "Good. Then no one else ever needs to know."

"Except the other nineteen people in the room," he said drily.

"If they squeal, they'll get their asses kicked to jail. Kind of delicious, isn't it? The best drama of the night and they can't talk about it." I walked at a brisk pace, but he had no trouble keeping up.

We reached a red light. I hit the walk button with a force that surprised me.

"You're pissed at me," he said.

The light turned green. He held me back as I took a step forward. "Morgan, what did you expect?"

"A text to see how I was doing would have been nice." I couldn't believe the words slipped out. Had I really been sitting around waiting for him to text me? Crap.

He frowned. "Fuck. You probably wanted flowers."

"I was in the hospital overnight."

"I had my own shit to deal with." He swung me around so I faced him. He looked like I'd verbally slapped him. "Shit, I'm sorry. That was harsh."

I stared at him. "I'm the villain," I said. "Do you know what it's been like around the house? Seth is the only one who understands, and everyone glares at me whenever I talk to him. Like I'm corrupting him or something."

"Maybe if you didn't try to scare the shit out of everyone they would work up a little sympathy for you. You're scary when you want to be, Morgan. You can lie to me if you want, but you can't lie to yourself. You've been bitchier than normal, especially to Alexis."

"What do you care?" My breath caught. "I forgot who I was talking to. You *would* take her side. You're a fool, Dak."

"She's your little. You could take pity and show some sympathy."

I couldn't believe what I was hearing. "Be as sympathetic as you want. You're not going to win her back." I took a deep breath. "Grow a pair. You were being two-timed."

He just stared at me until the silence was painful.

"Seems like we could have come to each other's aid. Two villains are stronger than one. At least we'd have each other to talk to." I laughed, but it was at myself. My love for Zach may have died, but the embarrassment lingered.

Dakota stared at me like he was trying to determine whether he could trust me. I liked that he didn't offer me platitudes. "You think we should stick together?" He sounded almost amazed.

I shrugged. "As two wounded parties, why not?"

He was quiet a moment. The light changed and the traffic streamed by.

He held my gaze. "It's nine o'clock on a Friday night. Do you really want to go home?"

"What makes you think I'm going home?" I looked him in the eye.

He grinned. "Can it, Morgan. What kind of a fool do you think I am? You can't afford to be caught drinking. Which means partying is out. At least until this damn class is over tomorrow. And unless I miss my guess, you're on social probation."

If he expected me to blink, he was crazy. "Very perceptive."

"You're not denying it." He held my gaze.

"Why should I?"

He shook his head. "I'm not under the oath of ADIS right now. I could spread the rumor around."

"You're an ass." I tried to step around him.

"But I won't."

I stopped short.

"But. If you head back to the house now, the infamous party girl Morgan will give herself away. The way I see it, you'll either have to feign a headache or illness and hide out in your room. Or go to the movies by yourself and pretend you've been out on the party scene." He paused. "I'll save you the trouble. I'm taking you to the movies."

My mouth fell open. He took my arm, looked both ways, and dragged me across the street against a Do Not Walk sign.

"Living on the edge?" I said. "Won't a jaywalking conviction be three strikes?"

"Dream on." He grinned, and my heart did an unexpected, odd little flip. "I haven't been convicted of anything yet."

The movie theater was two blocks away down Main Street. We walked there in silence. At the box office, Dakota picked an action-adventure comic book flick and insisted on paying. Inside the lobby, he bought a huge-sized popcorn, two huge cups of pop, and a box of Nerds.

The theater was nearly full, but we found two seats in the back. As we made our way up the aisle, I spotted Brenda with a couple of her friends. She gave me the death glare.

Crap! I was already in her crosshairs. She had the completely wrong idea, I could tell. But that didn't matter. I couldn't explain. I wouldn't. Now it would be all over the sorority that I'd been out with Dakota.

For his part, Dakota ignored her. He made his way to the far center of the row and lifted the armrest separating two seats. When we'd settled in, he rested the popcorn on his leg and mine between us.

The previews had already started. Neither of us spoke. Our hands brushed as we reached for popcorn at the same time. I felt almost like I was on a junior high date. Everything was so innocent. But I was nervous and out of my element. Like, what were we?

Frenemies. That was all I could think. But every time our hands accidentally brushed, I felt a spark. And almost shy, like he thought I was doing it on purpose.

At one point, I half expected him to put his arm around me and try to cop a feel of my breast. But he kept his hands, arms, and all appendages to himself. And stupidly, I was disappointed.

When the movie was over and the credits started to roll, Dak popped right up. I stayed in my seat. I wanted to give Brenda and company a chance to exit before we did. The last thing I needed was a run-in with her.

Dak looked at me quizzically. "Coming? The movie's over."

"No, it's not." I stared straight ahead at the screen. "It has a stinger. You know, one of those little surprise scenes at the end of the credits? Victoria saw this movie last week. She said the stinger's awesome."

"Oh. You're one of *those*." He sighed like he was resigned, and sat down. "Irreconcilable differences."

"You're not?" I actually turned to look at him. "Stingers can make the whole movie. Either they set up a sequel or they highlight the whole point of the film. Worst case, they just give you a laugh."

"Or they irritate the cleaning crew."

"Shut up! Stinger haters miss the point. We paid to see the movie. The whole movie. Don't sell us short. You should be looking for the fun surprises in life, waiting patiently for them. Not cheating yourself out of them."

The theater was nearly empty. Brenda gave up and left, shooting me a glare over her shoulder before she disappeared from sight. Only the half-dozen hardcore stinger lovers remained. And the cleaning crew was already sweeping up popcorn.

"But—"

"Shhh! Here it is."

He shut up and watched it with me. When it was over, those of us who were left clapped.

I turned to Dak.

His eyes were wide. "Awesome!"

"See!" I said. "Made the movie." Then I nearly did something stupid and reached for his hand. I stopped myself just in time. "Can't wait for the sequel now, can you?"

We spilled out of the theater, laughing and picking apart the weak plot points of the movie.

"You're a harsh critic, Morgs," Dakota said with admiration in his voice.

"Not harsh. Just discerning. Despite its flaws, I enjoyed it. The storytelling swept me away."

"Me too." He stuffed his hands in his pockets as we walked up the street toward campus.

There was no way I could grab it without thinking. He saved me from stupidity. But I was almost insulted by the clear message that he didn't want to touch me.

We took a different route back from the theater than we would have from the counseling center. No rape alley for us.

I didn't know what compelled me, but I had to ask: "Is your heart very broken, Dak?"

He stopped and stared at me, frowning slightly, like he was puzzled.

I didn't understand his confusion. I prompted him. "Alexis sleeping with your best friend?"

His face was dark and unreadable. "Yeah, it was a stab in the back. But then, he saved you. So I guess we're even."

My heart pounded out of control. Saved me? Like that mattered to Dak, other than he wasn't going to jail

for vehicular homicide. I felt myself blushing in the
dark. "That's an evasive answer."

"He and I are still tight. He asked the prosecutor for
leniency on my behalf. We've forgiven each other."

I didn't understand it. Nobody did. But he didn't
elaborate. I started walking again.

I caught him off guard. It took him a few steps to
catch up with me. "Alexis and Zach belong together."
His voice was soft and understanding, like he was trying to avoid a landmine that was me and my tender
feelings for Zach. "I'm over it." There was a long beat
of silence. "You?"

"I'm over him. I kind of have to be." I took a deep
breath and blew a white cloud of it out. "Being with
Zach was always just a fantasy, anyway."

We both let it drop. He walked me all the way to the
end of the walkway in front of my house. For an insane
moment, I wanted to kiss him, and he looked like he
wanted to kiss me.

His hands were still jammed in his pockets. "I'll be
by to pick you up at seven thirty tomorrow morning. Be
waiting for me."

On impulse, I leaned over and kissed him on the
cheek. His cheek was cold, and bristly with stubble. He
smelled like that damn cologne he always wore. I had a
flash of having sex with him and steeled myself against
the inevitable lust attack. I didn't want Dakota. I
couldn't afford to care about him. He wasn't my type.
Why did scent have to bring back memories like it did?

Without waiting for his reaction, I turned and ran
up the walk. At the door, I finally looked back at him.

He was exactly where I'd left him, waiting to make sure I was safely inside. How sweet. And I don't mean that cynically.

I called out to him and gave him a safe-arrival wave.

His face was in shadow. It was hard to tell, but I imagined he smiled. He did, in fact, nod before he turned and walked away.

A ridiculous smile popped up on my lips. I was grinning like the first time a guy had given me a secret Valentine. I was still smiling when I let myself in and nearly ran into Alexis.

I skidded to a stop, and she stepped out of the way just in time to avoid an embarrassing collision.

I knew from the look on her face she'd seen me with Dakota. What did she want from me? She couldn't have *both* Dakota and Zach.

I caught her off guard by smiling sweetly. "I've been a bad big. We should do coffee. Get to know each other better. Sunday morning. The College Grind. I'm buying."

CHAPTER FIVE

Dakota

When I got back to the frat, it smelled like Friday night, or maybe I should say early Saturday morning— of smoke and beer, sweat and perfume. The floors were sticky. Guys were passed out on the sofas. The pounding sounds of sex emanated from rooms along the hall as I made my way to the presidential suite and turned a blind eye to any infractions or underage drinking.

In my room, I felt guilty as hell as I pulled out my phone and called Jordan. "Hey, babe," I said when she picked up.

"Hey to you, too. You're back late from your class." Her voice held the edge of a frown.

"Yeah. Some of us went to a movie after." The truth. And a lie.

"What did you see? Was it any good?" Her voice softened.

"Ah, an action flick. It was okay." The company was better. The stinger was killer.

"And class?"

I could either lie by omission or come clean. "Boring. Surprising." I paused for a beat. "Morgan was in it."

"What?" She spoke the word harshly, coloring it with jealousy and anger. She inhaled like she was trying to get control. We'd had too many fights over Morgan in the past. "Awkward."

She had no idea. "Yeah." I had to defuse the situation and put Jordan at ease before the powder keg we were walking on exploded. I doused my voice with sarcasm. "She hasn't changed. She's still the same sweet girl."

I paused again. "She had the nerve to threaten me, saying she was going to see if she could get on the victims' panel I have to sit in on. She's determined to make my life hell."

Jordan gasped. "No? The witch!"

I winced, thinking of Morgan's warm, gentle lips brushing my cheek. "Yeah. Nice, huh?"

"She'll be there tomorrow? Can you avoid her?" Jordan's tone was so sympathetic, she was practically cooing, *Poor baby, baby* to me.

I felt like a jerk. I shrugged, even though we weren't on Facetime or Skyping and she couldn't see me. Which was intentional on my part. "I'll damn well try.

But it's a small class. And we have share time, you know, to get our demons out."

"No! That's awful," she said. "What did you share?"

"As little as possible. That's my plan going forward." I changed the subject. "I talked to Zach. He said you visited him."

She paused for so long, I wondered what I'd done wrong. Jordan and I had known each other long enough to sense each other's moods.

"Yeah," she said at last.

"How is he? Really. He says he's doing better—"

"He is!" Too exuberant. Like she was covering for something. "He looks almost like his old self."

I had to tease her. We'd all gone to high school together. Zach had been Mr. Popular. All the girls drooled over him. "Does that mean he's not as hot as he used to be?"

She laughed, but it sounded nervous and forced. "Dream on! He's hotter. Girls love a guy they can nurse."

"Shit." I laughed, too. "Guess I'll always be number two."

"Not with me, Dak." She sounded fierce again. "Never with me. You're always number one. *Way* hotter than he is."

It was like she was over stroking my male ego. Yeah, I knew girls sometimes thought us guys were fragile, but seriously? Something was off. Maybe my own guilty conscience was simply projecting. Maybe she was picking up the awkward vibes between us. Neither of us seemed to be into it tonight. Maybe we were both just tired.

"IloveyouDakota." She spoke quickly, slurring the words together.

It took me a sec to understand what she'd said. I knew the expected response. But I hesitated an instant too long, nearly tripping over the words. "Love you too."

She picked up on my reticence. "Is something wrong?"

Everything, I thought, pissed at myself for letting Morgan insinuate herself into my heart. I'd tossed Jordan aside for her once. My mistake. I wouldn't make it again. "No, just tired." My determination showed through as fierceness.

"Yeah." She let out a sigh. "Me too." Another awkward pause. "Call me after class tomorrow."

"Absolutely."

***

I was up and out of the house the next morning before any of the girls sleeping over left blurry-eyed for home in their shacker shirts. The place was trashed and littered with empties. Chips and popcorn crunched beneath my feet. The house smelled like the morning after. The pledges were going to have a fun time cleaning up today.

I left early enough to stop by The College Grind for a coffee to go. Even though the last thing I needed was caffeine. I was jittery enough and wide awake with the thought of seeing Morgan. Shit. On impulse, I grabbed a mocha for Morgan, too. Made just the way she liked it. Like ADIS was a date and I was trying to impress her.

It was cloudy and cold. A few flakes of snow were flying as I walked up Greek Row to the Delta Delta Psi house. Morgan was waiting for me on the steps of her house, dressed in skinny jeans and boots, and just a hint of makeup where yesterday she'd worn none. Not enough to look overdone. But enough to make me wonder if she'd fixed up for me. My heart skipped a beat at the thought. It was a damn traitor.

Her hair was curled and fell loose around her shoulders. She looked like the gorgeous freshman that had first stolen my heart. She spotted me and waved. As she bounced down the steps and came down the walkway toward me, I felt like that naïve guy just out of high school.

As she reached me, the breeze blew a strand of hair in her face where it stuck in her pale pink lip-gloss. She frowned as she pulled it free. "Stupid wind."

All I could think about was kissing her. Yeah, that was stupid shit. I handed her a cup of coffee. "The wind has a bite this morning."

She gave me a wondering look. "For me?"

"No, I'm handing you my second cup to carry for me. I don't want to look like a two-fisted coffee drinker. That's just sad." I shook my head.

"I deserved that." She sighed. "Crap, it's early. I could barely get moving this morning, and I went to bed early."

Our eyes met.

"You're not trying to sober me up? Just in case I've been secretly drinking in my room?" She sounded half serious.

"Shit, Morgs." I started walking. "Even you aren't that stupid."

"Even me?"

I grinned and kept walking. "That's what I said."

She came to a dead stop. "You think I'm a drunk?"

I stopped and stared at her. "I think you drink too fucking much." I hesitated. "There's having fun and there's being stupid. You drink for the wrong reasons."

Her eyes narrowed. "Shut up. Look who's talking."

"You asked," I said, holding her gaze. "All I'm saying is you don't need a buzz to be fun to hang with."

For a second I thought she was going to thrust the coffee back at me. Or throw it in my face. But the last part of what I said had stopped her short.

She looked at me like she was trying to see if I was playing her. I wasn't.

She stuck out her free arm and held out her hand. "See any trembling?"

Her hand was steady. On impulse, I grabbed it and stroked her palm with my thumb. Her eyes went wide, like I'd startled her.

"No tremors. Very good, Morgs. Feel nauseous? Anxious? Are you sweating?" I grinned at her, but I was half serious, too.

She pulled her hand free from mine, clasped it with the other one around her warm cup, and laughed. "Can it, smartass. So you paid attention in class. Stop showing off. This isn't ADIS. Save it for the day ahead. I'm not talking about it anymore." She started walking again. "We'll miss the bus."

I got in step with her.

She took a sip of her mocha and sighed happily. "Perfect! Just the way I like it." She glanced at me again. "Skinny?"

I nodded. "Of course. No whip, too. Not that *I* think you're fat. A shot of hazelnut, sugar free."

Her glance turned into a stare. "How did you know what I like?"

"I remembered." Maybe she'd forgotten, but I'd taken her for coffee in those heady early days of our freshman year.

Her face softened. She looked touched that I remembered. And puzzled by me. Like she expected me to be a jerk.

I turned straight ahead to avoid giving myself away. "Shit. There comes the bus. We'd better run or we'll miss it." I grabbed her hand and pulled her with me.

Morgan

I didn't tell Dakota, but I *was* a little nauseous. And super tired, like dead tired. It was early, but still. Was I worried? Maybe, but not about being an alcoholic. More about coming down with mono. That was the last thing I needed. As if I had time to slow down.

I'd woken with a headache. I hoped it was a caffeine headache. Even though the coffee didn't taste as good as usual, and made me a bit gaggy, I drank the whole cup.

A lot of things made me gag now. Some of them made perfect sense. Like I couldn't stand the sight or smell of orange juice after drinking too many screwdrivers the night Dak nearly ran over me. Though the smell of vodka, such as it was, was fine. Other things that smelled off made no sense at all.

By the time we got in our circle to discuss where we each were on the road to alcohol dependence, the headache had faded. So maybe it wasn't mono. Maybe I was just a hypochondriac.

We went around the circle, each talking about whether we were alcohol dependent or not. Whether we had any, or all, of the four symptoms—craving, tolerance, impaired control, and dependence.

Larry listened and asked questions. "Mr. Bradley, your turn."

Dak shrugged. "I'm not alcohol dependent. I drink to have fun. I can shut it off."

"That's why you ended up running over your best friend?" Larry's tone was gentle and probing, not judgmental.

Dak actually grinned. "I didn't say I had good judgment when I was drunk."

That got a few laughs. I had to stifle one myself. I admired his guts.

"I'm here to teach you to make good decisions."

And decide whether we need further rehabilitation, I thought.

Larry was studying Dakota. "Let's talk about the night you got your MIP. Why didn't you shut it off that night?"

"Morgan told you last night. Our houses were partying after winning the powder puff football game."

"Do you usually drink and drive after a party?" Larry said.

Dak let out a sigh, like what kind of a dumbass question was that? "Shit. No. I'm always totally responsible."

"Mr. Bradley, may I remind you I hold the power over whether you pass this course."

Dak rolled his eyes. "There were extenuating circumstances, okay? Seriously, I don't usually drink and drive. That night I just had to get away from the frat." His Adam's apple bobbed. He shot a quick glance at me. "When I started drinking earlier, it was cool. Everything was fine. I drank just enough to have fun.

"Then one of the Double Deltsie pledges drank too much." Dak glanced at me. "Morgan asked me to help her take the pledge home. So I did." His eyes grew hard. "When we took her to her room at the sorority, I caught Zach in bed with my girl. I raced out of there before I did something really stupid. Morgan followed me.

"We ended up at the frat together. Morgan was consoling me. That's when the drinking crossed the line. I got hammered and so did Morgan.

"News got around. Morgan left. The guys were ribbing me. I had to escape. I didn't think. Just grabbed my keys and a few buddies and headed out. It was a crime of passion, so to speak.

"I didn't see Morgan behind the car. You'd understand how I missed seeing her if you saw where and how I was parked. A sober person could have missed her.

"Zach was walking by, saw her, and jumped to her rescue. That's Zach all over. Always the hero." He sounded sarcastic and unhappy about Zach the hero. "I pulled out and backed over him. Not on purpose. I couldn't tell it was him." Dak's voice was soft, like it pained him to talk about it. He took a deep breath. "That's it. That's what happened. It wasn't your usual set of circumstances."

He took another deep breath. "I was furious. Zach always got the girl I wanted." He glanced at me. "I was fucking tired of coming in second."

It was so quick, I nearly missed it. But I was sure he had given me a look. My heart pounded like crazy. He was talking about Alexis. And *me*.

"It's not like it's going to happen again." He shook his head and laughed. "I *hope*." He somehow managed to grin.

But it wasn't funny.

"Dakota's right."

The class turned their attention from Dakota to me. I didn't know what made me speak up. It was like I wanted to protect him.

"It happened just like Dakota said. Neither of us had crossed the line until we walked in on Zach and Alexis." I swallowed hard. "It won't happen again. Zach is never going to leave Alexis."

Dakota reached over, clasped my hand, and squeezed it. I squeezed back, surprisingly touched. My hand felt good in his. I felt—stupidly, maybe—protected and comforted.

"You drink to numb pain?" Larry said.

If I had liked Larry at first, I hated him now. I wanted to scream at him to leave Dakota alone. I squeezed Dakota's hand tighter.

"No," Dakota said. "I drank to show I didn't care."

CHAPTER SIX

Morgan

Dak and I walked down the street to a local café for lunch, talking about nothing, really. The air had gotten colder. It looked and smelled like snow, which would make walking up the hill to campus treacherous. I had this insane desire to grab Dakota's hand and walk hand in hand down the street with him. Crazy. We were, like, frenemies at best.

Inside the café, we found a table and ordered. We were munching sandwiches before I finally found the courage to thank him for his chivalry. "You made me sound almost angelic in ADIS this morning. Thanks for not sharing my not-so-secret crush-on-Zach crap with the class."

He looked at me over his sandwich and shrugged.

"No, seriously." I bit my lip and screwed up my courage. "You're not second to Zach." I didn't know why it was so important for me to tell him that.

He froze with the sandwich halfway to his mouth, and arched one eyebrow. "Am I supposed to be grateful for that?"

I laughed. "Yeah!"

He shook his head. "Me, second to Zach, who's a houseboy? I'm president of the Tau Psi fraternity *and* Mr. University."

"Former houseboy. And you're full of yourself. Quit bragging." I grinned. "That Mr. University competition was rigged."

"Was not."

I ignored his protests. "Girls love bad boys. And badass jailbirds." I rolled my eyes. "You won their votes with a sympathy ploy. Poor baby, spent the night in jail."

He shook his head, rolled up his sleeve, and made a muscle. Crap, he had a nice bicep.

He pointed to it. "You gonna discount this gun?"

He'd caught me drooling. I laughed. "Stop showing off. There were some other fine guns in the competition."

"Yeah?" He held my gaze. "I didn't see you in the crowd checking them out."

"Oh," I said, playing coy and flirting just to pull his chain. "Were you looking for me?"

"No. Should I have been?"

I shrugged, hating the way my insides were turning to jelly. Over Dakota. "Maybe you just missed me."

"You're not the invisible kind, Morgan." His voice was low and sensual.

I swallowed hard. Who was this new Dakota? And why was he making my pulse race?

He was flirting back just to toy with me, no doubt. Or get laid. Once a hookup, always a hookup?

That was what my favorite sorority advice columns on the internet said. Run! Avoid them like the plague. And any other clichés you can think of to throw out there. Now that I was this new, un-party girl who was looking for an actual relationship, an attainable, achievable relationship with a decent guy, I had to be more selective. And platonic. Give the milk away for free...

I could cliché all day.

Getting involved with Dak would be totally airhead stupid. And just lead to more hookups, not a relationship.

When my traitorous pulse refused to slow, and I couldn't get the image of Dak's naked bicep out of my head, I changed the subject with a definite mood killer. "Larry is going to make us write an action plan this afternoon." I rolled my eyes.

"Yeah. What are you going to put in yours?" He was studying me in that penetrating way, like he could hang on my every word. The bastard. He was also subtly flexing that bicep.

I had to be imagining this flirting. Then again, the sex between us had been hot. "Not to lie down in strange alleys?"

"That one should be easy to keep," he said. "What were you thinking?"

I stared at him like he'd just asked the dumbest question ever. "You really think I was thinking?"

He half grinned. "I was giving you some credit." He paused. "Shit, Morgan. What's up with you this year?"

I played innocent. "What do you mean?"

He stared at me so intently, I caved under the weight of it and looked away like a coward.

"Being such a bitch about Zach," he said. "I have to give you credit. You've upped your game. I didn't think that was possible."

Alexis had clearly poisoned Dak's mind.

"Funny you're taking his side." I tried to play it cool. "Given the crap between you. And the way he stole your girl." Maybe that was meant to wound Dak. And maybe not. I was genuinely puzzled that he was so understanding.

"No one understands the shit between Zach and me. Least of all me." He shrugged. "I've given up. It's pointless to try. He's a complicated dude, totally beyond comprehension." There was that grin again.

I frowned. Was he insulting me? "What's that look supposed to mean? That I can't handle a complicated guy?"

"Hey!" He held his hands up, like *don't blame me.* "I didn't say anything. But, since you mentioned it, go for a simple guy, Morgs. They're much less trouble."

I made narrow eyes at him. "If Zach hadn't been leading me on since freshman year—"

"Leading you on?" He let out a hiss of disbelief, like I was a huge fool.

"Yeah." I glared at him. "He was totally into me when we first met."

"And you think he never got over you?" I could tell he was trying to keep a straight face, but he was failing. That damn grin kept threatening to pop up.

"He just strung me along."

Dakota looked like he was trying to keep his jaw from dropping. "Killed you with kindness?"

"What?" I wanted to slap that smug look off Dakota's face.

"I hate to be the one to tell you this—he was never into you."

I simply stared back at him, cursing him for the cruel bastard he was. I lifted my chin. "How would you know? You two weren't talking."

He snorted, shook his head, and leaned in close. "I'm a guy. We're not that complicated. Did he ever try to get in your pants?"

I glared at him, refusing to answer.

Dak shrugged. "I get it. He didn't. I was right. The truth hurts, doesn't it, babe?"

I balled my hands to keep from doing something stupid, like throwing my water in his face. "Shut up, Dakota Bradley."

"Hey, I call them like I see them. Right now, I'm the best friend you have. I'm the only one giving you the straight shit. Not the crap you want to hear. Don't like the truth? That's your tough luck." He lowered his voice. "Look. Zach's a red-blooded guy. If he'd wanted you, *nothing* would have stopped him. Certainly not some fucking job. Hey, he had the same opportunity to use me as a front back then, as he did with Alexis." Dakota's gaze was absolutely soul piercing and convicting. "He chose not to."

I'm as bad as Alexis, I thought. *In Dakota's eyes, for sure.* I had used him to get close to Zach. So maybe I deserved to be cut down a little. And maybe my little and I had more in common than I wanted to admit.

"That was freshman year silliness," I said, lamely defending myself. "We were all young and naïve."

Dakota was still staring at me like he expected an apology. Two years later?

His expression didn't waver.

"Crap. I'm sorry." I made flirty, pouty lips at him. I didn't know what it was about him that suddenly brought out my responsible side and wanted to please him.

"About what?" Suddenly, he was Mr. Nonchalant.

Call it vanity. Or call it social probation craziness. I wanted him to still care for me. "Do you want me to spell it out?" I arched an eyebrow and let out an exasperated sigh. "Fine. I'm sorry I played you freshman year to get close to Zach. I was a heartless little bitch who didn't know what a great guy she was throwing away. If I had known then what I know now, I never—"

"I get it. Nothing like a heartfelt apology to soothe my wounded vanity." He grinned again, and my heart did that odd little flip. "Once more with feeling?"

"Don't push your luck." I shook my head. "What would I do without you and your brutal honesty?"

"Hard to say. But you should have asked me for it sooner." He looked dead serious. "And saved yourself a fucking lot of heartache."

"I'm over Zach now." I blurted it out without thinking.

Dakota's eyes narrowed, like he didn't believe me.

My phone buzzed. I pulled it out of my purse, glanced at the text that popped up, and shoved the phone back in without replying.

"Mad at your phone?" He made it sound like a joke.

"It was just my dad." I rolled my eyes again. "Reminding me about the baby shower for my stepmom the day after Thanksgiving."

"Baby shower? You're going to be a big sis— congrats!" He gave me a sympathetic look.

I closed my eyes and took a deep breath, like *heaven help me*. "My little sister is due Christmas Eve. Isn't that sweet? Santa's leaving Daddy a baby in his stocking!"

"You won't be the baby anymore." Dakota sounded jokey. "That should make you happy."

I frowned at him and shuddered. "Yeah. Maybe it would have, like, sixteen years ago. But now? Dad's sixty-three and acting gaga, like a first-time dad. It's disgusting."

"You're sounding dangerously like you've described your older sisters. Are you going to call this baby your niece like they call you?"

I just glared at him.

"The older sibs must be petrified. They're about to have a grand-niece!" He stopped short. "Come on,

Morgan. You can see the irony in the situation?" He paused. "Oh, I get it. You *liked* being daddy's little princess."

"Shut up." I stared at him. "I haven't been Dad's little princess since he married my babysitter." I paused. "That sounded wrong. Like I'm a spoiled child or something." I forced a smile. "Since he screwed my *former* babysitter behind Mom's back right after I left for college." I took a deep breath. "Waiting to get divorced until the baby leaves for college is such a stereotype! Who knew I was the glue holding their marriage together. It's like my whole childhood was a lie."

"Look on the bright side—this could be a bonding opportunity with your older sisters. You finally have something in common with them," he said.

"Yeah, but they're not on my dad's blacklist right now like I am." I hadn't meant to tell Dakota my problems. "He's furious about my MIP. 'I don't have time for your crap, Morgan. You're an adult now. Act like one.'" I mimicked Dad.

"'I'm going to retire next year. I'll have a new baby to support soon. I'm too old and tired to handle your screw-ups. One baby in the family is enough.'" I snorted. "'If you even think about drinking or violating the terms of our agreement with the prosecutor, I will pull your college funds and drag you home to learn to be a good role model for the baby.'"

Dakota stared at me. "Serious?"

"Deathly." I sighed. I hadn't told anyone else.

"You do a pretty good dad voice." He paused. "You sound like mine."

I looked at Dakota, wondering how he could be so calm. "Your dad's threatening the same thing?"

"Yeah. Without the baby part." He smiled. "Says he'll drag my ass home if I don't stay out of trouble. He has a reputation to maintain. And I'm his son who's destined for politics." He smiled like he didn't care. "In our family, it's kind of like dedicating a son to the church. Second son is of no consequence unless he can prove himself in the arena of politics."

"That's crap." I bit my lip. "But I can see you as a politician."

His laugh was bitter. "That makes one of us."

"You'd be good at it."

He looked skeptical.

"My dad's coming to Dad's Weekend to check up on me," I said.

"Mine too."

"More things in common. We're on a roll. We should start a commiseration support group!" I winked at Dak.

His answering laugh was genuine, and he got a devilish look in his eye. "Yeah. Why not?"

"My grandma's coming, too," I added. "If she's well enough."

"How is your grandma? She must be doing better."

I frowned. "How do you know about my grandma?" I remembered too late. Me, sobbing in his arms. Blabbering to him about all my problems, crying over Zach.

He cleared his throat. "You told me about her heart. She's better, then?"

A wave of nausea crashed over me. The potato chips I'd eaten rolled over in my stomach. I pushed back from the table.

Dak frowned. "Morgan? You okay? You look green."

I took a deep breath and the moment passed. I looked up at him. His face was etched with genuine concern, or at least a well-faked version of it.

"She's fine," I said, cursing myself. I wasn't even drunk and I was spilling my private biz to him. "Out of the hospital and on the mend." For now.

He pushed a glass of water my way. "Take a drink. You'll feel better."

I wasn't thirsty. Even water looked suspect, like my stomach couldn't take it. I took a sip anyway, just so I wouldn't look like a bitch. The water sat in my stomach, but at least it didn't come back up.

He reached across the table and grabbed my hand. His was too warm, too nice, too comforting. "You have a lot of shit on your plate right now." He held my gaze. "That action plan—you and me need to stick together. Or we'll both do something stupid. Like end up in jail with our college and political careers in the toilet. From now on, you and me are on the buddy system."

I shook my head. "I'm on social probation. You really want to hang with me?"

He shrugged. "Like I'm going to be so much fun! Guys who don't drink are only popular as designated drivers. I'm not even fit for that. I can't get my license back until January. Guess I'm SOL."

I laughed. "That makes two of us. January? Your birthday?"

He nodded. "The eighteenth."

"Wow. Coincidence after coincidence," I said. "Our birthdays are back to back. Mine's the seventeenth!"

"Shit, I'm hanging out with an old lady." He winked. "You get your license back in January, too?"

"Yeah, and no more chance of an MIP/MIC. I'm going to have the best twenty-first birthday run in history."

He nodded like he fully understood. His eyes danced. "Enjoy your moment of fame. The next day, *I'm* making twenty-first birthday history." He glanced at his watch. "Time to get back to class."

***

The afternoon session was mostly about making our action plan. It seemed pretty straightforward to me—avoid alcohol, parties, people who drink, enablers, and stress. Basically, drop out of college and join a monastery. Wait a minute—don't monks drink wine? Monasteries were out, too. What did that leave? Get thee to a nunnery? Well, anyway, it sucked.

We rounded up our chairs into the infamous circle we had all grown to love. Right. Larry prompted us to share. Like I wanted to after last night's fabulous sharing and airing of my relationship with Dakota. Most of the plans were suck-up plans right out of the textbook. As if the makers of them had *any* intention of following them. The key was not to get caught. Dakota sat next to me. His turn to share popped up before mine.

He cleared his throat, like he was about to make an important speech. Politician in training. "I've watched a lot of TV shows, like *Elementary* and *Nashville*—"

Dakota watched *Nashville*? He had to be just pandering. He wasn't a country music or soap opera kind of guy.

"—where one of the main characters has to kick an addiction. They all have one thing in common. They rely on a good buddy to keep them straight. Someone they can call in the middle of the night. Someone who will jump out of bed and meet them at an all-night coffee shop and stop them from taking that drink or shooting that heroin at any cost."

Very dramatic.

He turned and smiled at me with his killer, heart-melting baby-blue eyes. Like I was about to be one of his conquests. Before I could react, he slid off his chair onto one knee and grabbed my hand as if he was about to propose. Something sinister. Even so, my heart beat way too fast.

"Morgan Peterson, will you do me the great honor of being my sobriety buddy?"

Larry nearly came out of his chair. "Mr. Bradley, stop making a mockery of this class and take your seat!"

The rest of the group sniggered as Dakota ignored him.

Dakota held up a finger. "Give me a minute. I'm serious here." For once, he actually sounded like it. "In return, I'll be your sobriety buddy, in sickness and in health, through problems big and small, and in moments of desperate need. Until we turn twenty-one or our sentences have been served. Whichever comes first."

The class actually went silent. The guys near me were literally perched on the edge of their seats, waiting for my answer.

"Does this proposal come with a ring?" I tried to look very serious and not laugh. Or give away my suddenly trembling hands.

"I thought my proposal had a nice ring to it. Isn't that enough?" Dak was still holding my hand.

I felt warm and flushed. And *happy*.

"Oh, come on! You can't turn the guy down in front of the whole class," the guy on the other side of me said.

"No fair!" someone else yelled as the class got into the spirit of it. "There aren't enough girls to go around."

Larry was lividly silent. But he had enough good sense to stand down and stand back to see what happened.

"'To the quick go the spoils." Dakota squeezed my hand. "Well? What do you say?"

I took a deep breath and quoted a line from *The Tempest* that I'd been studying in English Lit. "Misery acquaints a man with strange bedfellows."

I met a sea of puzzled looks.

"Shakespeare?"

Blank stares.

I rolled my eyes. "Do I have to spell it out? Yes! I say yes." There was no way I could have said no.

The class erupted in cheers.

Larry smiled. His eyes twinkled, like he was amused and pleased. With himself. Damn, the man was a good actor, like quicksilver with his moods. "Well played, Mr. Bradley. Miss Peterson, care to share your plan?"

Dak dropped my hand and slid back into his seat. My hand tingled, missing him already.

I pointed to him. "I'm on the abstaining, non-party, sobriety buddy, have-no-social-life, die-of-boredom plan. With him."

"Am I supposed to be flattered?" Dak's eyes sparkled.

"Hey, I wouldn't want to be bored and a social pariah with anybody else." I smiled sweetly at him.

He laughed. "I'll take it."

"All I can say is with all the parties I'll be missing, my grades had better improve." I laughed with him.

CHAPTER SEVEN

Dakota

After class, the weather had turned even colder, teetering between rain and snow. Some of the guys wanted to get together. Like we were suddenly buds. A couple of them were pretty cool. But what would we do? Go out for a beer? My fake ID was pretty much grounded along with my real one. We decided on pizza. I invited Morgan along. To my surprise, she accepted. But what the hell was she going to do on her own on a Saturday night, anyway? If only my damn racing pulse would get a clue she was hanging with us out of desperation and boredom and nothing more.

As Morgan sat next to me, her perfume wafted over to me. It smelled like sex. And made me horny as hell. I couldn't shake my awareness of her even as she ignored me and flirted with the other guys.

Any of them would love to have bedded her. Irrationally, that made me mad and protective.

At one point, one guy got slid his arm around her shoulder. Shit, I knew that move. Next he'd try the accidental breast brush. Or put his hand on her knee.

He leaned in to bend her ear. "Hey, babe, want to ditch this crowd and see a movie with me?"

Yeah, the way he caressed the word "movie," sex was the first thing on his mind. A movie was just a prelude.

I wasn't Morgan's abstinence buddy, but I jumped in without thinking, putting humor in my voice to cover my anger. "Lay off her and get your own sobriety buddy."

"Shit, man!" He laughed, but his eyes were hard. "You think you own her now?"

I balled my fist, almost aching for a fight.

Morgan flashed me a look, warning me to butt out. Her eyes were snapping. She turned and gave him a megawatt smile. "Thanks, but it's Saturday night and I have sobriety duty with this one." She hitched her thumb at me and rested her hand on my shoulder.

She sounded so sweet and flirtatious, the other guy looked almost placated.

"Another time?"

Damn, he wouldn't quit.

"Maybe." Morgan laughed in a way that left room for hope. She could string a guy along indefinitely. I should know. She'd practiced on me. It was easy to see how the Double Deltsies got their reputation as man killers. Morgan exemplified their technique.

She slid her hand down and rested it on my knee, squeezing it with the warning for me to cool it. All it did was give me a hard-on. She'd managed to defuse the tension, but not my irrational desire for her.

We settled the bill and the party broke up. I held the door open for Morgan as we left the pizza place. Was I playing gentleman to impress her? Who the hell knows? I didn't want to analyze anything too closely.

A blast of cold air swept in. Two guys stepped passed us.

Morgan looked out, shivered, and pulled up her hood. "It's raining." She stepped out onto the sidewalk and nearly slid on her cute little ass, screaming as she almost went down. "Crap! It's not just raining. It's freezing rain!"

I caught her by the elbow and pulled her into me until she was braced against my chest. There was an awkward moment when time stood still and I stared down into her wide eyes. It might have been my imagination, but I sure as hell thought I saw desire there. Like she wanted me as much as I wanted her. Her lips were moist and glossy and so damn kissable. It wouldn't be hard to kiss them, and kiss them hard.

"The buses won't be running," she said.

The spell was broken.

I let her go. "You're right. We'll have to walk."

She pulled away from me and took another tentative step, laughing as she slipped, and grabbed my arm to hold herself up, almost as if she was flirting with me.

I stared down at her. "Are you trying to take me down with you?"

She shook her head. "Trying to show you how crazy you are. We'll never make it up the hill. It's like an ice rink out here."

"Like hell we won't." I grabbed her hand to pull her forward.

She resisted.

"Come on. Trust me. I'm steady on my feet." I gave her another tug. "Hold on to me and you'll be fine."

I let go of her and took a step out to show her how steady I was. Not a slip in sight.

"See?" I held my arms out. "No hands. No problem." I held my hand out to her. "We'll walk on the grass where we can. It's not frozen over yet. Once we get to the hill, there's a covered breezeway that runs through that big apartment complex. I know my way around there. From there, we can cut through the engineering labs and the science building. Then we'll be on Greek Row."

She studied me. "You have it all figured out already? Done this before?"

I just grinned and wrapped her arm in mine. "Come on."

"What if the labs are locked?" She clutched me like I was a lifeline.

"What if, what if. Would you rather spend the night on the street?" I pulled her gently forward. "One small step for Morgan. One giant step for womankind."

"Shut up!" But she was smiling, and looking at me like a flirt. Giving me ideas I was better off not entertaining.

"I didn't think you were such a wimp, Morgs." I inched us along the sidewalk until Morgan relaxed.

"It's going to take us all night to get home at this pace."

"Not if we run." I took off, running, pulling her with me while she fought to break free, gliding on the ice with her hand tucked in the crook of my arm.

"Dak! No!" She stiffened.

"Relax! I won't let you fall."

"Famous last words!" She tried to pull free.

"I'm not letting you go." I took off again. Run. Slide. Run. Slide.

She squealed. She protested. "Let me go!"

Still holding her hand, I got up to full speed and held her at arm's length. "You sure?" I grinned at her and loosened my grip, daring her to let go.

She could pull away any time she wanted. I released her hand until our fingertips were barely touching.

She grabbed my fingers and pulled close to me. "Bastard!" But she was laughing as we reached the edge of the park between downtown and the big apartment complex up the hill.

I stopped abruptly. She slid into me. I caught her, holding her by both arms. There was a second when our eyes met and we had a real connection.

As I lowered my head to kiss her, she looked away. "It's a maze up there."

"One of my frat brothers lives in the apartments. I know my way through." My heart was pounding. Disaster averted.

I led the way as we cut up the hill, through the apartment breezeway, and came out behind the engineering labs. I held my hand out to her. "We're back on asphalt. It's slick."

She took my hand without hesitation. I walked to the back door, with Morgan clinging to me. "They never lock this door." I pulled it open for her.

A blast of hot air blew out.

"Toasty," Morgan said. The clang of the ancient heaters made her jump. "And scary."

I laughed. "Perfect pre-Halloweekend atmosphere."

"Don't remind me! The only Saturday Halloween of my college career and I'm on social probation." Morgan frowned and made a face. "This place should be condemned."

"Yeah, but it's warm."

"It's a maze," she said.

"Good thing I left breadcrumbs last time I was here." I didn't drop her hand. And she didn't pull it free.

"Lead on, Hansel."

"Whatever you say." I took off running, pulling her with me. We ran hand in hand, laughing as we ran around corners and past bare pipes. Past things that went bump in the night. Past the inner workings of the heat plant that generated the steam for the heated sidewalks around campus. By the time we reached the far side of the building, I was sweating.

I paused at the door, reluctant to let go of the mood. "Fifty feet and the heated sidewalks start. Think they've turned them on?"

"In our dreams." She looked at me with sparkling eyes. "What are you waiting for? You've taken me this far."

I wanted to take her, period.

"Do I detect a note of trust in your voice?"

She smiled. "No, that's hero worship." She linked her arm through mine and clutched my bicep.

Outside, the coating of ice was growing thicker and the heated sidewalks were off, as predicted. But we were up the hill and beneath tree cover as we hit the edge of Greek Row. It was just after eight, on the early side, but parties were gearing up, despite the bad weather. Guys were out, sliding down the roads and showing off.

"The frat's just ahead." I hesitated. "Why don't you come in for a while? Warm up. Wait for the storm to pass."

"This ice isn't going to melt until morning." She paused. "Are you inviting me to spend the night?" Her voice was soft, almost sorry, but it was hard to read her expression in the dark.

I swallowed hard against my desire for her. "We have beer, obviously. And I have an excellent selection of T-shirts at your disposal for a shacker shirt."

"Dak." She bit her lip. "As your sobriety buddy it's my duty to tell you that beer is off limits. Didn't you learn anything from class?"

She looked so damn hot with her pink cheeks and nose.

I leaned in close to her. "So come in and save me from myself."

"Dak." Her cold breath curled skyward on a sigh.

I knew from her tone what she was going to say before she said it. I waited for it anyway, feeling like a fool in the freezing rain.

"I'm your sobriety buddy, not your fuck buddy." She looked away. "I'm not that kind of girl." She laughed softly.

This was news to me. "Since when?"

She bit her lip and gave me a pointed look. "Since you almost ran me over."

"That's cruel."

"That's true," she said. "Take heart—you were my last hookup." She smiled again. "It's time to stop screwing around and find a real relationship. Obviously, as my dad says, I need someone steady." She waited a beat. "You can run for the hills now."

I stood my ground. "Why would I run?"

"'Cause that's what hookup partners do." Maybe she was just being coy. If she was, it was working. "Anyway, I don't mean *with you*."

"Thanks for that," I said. "I appreciate the concern."

She laughed again. "You're welcome. FYI, it's never wise to hookup with old hookups."

I sighed and shook my head. "You've been reading that fucking sorority advice website again. What's it called?" I tried to think of the name. "The one with great articles like 'Fifty reasons guys don't need blowjobs' and 'Ten ways girls with flat butts rule.'" I stared at her and tried to cover. "By the way, they're wrong."

"Girls with flat butts don't rule?" She grinned.

"Guys definitely need blowjobs."

"Why Dak, you actually read." The flirt was back in her voice, like she was trying to defuse, too. "Your choice of reading material, though. Are you trying to get in touch with your feminine side?"

"Just a confused guy trying to figure out the opposite sex."

"And?"

"Confused as ever."

She studied me. "The day we figure each other out is the day the mystery of love dies." She shook her head. "If you really have read that article, then you know it's true. Guys don't need a blowjob to get them excited." She held my gaze, but her lips twitched like she was trying not to laugh. "I've never seen a limp dick."

"That's purely anecdotal evidence. I've seen plenty of limp dicks."

She held my gaze. "Prove it. Show me yours right now." She reached for my crotch.

I arched away and grabbed her hand. "Come inside and I'd be happy to. Not out here. It's too cold. I don't want to risk shrinkage and have you get the wrong idea."

"I've seen it all before. I know the size of your package."

"Don't tell me you're not tempted."

She just smiled. "Relationships only work when both parties know and respect the boundaries. We're sobriety buddies, Dak. I'm here for you, in a sobriety sort of way. I gotta go."

"Damn. I was going to show you my new video game." I leered at her for effect.

"I'm sure you were." She turned.

I caught her arm. "I'll walk you home."

Morgan

At the sorority house, Seth and Dillon were spreading sand and de-icer on the front walkway.

Dakota paused where the walkway to the sorority house met the sidewalk that ran along the street.

"I think I can make it by myself from here." I shook my hand free from his as I caught a glimpse of Alexis in the front window. What was she—the house police?

Dakota waved enthusiastically to her. I didn't know why I should have been jealous, but I was. Their relationship was off kilter and odd. After he'd caught her in bed with his best friend, how could they still be friends?

He turned back to me. "Sure? It's slick. I don't mind."

I nodded, suddenly possessive and reluctant to let him go. "Seth and Dillon will rush to my aid if I need them." Well, Seth might. Dillon would love to see me land on my butt. "Thanks."

Before Dakota turned to leave, I kissed him. Lightly. A bare brush of my lips on his that rocked me all the way to my toes with the innocent pleasure of it. I didn't know why I did it. Sudden impulse, I guessed. To protect Dakota and show Alexis that he was over her.

I turned before he could react, or I could see it. I was weak and liable to tumble into his bed again too easily. But I was through with my lusty-hookup phase and my-longing-for-a-guy-I-couldn't-have phase, and on a quest for true love. Yeah, that sounded sappy. But whatever. I slid up the walkway to the house, trying to mask my expression.

Seth looked up from his work, catching me by the elbow as I wobbled near him. His eyes narrowed as he studied me. "A little early to be coming home, isn't it?"

He was teasing, yet he sounded relieved. There was no love lost between him and Dakota. Seth was firmly in Zach's camp and not fond of frat boys in general.

"On the contrary, it's a little slippery to be out." I winked at him, giving him the impression it was dicey being with Dakota. "And getting worse by the minute."

I had to force myself not to turn and watch as Dakota walked away. I stretched out my hand for Seth to help me up the steps. "Have you de-iced these?"

"First thing." He took my hand. "But it's a losing battle. At the risk of sounding like our dads, we've been warning the girls to stay in tonight."

"That's a fool's errand."

"Yeah, you're telling me." Seth held the door open for me.

Inside, the house was warm and toasty and filled with two kinds of girls—those who weren't going to let a little freezing rain ruin their Saturday night, and those who valued their lives. The latter group being the smaller of the two.

Alexis was sitting on the sofa in the living room with her arms crossed, glaring at me like I was public enemy number one. In her mind, I was. Never one to cower, and remembering the admonition to get along with her, I walked over and plunked myself next to her.

"Lovely weather we're having." I made a point of evaluating her outfit. "Yogas and a sweatshirt. You'd better get dressed and join the partying marauding hordes before they've all departed. You don't want to miss all the best parties."

Since Zach had gone home to recover, Alexis had been a regular bore. She never went out. I was poking at a raw wound and I knew it. But sometimes you had to do what you had to do. As her big, it was my duty to make sure she behaved like a proper Double Deltsie. She was only a few months into her freshman year. She needed to get out and live a little while she could. Before she became an upperclassman and the pressures of studies wore her down and took the sheen off her party edge.

She gave me a pointed look. "Look who's talking."

I flashed her the evil smile I was famous for, the one that put fear in the heart of every pledge. Sometimes being the wicked witch of the house was a power trip. "I've been out."

If you're an upperclassman you really should master that stare for your own good. It's never wise to let freshman have the upper hand.

"I noticed," she said. "Stay away from Dakota."

"Are you offering me unfriendly advice?" I laughed. "Take it from me, I won't heed it. It's not in my nature. Not even if it was friendly advice. I'm odd like that. And as for Dakota, you forfeited any claim on him when you slept with Zach behind his back. You can't have them both. I should know." I laughed, unable to hold back my bitterness.

Alexis' eyes snapped. She was supremely peeved. I recognized myself in them. I didn't like what I saw.

"Dakota doesn't forgive girls who use him to get to Zach." I had firsthand experience there, too. I was curious about how he and Alexis could still pal around together. And suspicious. Something wasn't right about it.

"I wasn't using him—" She stopped short. "Dakota and I are still friends."

"Then that's something we have in common," I said. "He and I are friends, too."

She shot me a look oozing with skepticism.

Victoria and Kelly bounded down the focal staircase, laughing and joking. They were dressed in tight jeans and full makeup, obviously on their way somewhere. Vicki spotted us sitting on the sofa. Her face lit up.

"Look at you two—big and little hanging out together. It warms my twin heart!" Vicki clutched her hands in front of her heart for emphasis in a corny gesture designed to make me gag, and flashed us a big smile.

I knew that smile. She was warning me not to botch things. The standards board wasn't going to be appeased until I ate crow and made up with Alexis. If you can make up with someone you've never been close to in the first place.

"Awwww, that's sweet." Kelly, the house president, gave us a thumbs-up. "Are you two staying in?" Her gaze flitted over our outfits. "You should come with us. The Zeta Nus are having a freezing rain party."

Kelly sounded so sweet and innocent. But she had to know I was on social probation. So was she dangling forbidden fruit in front of me on purpose.

My heart pounded, but I smiled sweetly and nodded toward Alexis. "We're staying in. Having a girls' movie night together. A little big/little bonding. I'm going to shower her with popcorn and share my favorite Halloween movie with her, *Van Helsing*."

I felt Alexis stiffen beside me, but I wasn't about to give her an out. She and I were going to bond, damn it. Not like I was terribly thrilled about it, either.

"That's a cornball movie," Kelly said.

"Hey!" I said. "Hugh Jackman looking hot and killing vampires." I gave her a look like, *come on!* "Do I insult your movies?"

Kelly laughed. "Point taken."

Victoria winked at me like she knew what was up. "Well, have fun, then."

"Don't break your necks." I waved cheerily at them.

"Thanks, Mom."

Kelly and Victoria headed for the door. I felt the cold blast of air seconds after they opened it. But it was nothing compared to Alexis' frosty demeanor.

Okay, I was the big. So I had to be the bigger person. There was sound logic in there somewhere. Plus I had the most to lose. "You and I got off on the wrong foot," I said. "How about we start over?"

Alexis' eyes narrowed, full of distrust. But I had her right where I wanted her—trapped into accepting my overtures of big/little bonding. I was going to get out of this social probation mess and get back on track if it killed me. As much as Alexis and I disliked each other, that might very well be the case.

"I'll get the popcorn and the movie. What do you want? Original or kettle corn?"

CHAPTER EIGHT

Morgan
So the movie night was a huge success. I got points for being the bigger person and trying to make up with Alexis, as ordered. Even though the atmosphere between was thick with distrust, about like the relationship between the vampires and the vampire hunters in *Van Helsing*. I was Anna, the heroine. She was Aleera, out for my blood.

A dozen other girls joined us. Drinking wasn't allowed in the house, certainly not in the common areas. So temptation, and suspicion, avoided.

I slept in past ten on Sunday and woke thinking about Halloween and Halloweekend coming up next weekend. How was I going to deal with those? If I came up with a clever enough disguise, then maybe...

And what about Dakota? Why did he keep invading my thoughts? And why did my heart race when I thought about him and a smile threaten to erupt? I knew the deal, just like I'd told him—hookups didn't make good serious boyfriends. But my heart refused to listen. The way my head and heart were playing ping-pong with my emotions and reason, I was beginning to think I was getting a crush on Dakota. Which was crazy, but the signs were certainly all there. He'd never been anything but second to Zach. Logic said I should stay away from him. But my heart wanted what it wanted. I resigned myself to being conflicted.

I took Alexis to coffee, as I'd promised earlier, and spent the early afternoon expecting a text from Dakota. And Facebook stalking him. Nothing. Screw him.

Around two, I was in the middle of reading for English Lit when my phone rang. When I read, I get so absorbed that I close the world out. The phone startled me. I grabbed it and glanced at the screen. Dakota was calling. Not texting, calling. My fingers trembled as I answered.

"Halloweekend," he said.

"Halloweekend to you, too," I said. "But 'hallo' would have done."

His answering laugh sounded richer and deeper than it had before. And made me smile. I was letting myself get in too deep.

"No, this is serious shit," he said. "On Halloweekend, the booze will flow like water. Temptation will abound."

"Abound?" I smiled.

"Thrive. Sobriety buddy, this is our holiday to stick together. Morgan, I need you more than ever."

Did his voice just crack? Or was that laughter? It didn't matter, because my heart had started dancing.

I goaded him. "I didn't know you needed me at all."

"Of course I need you! I need you desperately."

"Only desperately?"

"Tragically."

"That's better. I like tragically. It has a nice ring to it." I couldn't wipe the stupid grin off my face. Involuntary smiling. I was in trouble. "What were we talking about again?"

"Partying. An epic, once-in-a-college-years Saturday Halloweekend that we can't miss."

"No need to miss it. Just stay at the frat and hand candy out to children," I said in my most helpful tone.

"Funny, Morgs! As if parents are going to trust us to provide wholesome treats to their babies."

"You mean non-alcoholic, non-spiked treats," I said.

"Yeah, that too."

"No problem. You'll have a steady stream of sorority girls drop by for trick or treats. You always do. They expect alcoholic goodies. I'm sure you can find one you can trick into showing her treats to you." I sounded pert and teasing. But I was holding back a wave of jealousy at the thought. I had to beat this craziness.

"You'd think," he said. "But they'll all be expecting a drinking party animal. I have a rep, you know. It's not fun being the only sober guy in the house. Nothing's as funny as everyone else thinks it is. And you get tired of holding girls' hair back as they puke."

"Nice. You make a good point."

"Damn right I do. And what kind of a sobriety bud would I be if I left you out of the action, alone, fending for yourself against nearly insurmountable odds?"

"You're laying it on a bit thick," I said.

"I'm making a point. I have as much duty to you as you do to me. Because you're banned from any Greek parties—"

"Not if I go in disguise." It was a relief to be able to be honest with someone.

"Shit, Morgan. That's a bad plan." There was real worry in his voice.

It was sweet, and I liked it. "Why? Everyone will be dressed up. I was thinking of going as a one-night stand." I didn't know why I threw that barb out there. Sometimes my evil nature would not be quashed. Dressing like a nightstand was no big deal.

"Having a lampshade on your head would be appropriate for a convicted MIC like you."

I sighed. "I set myself up for that one. But seriously, I'm going to wear a mask—"

"And disguise your voice? Change your personality?" He sighed. I pictured him shaking his head. "Your standards board will have spies everywhere."

"Victoria is my twin. She'll look the other way."

"And Brenda?"

"How do you know about her?" I asked.

"It's my business to know things," he said. "The girl's hot for my bod."

"Egomaniac," I said. But he was spot-on.

"I can see I'm going to have to save you from your-self. I have a better idea. Much better. Wait for it." He paused a beat while I shook my head. "You and me in matching Halloween costumes. We won't even need masks if we don't want them."

My pulse raced as I got irrationally hopeful about a plan that included me and got me out of the house on Halloweekend and into the party scene. With Dakota. Wearing matching outfits, like a couple. "What's your idea?"

"Party refs," he said.

"Party refs?" I frowned.

"We dress as party refs and crash the Geed parties at the apartments."

"I don't know—"

"It's perfect, Morgan. You and me dressed in referee costumes showing up as a team of party refs, going to all the parties and calling the shots. Literally if we want to."

"Will we have whistles?"

"Whistles. Hats. Whatever you want, babe."

Babe? I let it slide.

"You can't refuse. As your sobriety buddy, I insist on this brilliant plan. The roads are clear. The ice has melted. I'll be over in fifteen to pick you up. We're go-ing costume shopping before all the good stuff is sold out."

"You're picking me up? On what? Your bike? How cute." I shook my head, but I was smiling.

"We're walking."

I cursed beneath my breath.

"I heard that. When did you become such a lazy ass? Walking's good for us. We're going to be in damn fine, hot shape by the end of this probationary period."

"Bring your bus pass," I said.

Dakota

When Morgan came out of the dressing room to model the sexy ref costume, my mouth went dry. Her short shorts were tight. A glittery silver belt was slung over her hips. And her breasts were pushed up and spilling out of her striped, form-fitting black and white tank top. I had a hard time not staring. I had a hard time all around.

"Well?" She turned her back to me and looked over her shoulder at me with a coy look.

The short shorts rode up in the back, revealing perfect, grab-able butt cheeks. The girl was hot. I was playing with fire.

"What do you think?"

What I thought was X-rated. "You need a whistle and a pair of striped athletic socks. I have a pair you can borrow." I was standing there in black pants and your standard referee shirt. "And some smoking heels."

She spun around to face me. "I have a pair of black high-heel boots that will be perfect. They're cute. From the front, they almost look like hiking boots or maybe black tennis shoes. From the back, you see the heel. They're awesome." Her gaze ran over me, like she was inspecting me.

Before I could move, she stepped forward and ran her hands over my shoulders, smoothing my shirt. "There. You had a wrinkle."

I had more than a wrinkle. I was completely creased. Morgan was going to be my undoing. We stood almost breast to chest, just inches away. Her shirt zipped up the front. On impulse, I grabbed the zipper and pulled it down a few inches, letting her breasts spill out farther. "Too modest."

She held her ground and smiled up at me provocatively. "Are we done here?"

"Yeah. Go change." I could have stared at her all day. "We'll stop by the sporting goods store for a whistle. If you're good, I'll take you to the candy store after."

"Oh, I can be very good." She winked and bounced off to the dressing room to change.

What was going on here? Were we still flirting with each other?

It took less than five minutes to buy the whistles. This college town was a small town. For years it had resisted any chain stores. That had changed, and the Walmarts and fast food chains of the world had invaded. But the shops on Main Street were still quaint and locally owned, throwbacks to a bygone era. The candy shop, with its jars of confections in bulk, was the place to impress a girl with your sweetness. It was the kind of shop that girls just went *Ah* to.

For Halloween it was decked out with witches, spider webs, black cats, and cauldrons, and every type of Halloween candy imaginable. Inside smelled like sugar and cinnamon, chocolate and licorice. And everything nice.

I held the door open for Morgan.

"I love this place!" She sighed in a way that reminded me of sex.

Around Morgan, everything reminded me of sex. But she more than turned me on. She lit me up. I enjoyed being with her. But how much did I trust her?

"Chocolate frogs!" She pointed to the candy counter. "Jelly beans. Candy corn in school colors. That's cool."

We wandered around the shop.

I picked up a candy necklace. "Can I buy you some jewelry?"

She laughed. "Big spender!" She was snooping around the jars of hard candy. "Green apple. Cinnamon. Sour balls."

"Yeah, they have about every flavor."

"I'm looking for something specific." She was squinting, reading labels. In front of the jars, there were cellophane bags of pre-bagged candy. She came to an empty jar and frowned. "They're out of tiger eyes. How can they be out! They only get them at Halloween."

My eyes were sharper than hers. I spotted one last bag, grabbed it, and held it up. "You're in luck."

"Yay! My hero." She snatched the bag from my hand. "I'm getting these." She took them to the counter.

I pulled out my wallet as she waded through her purse for hers. "I said I was buying. What else do you want?"

"Nothing." Her eyes shone.

"No chocolate? Don't girls want chocolate?"

"Stereotyper! Get some for yourself if you want it."

I laughed, paid for her candy, and bought a couple of things for myself. I handed her her bag. Saturday had been full of freezing rain, but today was sunny and surprisingly warm for this time of year. Out on the sidewalk, she opened her bag of tiger eyes and slipped one round ball into her mouth. She rolled her eyes and sighed as she sucked on it. "Delicious."

I imagined her sucking something of mine. "Are you going to share?"

"No." She shook her head and held the bag of candy behind her back. "I'm just going to tantalize you." She stuck her tongue out at me with the tiger eye balanced on it.

Shit, she was succeeding. Egging me on. I wrapped her in my arms, held her against me so tightly all she could do was squirm, and pressed my mouth to hers, taking possession and wrestling that candy free from her mouth and into mine.

She fought me. Feebly. I released her and stepped back, making a show of sucking on her candy. "You're right. It's delicious." I held it out on my tongue for her to see, just like she had to me.

"If you think I'm going to come get that back, you're crazy." She was breathing hard. Her eyes were dark and wide. Her lips were pink and puffed from cold and kiss.

I shrugged. "My gain."

She narrowed her eyes at me. "That was a kiss, so-briety bud."

"No, that was theft."

Fuck, I wanted her.

***

I was lying. Stealing her tiger eye was an excuse to kiss her. Tasting her like that, pressing her up against me, gave me ideas I shouldn't have. I had a girlfriend who loved me. Why the hell should I risk that relation-ship? That was what my mind said. But my heart was a smooth-talking son of bitch who didn't have any prob-lem pursuing Morgan. My body was a traitor, too. I lusted after her. I couldn't get the picture of her in the slutty ref costume out of my mind.

I'd thought screwing her that night we walked in on Zach and Alexis would get her out of my system. I was wrong. I only wanted her more. But I also liked hang-ing with her.

I did the thing every self-respecting guy does when he's trying to get a girl out of his system. I didn't text or call her. I buried myself in my studies. But Saturday and our party ref plan was never far from my mind.

Thoughts of Morgan popped up at the most incon-venient times. Like in the communal shower in the frat, which was nothing more than a huge shower stall with showerheads sticking out at random intervals. Like PE showers at high school gyms. Shit, getting in the show-er every morning without getting a hard-on was hard enough without Morgan on my mind. The walls of the shower were covered with pictures of hot naked girls that had been decoupaged to the walls over the years.

It was epic watching the pledges hit the showers the first time. But I was a seasoned junior. I couldn't afford to be caught with my dick up.

I talked to Jordan daily. On Thursday, she called while I was studying and grumpy to begin with.

"Halloween is on a Saturday, Dak. You have to come home." She'd gone from having a sexy pout in her voice earlier in the week to just nagging.

"I can't, babe. I can't drive."

She swore beneath her breath. "Take the bus or catch a flight home. I'll pick you up."

"I can't. I just can't. I have too much studying and too much to do at the frat. I can't break away right now."

And I had too much to do with Morgan.

"Fine, Dak. Be that way." The line went dead.

Shit.

Morgan

Sometimes I wanted to scream at myself for being stupid. Any girl who waits for a guy to text her was being just the kind of stupid I was talking about. And whether I liked to admit it or not, I was waiting for Dakota to text me. I mean, friends text each other, right?

But no. He kissed me and then nothing but silence. He was obviously the smart one here. People thought girls were hard to figure out. They had nothing on guys.

Sure, I could have manufactured an emergency to draw Dakota out. But I was damned if I was going to.

The week slid by slowly. The big news on campus was a prank that someone had pulled on that awful Dr. Rogers I'd had for Chem my freshman year. Someone had put a smoke bomb in her ancient overhead projector and given her the scare of her life. It was the best trick on campus and it wasn't even Halloween yet.

Finally, on Friday afternoon, he texted to confirm our party-crashing date.

Pick you up at ten tomorrow night.

Brief. To the point. Totally frustrating. What could I read into that?

I amused myself by reading my favorite blog. An article on why a straight male best friend was better than a gay one caught my attention. Perk number one—straight guys had straight friends. And there were no competition issues.

Dakota had some hot friends. I decided I would take advantage of that. All I needed to get Dakota out of my mind was one hot, straight guy who was ready for a relationship. In other words, a unicorn. Then I could stop imagining something was, or might be, going on between me and my sobriety buddy.

Saturday at the sorority was totally dedicated to getting into costume. Every girl in the house was going as a slutty something—slutty cop, slutty maid, slutty colored candies, slutty witch. Looking appropriately slutty was no easy feat. It took skill to apply the perfect smoky eye makeup or paint your face to look like a slutty kitten.

Excitement ran high. As I got ready with the rest of the girls, I felt Brenda watching me.

She came up to me in the bathroom, so close she was in my face. "Going out tonight?" What was she? A personal Breathalyzer? Her gaze ran over my costume. "Or is this just for show?"

"I'm not chained to my room." Shaking, I brushed past her and out the door.

Halloween was when the weather here changed from fall to winter. We often got our first snow of the season. This year winter had threatened to come early. We'd already had a bout of freezing rain. But no one wanted to put a coat on over their slutty costumes. So it was tradition to put on an alcohol blanket. Meaning, you took a few shots before heading out. Not in the house, of course. That was an alcohol-free zone. Just outside, out of view.

That wasn't happening for me tonight. I couldn't afford another MIC.

I was still upstairs when Dak arrived to pick me up. Victoria called up to me before Dak could text that he had arrived. "Your fellow ref is here, Morgan."

Dak had texted me he was on his way. But I was running late.

When I came downstairs, Brenda was batting her eyes at him and laughing in that giggling, flirty way that means, "I'm interested." It was bad form to poach another sister's escort for the evening. And she knew it.

I made my grand entrance. "Hey, partner." I neatly divided Brenda from him, stepping between them as I hugged him.

He'd gotten a haircut and shaved. His cheeks had that freshly scrubbed look that made me want to rub them with mine. And he smelled good enough to snuggle up to. *Must resist urge to hook up.*

He held me at arm's length, ignoring Brenda and studying me. "You look good enough to eat."

"Do I look good enough to rule a game? That's the question."

Next to me, Brenda was dressed like a slutty green candy-coated piece of chocolate. I could tell by her scowl that she thought she was the one who looked delectable enough to consume. Too bad for her.

Alexis came into the foyer from the living room just then. She threw herself at Dakota. "I thought I heard your voice!"

Odd. Strange. Totally uncommon for exes to be this friendly. Their behavior kept everyone gossiping and guessing about the true nature of the relationship between the three of them—Zach, Dak, and Alexis.

Dakota smiled at her. "Why aren't you in costume?"

"I'm not going out." She bit her lip, prettily.

Ah, poor innocent child. I wanted to scowl at her, but I made myself play nice.

"What?" His eyes were wide.

For a second I feared he was going to invite her along with us.

"I'm Skyping Zach later. And I have a bowlful of candy and a bunch of Halloween movies to watch. I'll be fine."

Dakota wore a black microfiber referee jacket over his uniform. It emphasized his broad shoulders and narrow waist. He was by far the hottest ref I'd ever seen. I pushed the thought out of my mind, telling myself the attraction I felt was simple transference. He was a lot like Zach, and I guessed I had a type.

"Get your coat and let's go," he said to me.

"I don't have a coat."

He looked at me like I was crazy. "Then get one. I'll wait."

I shook my head. "And ruin my outfit?" I looped my arm through his. "I don't have a cool ref jacket like yours." I nodded at the two girls next to us as I pulled Dakota toward the door. "Alexis. Brenda. Happy Halloween!"

"It's freezing outside," he whispered to me. "I don't have a car, remember? And we're alone on this mission, just the two of us. No one to carpool with."

"I'll be fine."

He looked skeptical. And rightly so. It was freezing outside.

I immediately started shivering. "So what's the plan? Where are we going?"

"My friend Collin is throwing his usual big Halloween bash at his apartment. I've never been before. Let's start there."

I wrapped my arms around myself. "Let's go."

"Your teeth are chattering." He slid his coat off. "Damn it, Morgan. You're going to freeze to death." He put the coat over my shoulders.

I slid my arm around his waist and cuddled in to him. "We'll share." I was just huddling for warmth, so I told myself. But it felt surprisingly good to be tucked against him. Safe.

He put his arm around me, too, resting his hand on my hip. Walking with him like that shouldn't have been so exciting. But it was, and nothing I told myself made the surprisingly giddy feelings go away.

Dak insisted on taking the bus. We got lucky and didn't have to wait for one. Five minutes later we were in the parking lot of Dak's friend's apartment in the middle of a brand-new complex on the edge of the wheat fields surrounding town. The apartments weren't much different in atmosphere from the frats. They pulsed with music and the air smelled like booze. People spilled out on the lawn and cluttered the clubhouse.

Dak knew where he was going. He led us directly to his friend's place.

At the door to Collin's apartment, I reluctantly released my grip on Dak and handed him his jacket. "Put this on. You look hot in it."

"Is that a come-on?"

"You wish." But, yeah, it could be. It would have been in the old days.

He pulled two masks out of his jacket pocket. "What do you think?"

I grabbed one from him and slid it on. "You can never be too careful."

The party was in full swing. Dak grabbed my hand and pulled me inside. "Where's our host?" Dak looked around the party. "Ah. There he is!" He pulled me through a throng of monsters, witches, and assorted characters. "Collin!" He slapped him on the back.

Collin turned. His eyes lit up when he saw me. "It's about time the refs arrived! This party is getting out of hand. And you brought a lady ref." He whistled.

I laughed.

"You know where the beer is." Collin hitched a thumb at a nearby keg. "We have the harder stuff. In the kitchen." Just then, another guy walked by. Collin grabbed him. "This is my roommate, Zave."

I stretched my hand. "Morgan."

"Delighted," Zave said. "This party needs more hot chicks." He gave me one of those undressing looks. "Gotta love a woman in uniform."

"Hey!" Dak put his arm around me. "My partner's on duty."

His possessiveness was cute.

"Logan, my other roommate, is around here some-where." He looked around. "There he is. In the corner. You'll have to forgive him. He's not himself tonight." Collin rolled his eyes. "Girl problems." He shrugged and slapped Dak on the back again. "Help yourself. And liven this party up!"

Dak yelled in my ear over the music, "Thirsty?"

"Terribly. But not for mixers."

He laughed. "Let's get to work." He pulled me into the middle of a group of dancing people. He watched the crowd like he was waiting for an opening. His face lit up. "Our first violators!"

He stepped between a dancing couple and blew his whistle. "No personal foul! Ten-yard penalty for danc-ing too far apart." He stepped out from between them and shoved them together. "Dude, you have a hot—"

He looked at her costume and frowned. "What are you supposed to be? A fairy?"

The girl wiggled her shoulders and flapped the wings she wore. "A butterfly!"

He put a hand on the guy's shoulder. "You have a hot butterfly here. Rush her before she flits off and finds another zombie to land on. Do some man-to-woman offensive. Net this girl. Got it?"

The guy nodded. The girl laughed.

Dakota slapped the guy on the back and grabbed me. "Let's show them how it's done." He stepped close to me and grabbed my hips as I shook them and shimmied to the music with my arms over my head, laughing.

"Twerk it, baby, twerk it!" Dak's eyes shone.

I caught him staring at my bouncing breasts and felt a tingle all the way to my toes. "My eyes are up here."

"Want to call a foul on me? Take me to the penalty box?"

"Shut up and dance."

I loved dancing. But I was surprised how thrilling dancing with Dakota could be. He was smooth. And sexy to watch and touch. He could be tender. And funny. And totally brutal. He tantalized me with a touch here. A touch there. The whisper and heat of his breath against my neck. A whiff of his cologne. A brush of my breasts against his chest.

Just when I thought I couldn't take it anymore, one more song and I'd have to make out with him in the corner, he leaned in and whispered in my ear, "Enough dancing. Come on. Let's play ref again. Look! Over there. Party poopers. Teetotalers. We can't let that stand."

He pulled me toward a coven of slutty witches. "Ladies, you aren't drinking. Am I going to have to put you in the penalty box?"

One of the witches smiled at him through her green makeup. "I'd rather you make me a drink. Before I have to make you a toad. Be a shame to turn a hot guy into something repulsive."

"Overpowered and outranked." Dak grinned at her. "What can I get you ladies?"

I lost him as he played bartender. And let the girls flirt with him. And it looked like he was enjoying the attention. Too much. Green didn't go with my outfit. I wandered off to get something non-alcoholic to drink. I was parched. The guy called Logan sat in the corner next to a table with a bunch of two-liter bottles of pop. He was hot in a helmet and Viking skirt, no shirt, watching the partying. Too hot to be sitting alone. If Dakota was going to ditch me...hey, straight friend, right?

He might have scared the other girls away with his Heathcliff brooding. But not me. I shook my whistle at Logan. "Timeout's over, player. Off the bench. Back in the game with you."

He didn't move, just grinned.

"Are you going to make me blow this?" I shook my whistle and glanced at the heart of the party in the living room and back at him. Dakota was still entertaining the girls with his sparkling wit and referee antics. "Or are you going to get out there and party?"

Logan took a gulp of beer. "I'm an introvert. This is partying."

It was hard to hear and talk over the music. I had to yell. "Introvert?" I slid my gaze up him. "Really, Viking? Must be hell during marauding."

"I'm not a Viking. I'm..." He named a character from a video game. He shook his head and smiled sadly.

"Then get out there and kick some butt."

"And leave my post as guardian of the mixers?"

Figured. I couldn't tease him out of his mood and into full party participation. He really was heartbroken and unavailable. And adorable. Too bad. Too soon. Timing was everything.

Dakota blew his whistle. "Strike three!" He handed a guy a shot. "Drink up!" He moved to another guy who was hitting on a sexy nurse. "Ball four." He shoved them together. "Runner, take your base. See if you can get to second at least, dude."

Logan nodded toward Dakota. "What's up with you and your fellow ref?"

I shrugged. "We're friends."

"Looks like more to me. Why are you letting the other girls hit on him?"

I shrugged. "Long story." I didn't feel like explaining.

"Ah." He sounded sympathetic, like he understood my reluctance. He took another drink of beer. "You look thirsty. Can I get you something?"

"Wow! I've made it past the guardian." I winked at him. "Diet cola if you have it."

"You got it." He grabbed a two-liter bottle on the table next to him and a plastic cup and poured me one. "Nothing stronger? I can add a shot of rum. No extra charge."

I sighed and made a partial confession. "I don't drink. For now."

"MIC?" He grinned. "Don't answer. I get it. Been there myself. When's your twenty-first?"

"January." I liked him, this Logan.

The shrill call of a whistle silenced the party. Dakota jumped up on a chair and looked right at Logan and me, his eyes snapping. "I call a foul on this whole party. Everyone get a drink, or I'm going to have to eject you all from the game!"

The crowd erupted in laughter. Dak jumped off the chair and started toward me.

I needed a second to get my jealousy and anger at him under control. "It's been a pleasure, Logan. Anyone gets out of hand over here and gives you grief about the mixer situation, call me. I have a whistle." I raised my glass to him and headed for the bathroom before Dakota could catch me.

Fortunately, it was empty. Inside, I locked the door and took several deep breaths to ward off a wave of nausea. Crap, I hadn't even drunk anything. When had I gotten so anxious over a guy?

When I came out of the bathroom, Dakota was nowhere in sight. If he'd left me alone here, I was going to kill him. Hey, he'd tried to kill me. It was my turn for a murder attempt.

In the corner, a girl was doing a keg stand, with two buff zombies holding her by the legs. She slapped the keg. Someone pulled the beer hose out of her mouth. The two zombies helped her off. And spotted me.

One of them pointed at me. "Human! Must catch and infect her with beer." He lumbered toward me, doing a zombie walk.

For zombies, they were surprisingly fast. I couldn't outrun them. It didn't help that my path was blocked by a couple of football players.

One of them grabbed me. "Hey, ref. We need an official ruling on the keg. Is it regulation?"

The zombies grabbed me and hauled me off.

"No!" I laughed and shook my head, protesting too feebly. Loving the spotlight. "No, I can't." A beer sounded so good.

They overpowered me and pulled me to the keg. "Up you go!" One of the football players grabbed me and threw me over his shoulder.

Before I could protest or escape, two zombies were holding me upside down by my ankles over the keg. Someone else was grabbing the spout and the line. I wanted a drink in the worst way. I grabbed the top of the keg and opened my mouth for the spout as the blood rushed to my head.

"Roughing the ref! Automatic ejection." Dak elbowed his way through the crowd, fire in his eyes. He was ready to fight. He grabbed me by the waist. The guys holding me let go as Dakota flipped me over his shoulder.

"Hey, man, we were just helping a lady to a drink."

"Shut the fuck up." Dakota held me tight.

I wrapped my legs around his chest and straightened up, with my arms around his neck. He had the most gorgeous eyes. Flashing with anger, they were as intoxicating as a rush of beer.

I was seated high enough on him that I looked down at him, breathing hard. Wanting him. Happy.

I didn't know if he saw it. In that moment, he was my hero.

Stone-cold sober, I leaned down, pressed my lips to his, opened my mouth to him, and kissed him with all the heady passion I was feeling.

CHAPTER NINE

Dakota

Morgan's perfume filled my senses. Her naked butt cheeks felt round and firm in my hands. My pulse raced. My head spun. I lost my senses and kissed her back. Hard. If she was going to play this game with me, I was going to engage. Her hair tumbled around my face. The tops of her breasts teased my chin. Damn, I wanted to touch and kiss them.

She kept me otherwise engaged, kissing me back, tickling the top of my mouth with her tongue until I shivered with pleasure. Nibbling my lips playfully.

"Referee PDA. Break it up! Break it up!" Collin came out of nowhere, suddenly beside us. "Get a room." He slapped me on the back. "You can use mine." He was laughing.

People around us clapped.

I was breathing hard as we broke the kiss. Morgan slid down me like I was a stripper pole, until her feet touched the ground. Her lips were puffy from being kissed and her eyes round and wide. She looked sexy as hell.

There was a moment where I was tempted to take Collin up on his offer. Then I remembered Jordan. I shook my head and grabbed Morgan's hand. "Thank you for the offer, dude. We'll have to pass. Other parties to referee." I winked at him. "I have my own room."

I pulled Morgan through the crowd to the exit and grabbed my coat out of a pile by the door. At the door, I paused and blew my whistle. "Party on!"

I grabbed her hand and pulled her down the stairs and outside the building to the parking lot. It was freezing outside. She immediately began to shiver.

I wrapped her in my coat and took her by the arms. "A keg stand in front of all those people? What the shit were you thinking in there?"

"The zombies got me. They dragged me to it. What could I do?" She smiled and made her flirty, pouty face at me.

I swore beneath my breath. She could twist me around her little finger. Make me forget Jordan. Make me do something stupid. "I can't leave you alone for a minute. I'm taking you home before we both do something we'll regret."

She stared at me. "What will we regret, Dakota?"

"Stop it, Morgan." I propelled her through the parking lot. "You know damn well what. I thought you weren't into hookups anymore."

She grinned back at me. "I'm not."

Fickle woman. Cock tease. I could have called her a lot of things. "You're right, Morgan. I'm not boyfriend material."

I sure as hell wasn't being a good one to Jordan.

Morgan

Late. Late. Late. Late! For a very important date—with my period. Where was Aunt Flow? And why wasn't she visiting?

On Sunday morning, I felt hung over and desperately tired. My breasts were sensitive to the touch. The houseboys cooked breakfast on Sunday mornings. Seth made scrambled eggs. His weren't as good as Zach's. But he was a pretty good breakfast cook. I gagged at the site of the eggs when he plated me up a bunch.

"Not you too, Morgan!" Seth shook his head. "Why do I even bother cooking the morning after Halloween?" He handed me a piece of dry toast. He leaned in and whispered, "I thought you were on probation and not supposed to be drinking."

I wasn't in the mood to explain, so I shrugged and let him think what he wanted. For not having had a single drop of anything stronger than pop, I was doing a great imitation of a hangover and keeping up my party rep without any effort.

Sunday slid into Monday and Tuesday. No period. Radio silence from Dakota. It was like he was avoiding me after that kiss. Fine. Screw him if he couldn't recognize what a good time we'd had together. Yes, I was being irrational. Yes, I knew I was the one who'd said getting together with former hookups was a bad idea. But there had been something between us on Halloween night. A spark. Chemistry. I'd had so much fun with him. I couldn't get him out of my mind.

He saw it. I knew he did. And he was running like a scared chicken from anything more serious than a casual boink. Verifying my reasoning to stay away from him. Sadly, being right wasn't the same thing as being happy.

I'd finished my active birth control pills six days before. I'd taken every one. I couldn't. It was unthinkable. And then I remembered the night of the powder puff football game. All the drinking and throwing up I'd done. I'd taken my pill the next day. Had I thrown it up, too?

I was scared. And alone. I walked past the Tau Psi house, Dakota's frat, hoping to get a glimpse of him. It was stupid. I was being stupid.

He could be so funny and sweet. He could be so totally aggravating. Just when I was beginning to really want him, maybe, he'd met my low expectations. Now I might be pregnant—with his baby. He was the only guy I'd been with. It had to be him.

I'd been late before. Sometimes, even on the pill, stress delayed things. I could have bought a home pregnancy test and found out for sure. If I wasn't pregnant, finding out would bring the menses on in hours. At least, that was what had happened in the past.

If I was pregnant...

I couldn't face it. I didn't want to think about it. Dak would think...

What did I care what Dak would think? He'd brushed me off.

In class that afternoon, I overheard two girls whispering. "At least you can tell Brad and he'll stand by you," one of them whispered to the other. She paled and stared into her lap. "I'm not even sure who."

You know how when something affects you, you seem to notice it everywhere? Where before it was invisible to you, a non-issue?

Everywhere I went, it was the same. I stopped by The College Grind to get something to wake me up. A girl in the corner booth was crying. "I've already had one abortion. My parents will kill me if I'm pregnant again. I'm two weeks late."

I wanted to cover my ears and run. I went to the store to get toothpaste because the brand I had made me gag. Yeah, bad sign. Like maybe it wasn't the toothpaste. Denial was a powerful thing. Right now, I was the queen of it.

I tried to avoid it, but I had to walk by the row with the contraceptives and pregnancy tests. A guy was helping his girlfriend pick one out. He studied the boxes, reading them with a serious look on his face while she bit her nails and held his hand.

I went back to the house to study. In the living room, one of the sophomores was consoling another. "I'm late," I heard as I walked by. And she didn't mean with a paper.

It was like the world was sending me one huge, cosmic message. *Morgan Peterson—you're late. Too late for everything.*

I went too my room and plunked onto the bed. Seconds later, Victoria tapped on my door. "Morgan? How are you doing?" She slid in and plopped onto the bed next to me.

"Hanging in," I said. "You?"

"Late."

"What?" I sat up. Her ominous tone gave her away.

She nodded. "As my twin, you're sworn to secrecy."

I nodded my agreement.

"I know of half a dozen girls in the house who are in the same boat. It's like everyone I know is worried. It's an epidemic." She pursed her lips.

"I know," I said without thinking.

"Not you too?" Her eyes were wide with sympathy.

"Just a few days," I said, covering. "It's nothing. I've heard the whispers. We've probably just all synced up."

Victoria shook her head. "Menstrual synchrony is a myth based on one faulty study from the seventies. The methodology was all flawed. I could bore you with the details."

"Spare me. I believe you." I forced a smile. She couldn't know she'd just crushed one of my best denial rationales.

"Periods are random and randomly sync up as a result. Anyway, that doesn't affect us here. Most of us are on the pill. You want to know the real culprit?" She sighed. "Too much celebrating on Homecoming Weekend." She paused. "Sometimes I wish we'd never won that powder puff tourney."

Celebrating had only tangentially been the cause of my problem. But I agreed. "What are you going to do?"

"Wait a week and hope for the best." She sighed. She had a serious boyfriend and could lean on him. "See what happens."

"Are you going to tell Darrel?"

She shook her head. "Not yet."

My cell phone rang the Dad tone. I rolled my eyes. "My dad. I have to get this."

Victoria rolled her eyes, too, and laughed. "Making his plans for the weekend. Dads! Last minute."

I sighed. "Fortunately, he's had his room booked for a year." I grabbed the phone as Victoria let herself out.

"Dad."

"Morgan. How's my girl?"

He used to say, *How's my baby girl.* I missed that, but I was glad to hear his voice.

"Staying out of trouble?" He didn't sound like he trusted I was.

He had good reason not to.

"Of course," I said.

"No drinks over the Halloween weekend?"

"Dad!"

"I have to check. It's my duty as your father. You have a great future in front of you, little one."

It was like he'd slipped and used his pet "little one" phrase with me. Soon I wouldn't be the little one anymore.

"I don't want you to ruin it," he said.

Like I did. Would getting pregnant in college count?

"Your grandma and I will be there Saturday morning around eleven. Your stepmom reminded me we'd better make reservations for dinner on Saturday or take our chances with fast food. Pick someplace nice. Someplace with a good bar. I'll need a drink if I'm going to have to deal with your grandmother all weekend."

I didn't think Dad realized what he was asking of me. "Will do." It was like him to dump the task on me. "I don't know why you don't get along with Grandma. She's great."

"She's not your mother." He sounded grim, almost like a chastened boy.

Sadly, I did know what he meant.

Dakota

My dad called while I was walking out of CRJU 301, Criminal Law and Judicial Practices. "Hey."

"Hello, Dakota. Your mom reminded me to call and confirm our plans for the weekend. I had my admin make dinner reservations for Saturday. I'll be arriving too late for dinner on Friday. But I expect a good frat party. The Tau Psis know how to party, I hear."

That was a jab at me. "So I hear."

"Well, good. It's been ages since I've played a rousing game of beer pong." He paused. "We have good seats for the game. Forty-five-yard line. We'll pregame at the university tailgate in the field house. President Lawrence will be there." He paused. "How are you doing, in the girl department? Moving on?"

Dad asked the most inappropriate questions. What he meant was—was I seeing anyone new and suitable? To his credit, maybe he didn't want me to be broken-hearted forever. When a girl stomped on my heart, in his limited view, I tended to run over innocent friends and drunk girls.

"I'm doing okay." I hesitated, thinking of Morgan. "I'm making a friend or two."

"Are you? Great! I'd like to meet one of these friends. They're pretty, I hope."

"Totally hot, Dad."

"That's my boy!"

We talked while I walked for a few more minutes before we hung up. I stared at my phone, thinking. I'd been avoiding Morgan again. But now, I was a weak fool. I hit her number before I could think too hard on it.

"Hey, stranger." The sound of her voice made my heart race.

"Hey, yourself," I said. "You've been quiet. Fingers broken? You haven't texted me."

"I haven't had any sobriety emergencies." Her voice had a smile in it.

"Do we need them for an excuse to talk?"

She laughed. "We've moved past frenemies and are friends now? Is that what you're implying?"

"Maybe."

"I like a decisive man." She laughed again. "So why are you calling now? What's up?"

"Sobriety emergency."

"You're horrible! Lead me on that we're friends and then hit me with a sobriety emergency."

"This call is doing double duty. I have an emergency and it was a great excuse to call a friend."

"What's your emergency?"

"Dad's Weekend," I said. "My old man wants to party and play beer pong. We're having a tourney at the house Friday night. Part of the Dad's Weekend entertainment."

She laughed. "Mine told me to make reservations at a restaurant that has a good bar. Do you think they realize what they're asking? Or are they totally oblivious." She put on a dad voice. "Do as I say, not as I do."

I laughed. "You sound just like my dad. Scary."

She laughed too.

"Who knows how the dad brain works?" I said. "With fathers like ours, we need to stick together." I smiled to myself. "The booze will be flowing and temptation will be everywhere. I need the sobriety buddy system more than ever."

She paused. "You realize what you're asking? I can't hang with you and ditch my dad and grandma. Your plan means introducing each other to the dads. And you to my grandma."

"Dad said he wants to meet my friends."

"He doesn't know them?"

"He meant my friends who are girls. My new friends who are girls, if you get my meaning. He hasn't met you."

"Oh."

"It's nothing serious, Morgan. He's afraid I'll slip into a dark depression over Alexis and screw up again. All he wants to see is that I'm hanging with other girls, even if they're just friends."

"I hate to bring this up." Her voice dripped reluctance. "But you do know what you're asking, right?"

"What?"

"Do I have to spell it out? You almost ran over me. Even as distracted as he is with the new baby coming, you're not exactly my dad's favorite person. I mean, for me, it's fine. Hanging with you will keep the heat off me. It will all be directed at you."

"I thought of that. It's worth the risk," I said. "I want to make amends. Let him see that I'm not a bad guy. I made a mistake and I'm correcting that."

"I don't know." She hesitated. "Dad can be pretty mean when he's in protection mode.

"I can handle him, Morgs. I promise. It's an awesome plan. Our dads will see how mature we're being. Forgive and forget. Maybe we'll even get written up in the campus newspaper as a human interest story. One of those stories that bring tears to people's eyes and reaffirms their belief in the innate goodness of human nature. He could have killed her. Now they're best friends."

She laughed again. "Right. I never knew you were such an optimist."

"Not an optimist. Just a positive guy. What do you say?"

"You're going to the game, I assume. What about the tailgate party at the field house?"

"VIP tickets," I said.

"Us too. Dinner?"

"Just Saturday night. Dad's admin got us reserva-tions. I can text her and ask her to add three to it. Your grandma will be joining us?"

"Yeah." She paused again. "You're sure about this?"

"Sobriety buddies till the end, Morgs." I cleared my throat. "Which reminds me—how would you like to ref our beer pong tourney Friday night?"

"What?"

"I'm asking as a sobriety buddy favor. You already have the outfit and the whistle. Your dad's invited to the tourney, too."

"He and Grandma aren't coming until Saturday morning and are leaving right after dinner Saturday night."

"Excellent. Then you aren't busy Friday night."

"I didn't say I wasn't busy. What gives you that idea? Maybe I have a hot date."

My heart lurched at the thought of her out with someone else. "Hot date, with a guy and his dad?"

"Not everyone's dads are here. Besides, how do you know? Maybe I like older men."

"You mean you're looking for a father figure? Dad's Weekend is a great time for you, then." I was getting grumpy. If she was toying with me on purpose and try-ing to make me jealous, she was doing a damn fine job of it.

"Actually, I like guys *my* age."

The way she emphasized "my" gave me hope. We were almost exactly the same age.

"I'm pulling your chain. No date for me. Tell me why I would give up a quiet evening at home to be sober among a bunch of drunk guys hitting on me?"

"Because you can't resist the opportunity to reprise our excellent ref act. We'll be a team again. I'll wear my costume if you wear yours."

"You want me to wear that skimpy costume around your dad? He'll think I'm a slut."

"Aren't you?" I couldn't help teasing her.

"Shut up! You're not helping your case. Do you want my help or not?"

"Dad loves eye candy. He'll be impressed by what a hot friend I have." I didn't give her a chance to refuse me again. "The tourney starts at nine. Want us to pick you up? Dad still has his license."

"Now there's an enticement." She laughed. "See you at nine."

My heart raced and I smiled like an idiot. I was getting in too deep.

CHAPTER TEN

Morgan

Late Friday afternoon, the steady stream of incoming dads began. The house quickly filled with the deep tenor of middle-aged male voices. I liked Dad's Weekend, and picking out which Dad went with what daughter was a game I liked to play with myself. Sometimes it was surprising. My dad, for example, looked more like my grandpa than my dad. Think how old he'd look for my soon-to-be-born baby sister's Dad's Weekend. If he was even still alive. The thought depressed me. I pushed it away.

The thought of meeting Dakota's dad sent a shiver of nervous anticipation over me. What was Dakota setting me up for?

I walked past the bathroom, where Seth and Dillon were fixing a toilet that wouldn't stop running.

"Zach will be back on Sunday afternoon, man. Can't wait to see him," Dillion said to Seth.

Seth was installing a new toilet chain. "Yeah, you and me both."

I ducked my head and hurried past, hoping they wouldn't see me. Sober, and out of party mode, I was nervous about him coming back. Guilty. Hanging with Dakota, and fighting the budding feelings that I tried to deny, but were growing for him, made me realize more than ever that I'd had blinders on regarding Zach. I'd been mistaken—he wasn't the guy for me. I genuinely was out of crush with him. I'd made him into a fantasy man. But the reality didn't match the easy way I got along with Dakota.

It still astounded me that he and I had gone from enemies, to frenemies, to friends. And maybe more.

The way I'd flirted with Zach for two years embarrassed me now. In hindsight, I'd seemed so desperate. Which was the way it went when crushes died. You could suddenly clearly see what everyone else had always known.

I was relieved my dad was only coming for the day on Saturday. And nervous about how he would react to Dakota. Hoping he would give Dakota a break and see past that one bad incident. Eager to see my grandma and determine for myself how she was doing. I lived in dread of getting a call that she was in the hospital again.

Just before eight thirty, I was dressed as a ref and ready and way too eager for Dakota and his dad to pick me up. I walked by Alexis' room. Her door was open.

Remembering my promise to be a better big, I popped my head in. "Your dad's not here?"

She was lounging on her bed. She looked up from a book she was reading. "He called this morning. Some emergency. He can't make it."

I tried to gauge her reaction to his last-minute cancellation. Was she disappointed? Upset? I stepped into the room. "That sucks."

She shrugged. "He has to cancel his plans a lot. I'm used to it. Actually making it here was always a long shot. He's not much into football or Dad's Weekend things. I think it was a convenient excuse. Anyway, it takes the pressure off me. Dad still hasn't fully come to terms with me dating a houseboy." She grimaced so slightly I almost missed it.

"*Former* houseboy." I smiled at her and tried to sound jokey and sympathetic. "Thanks to me."

She looked at me, surprised by my attitude.

"You should thank me for saving him the embarrassment and getting Zach back into your social class." I tried to make myself clear by my tone that I wasn't being serious or arrogant. I was trying to let her know, in my own way, I was sorry.

I twisted my hands in my lap. "When Zach comes back, he'll be a Geed with his own place in one of the ritziest, priciest new complexes in town. That's status. That's a boyfriend your parents can brag about right there."

Her surprised look turned into a hint of admiration as she studied me and smiled. "That's one way to look at it."

"That's me, always pointing out the sunshine."

"Where's your dad?" Her gaze traveled down me. "And why are you wearing your Halloween costume?"

"Dad and Grandma aren't coming until tomorrow morning. Grandma can't take more than a day on campus. She's been sick. Heart trouble." I bit my lip and inhaled deeply. Why was I sharing this with Alexis?

"I'm sorry." Her eyes were soft with sympathy.

People liked Alexis. She had a way of engaging and caring about people that used to rub me wrong because I didn't like her. I appreciated her concern now.

I shrugged. "One day will be tiring enough for her. I hope she's up to it." I put on a happy face. "Since I have nothing else to do tonight, I'm refereeing the Tau Psi beer pong tourney. With Dakota." I indicated my costume. "Hence the referee's uniform. Double bang for my Halloween buck."

I had to force myself not to smile at the thought of Dakota. I was being stupid. Why hadn't I noticed how great he was in the first place, freshman year? Why had I ever wasted time on Zach?

Maybe it was hormones. My period still hadn't started. Maybe Dakota's baby was growing inside me and predisposing me to like him for its own nefarious purposes. Like it wanted a daddy. Maybe I was just stupid.

"Dakota?" Alexis frowned.

I took a seat in her desk chair opposite her and shrugged. I decided to level with her. "Why not? We're helping each other stay out of trouble." I paused, trying to be a considerate people person, like she was. "I'm sorry. I shouldn't have brought him up."

She shrugged. "Why? There's no bad blood between us. We're friends."

Which was true and totally confusing. She and I were getting along, actually bonding. If ever there was a moment...

I seized my opportunity to do a little digging. "Yeah, and no one understands that. What's going on with you two? You should help us all out and give a workshop on how to become best friends with your ex. I mean, given the way things ended between you, you can understand everyone's confusion."

Her smile was devilish, but it lit up her face, highlighting how pretty she was. "It's simple, really—Zach is important to both of us. Dakota is smart enough to realize he and I don't belong together and Zach and I do. He wants the best for us." She paused and her voice became soft. "He's a great guy."

Oh, I knew that. *Now.*

"Still confusing," I said. "Are you guys really aliens?"

She laughed.

"What time will Zach be here on Sunday?" I asked.

"Late Sunday afternoon. After most of the dads have left town. He's leaving Seattle around ten or eleven." She looked wistful.

"You can't wait, can you?"

She grinned. "That obvious?"

"I'm over him." I spoke without thinking. "I want you to know that. I owe him my life. I'd like to be his friend. And yours. I won't try to come between you again. I mean it."

My phone buzzed. I had a text from Dakota telling me he and his dad had arrived to pick me up. My heart suddenly pounded and I got a ridiculous smile on my face. I simply could not hide it. "Gotta go. Dakota's here to pick me up." I stood.

"Have fun."

I walked to the door.

"Morgan?"

I turned over my shoulder to look at her. "Yeah?"

She was studying me with an uncertain look on her face. Like she had something she wanted to say, but wasn't sure she should. "Be careful around Dakota. I mean this in the kindest way possible. No ulterior motives. You're my big. I want us to be friends." She fiddled with the pages of the book next to her. "Don't lose your heart to Dakota. Not that I'm saying you are. Just guard it, okay? He's not what he seems."

She looked so genuinely concerned, I almost laughed. "Not what he seems?" I said. "Don't tell me he's gay." I knew for sure he wasn't. "And you were his fake cover girlfriend."

It might have been my imagination, but I thought she paled slightly. She shook her head. "Absolutely not. Go. Have fun."

With her puzzling warning ringing in my ears, I slid my coat on and bounded down the stairs to meet Dakota and his dad.

They waited for me in the entry, bundled in jackets that emphasized their broad shoulders and masculinity. Dakota had grown a stubble of a beard since I'd seen him. He was like that. He could grow a sexy shadow overnight. Seeing him, my heart did a happy little flip. I willed my stomach to keep calm and hoped the periodic waves of nausea would stay at bay.

His dad was clean-shaven, but I was immediately struck by the resemblance between father and son. Same height. Same broad shoulders and build, his dad's tarnished by middle age. Same sandy blond hair. His dad's highlighted by shades of gray. Same intelligent, snapping blue eyes. His father's were undimmed, as youthful as Dakota's, and leveled on me.

I swallowed hard. *Buck up,* I told myself. *How bad can his dad be? I can stand up to his scrutiny.*

But I felt suddenly shy. And like I should have worn something more conservative. Then again, Dakota and I were just friends. That was the way Dakota and I both wanted it. That was the lie I told myself. I didn't have to try to appear like girlfriend material to Mr. Bradley. I could be party girl, fun friend of his son's, without worry.

"There she is!" Dakota's face lit up.

Which lit up mine. He was killing me. I ran to him and hugged him.

He slung his arm around me. "Dad, this is Morgan. The girl I've been telling you about."

Telling him about. The words echoed in my mind like they meant something more. Silly.

With as bright a smile on my face as I could manage, I offered my hand to Mr. Bradley.

"Morgan, nice to meet you. You can call me Al." His voice was a deeper, more mature version of Dakota's. He held my hand in his and squeezed it. "Nice to meet anyone who can keep my boy on the straight and narrow. How do you manage?"

"We're keeping each other out of trouble." I turned to Dakota. "What have you told him about me?"

"That he nearly killed you," Mr. Bradley said. "I can't tell you how glad I am that my son didn't remove such a gorgeous girl from this world." His voice was deep with flattery.

Dakota took my arm. "Stop flirting with Morgan, Dad." Dakota was smiling and sounded like he was teasing, but there was an edge to it. "Remember, I have Mom on speed dial."

A little father/son competition?

His father laughed. "Around such beauty, how can I help myself?"

Dakota rolled his eyes and took my hand. "Let's go." He walked me to his dad's BMW.

Dad's Weekend was like the Cinderella story in reverse. On Dad's Weekend, a great many dads reverted to the partying frat boys they used to be. Sunday at noon, they would return to their respectable middle-aged selves. But on Friday night, they were eager to win at beer pong and flirt with their sons' dates.

At the frat, I felt suddenly shy when Dak asked if he could take my coat. I was more than a good-time party girl. I wanted him to see that. As irrational as it was, I wanted to make a good impression on his dad, too. But there was nothing I could do now but roll with my role.

I knew most of the guys in his house. As we walked to the game room, we were stopped and introduced to too many dads to keep track of. I got the up-and-downs and the leers from way too many fathers, the sweet old lechers. Like I said, they were young studs again. In their own minds.

Dak led us to the game room and blew his whistle to quiet the competitors who had gathered and already tapped a keg. "The refs have arrived! I'm Dakota and this is Morgan."

Whistles. Catcalls. Hoots. Typical frat boy behavior. I winked at one of the dads. Hey, I knew the role I was supposed to play.

Dakota blew his whistle again. "Settle down. The official rules have been laminated and are posted around the room. Before we begin, I'll hit the highlights of the house rules.

"It should go without saying—all elbows and wrists must be kept behind the table at all times or the shot doesn't count. Every team can ask for the cups to be re-racked twice per game at the start of their turn.

"Finally, you've all heard the saying, *Guys finger, bitches blow.* Neither fingering nor blowing count, gentlemen." He glanced pointedly around the room. "I don't see any ladies to warn."

I elbowed him. "Hey!"

"What?" He grinned. "You're not playing. One last rule. No flirting with the refs and trying to get favors."

"Who the hell would want to flirt with you?" Dakota's big yelled out to him.

The crowd laughed.

"Shut up, Brady." Dakota glanced at me. "I have my admirers." He took a deep breath. "We've randomly assigned the schedule." He called two teams to the table. "Let the drinking—I mean, the tournament—begin."

Dakota had paired his dad with the best beer pong player in the frat. It had been fortunate the beer pong champ's dad hadn't been able to make it.

I did my job, flirting, enforcing the rules. Blowing my whistle and smiling coyly while reprimanding. "Elbows over the table. Shot doesn't count!" Laughing while the offenders pleaded for a review.

Dak stepped in. "The ref's decision is final. Keep protesting and I'll have to eject you from the tournament. And the house."

"You can't do that!"

"I'm house pres." Dak slapped the guy on the back. "I can do anything."

I suffered endless innuendos. A few butt pinches. And more than a few lewd stares. Dakota kept popping up, joking, relieving the pressure. Watching out for me. Flirting. I caught him staring at me.

"I want a re-rack" was a frequent request.

I would lean over the table so my cleavage was in full view, and re-rack while they stared at mine. Again and again throughout the night.

The guys and dads got drunker and drunker. Louder. Ruder. Dakota's dad and his partner Brett lost the tournament championship in overtime around midnight.

The winning dad grabbed me. "Time to thank the refs." Instead of shaking my hand, he planted one on me. A big, sloppy, wet one.

Dakota intervened, pulling him off me. "That's enough thanks for one night."

"Killjoy," the dad said as Dakota hovered over me like my big, bad protector.

It was kind of sweet of Dakota, actually.

"I'll drive you home," Al said to me after he was presented with his second-place prize—an oversized Tau Psi beer mug. "Or are you spending the night?" He shot Dakota a meaningful look.

"I'll walk her home, Dad." Dakota took my arm and got my coat.

He took my hand as he opened the door for me. His dad was watching. I caught him smile. It was almost as if Dakota was making some kind of statement. The thought made me way too happy.

Outside, the air was crisp and brisk.

"Don't ever ask my to do something like that again," I said to Dak.

"Why? You were good at it. The guys loved you."

I rolled my eyes. "I'm going to have to brush my teeth half a dozen times to get the taste of that dad out of my mouth."

He stopped and stared at me, his eyes hard. "He used tongue?" Then his face lit up. He looked like he was about to laugh.

I gave him a playful shove. "Yeah, white knight. I nearly gagged. You could have intervened earlier and it wouldn't have hurt my feelings." I took a deep breath. "Do boys ever grow up?"

"Never," he said.

"I can just see you at forty-five sticking your tongue down some young coed's throat. Thinking you're still a stud." I shivered. "Remember teasing me about looking for a father figure?" I shook my head. "Total turnoff."

He squeezed my hand. "When I'm forty-five, your words will haunt me. I'll keep my tongue to myself."

There was something simple and wonderful about holding hands in the dark, starry night. I was afraid to hope it meant something more than kindred spirit between referees. I mean, a guy and girl holding hands, that was a proclamation of togetherness, if only for the night. We laughed about the tournament as we walked to Delta Delta Psi.

He paused at the front door while I fumbled for my key. I had this crazy first-date feeling. Fumbling for a key was a way to give a guy time to work up to a goodnight kiss. An age-old feminine trick.

Dak had let go of my hand and stuffed his in his pockets. If I was throwing hints, he was letting them pass.

Finally, I laughed at myself. "For some reason, it feels like this is the time I'm supposed to tell you what a great time I had tonight."

"Did you?"

Did he sound hopeful? He still wasn't angling for a kiss. He was taking this no-hookup thing way too seriously. Maybe there was hope for him. But I was beginning to think he'd turned into a eunuch. He'd been flirting with me all night. And playing protector of my virtue. And now nothing. Yep, eunuch behavior.

I arched an eyebrow. "Being pawed by middle-age men? What do you think? I think you owe me one." I jabbed my key in the lock.

Still nothing. Okay, I got the message. It was depressing, but I got it. I turned the key. "Goodnight."

He caught my elbow as the door swung open. "See you tomorrow at the tailgate?"

"Partying in the field house isn't really tailgating, is it?" Two could play the disinterested game. I slid into the house and closed the door before he could see how disappointed I was. That blog had it all wrong. Former hookups gone friends were absolutely the pits.

I was doing it again—falling for a guy who was unobtainable. Alexis' warning rang in my ears: "Dakota isn't who he seems to be."

Maybe he wasn't.

CHAPTER ELEVEN

Morgan
Dad and Grandma arrived on Saturday just in time for coffee and cookies at the house before heading out to pre-game at the VIP university tailgating party. I was surprised by how tired and frail Grandma looked. She walked so slowly, it was like she wasn't even moving. But her mind was sharp again. She'd been out of it the last time I'd seen her, too tired to lift her head and talk. Seeing her doing any kind of walking, no matter how slowly, was encouraging. And made me crazy happy. I was suddenly Little Miss Optimist. Grandma was one of my favorite people. I couldn't bear the thought of losing her.

Making small talk at the house kept the focus off me and the queasy way I felt. Part of it was nerves. I hoped all of it was nerves, but I feared worse.

"We have dinner reservations right after the game with a friend and his dad," I told Dad and Grandma between sips of coffee, not making a big deal of it.

To my pleasant surprise, he didn't question me further. Grandma was in her element. She winked at me. I couldn't stop smiling at her. I was thrilled she'd come.

"I'm sorry there aren't more girlie things to do." I handed her another cookie. "You'll have to come back on Mom's Weekend. It's much more fun. We could get matching pedis. I know the best place in town. The girls there paint the best flowers on your toes for no extra charge." I grinned at her.

"Have you seen my old toes! No amount of flowers will save them." She laughed. "I couldn't wait for Mom's Weekend, Morgan. I wanted to see my favorite granddaughter at school now. At my age, the future is almost a foreign concept. Live for the moment." She squeezed my hand.

We both knew what she was saying. I pushed the thought to the back of my mind.

"You're all better now." I gave her a shaky smile, unable to imagine my world without her.

"Yes, all better." She smiled, but it looked tired.

Dad looked at his watch. "Time to be going. Sure you're up to this, Mom?"

"You'd have me in my grave." She took the arm he offered her. "My heart may only be working at half capacity. But I've always had enough verve to live on less."

Dad drove us as close to the field house as he could, and parked in the lot at the top of the hill. He'd arranged for a motorized cart to pick Grandma up and drive her to the pre-game function. It was waiting for us. He helped her in. He and I walked down together as the cart pulled away from us.

"Tell me about dinner. Why are we dining with an unnamed boy and his dad?" He paused, like the silence would pull the truth from me.

I wasn't playing. "I called around and all the good places were booked solid." I shrugged. "I wanted us to have a nice dinner. This guy had reservations he said he could add us to."

Dad frowned. "I see, a mysterious friend with connections. Why haven't I heard you mention him before?"

I glanced away. "Maybe you weren't listening." That was an intentional dig at Dad. To let him know he hadn't been paying attention to me lately. I'd noticed the distance between us.

"This friend has a name, I assume?" Dad was always straight to the point. And scary when he used his firm voice.

I lifted my chin and faced him. "Dakota Bradley."

Dad stopped short and stared at me, his face a mask. You'd think a mask would be good. In this case, he was hiding his fury. "Dakota." He stared at me like I was crazy, and in deep trouble. "The boy who almost ran over you? And got you in all the trouble?"

He didn't know the half of the trouble Dakota might have gotten me in. I bit my lip and looked at the ground like a chastened child.

"Morgan? Answer me."

I forced myself to meet his eye. "Yes, Dad. *That* Dakota Bradley." Like there was more than one on campus. "To be fair, he didn't get me in trouble. He didn't ply me with alcohol and force me to lie down behind his car where he couldn't see me. We became friends at Alcohol and Drug Information School."

I explained to him about Dakota and me meeting in ADIS and becoming buddies to keep each other from drinking and getting in trouble. I thought Dad would appreciate that.

Instead, he looked blatantly unhappy and worried. "Whatever you do, don't let your grandma know who he is or what he did." Dad took my arm.

"So when I introduce them, I just call him 'hey you' or 'boy'?"

"Don't be a smartass." He frowned at me. "You know we've kept the details of your MIC from your grandma. There's a reason I insisted you not mention almost being run over and ending up in the hospital."

He took my arm. "I'm serious, Morgan. Her heart is weak. Seriously weak. She can't even watch her favorite Masterpiece Mystery shows anymore without her heart going into arrhythmia. If she finds out about him, she'll literally make herself sick with worry."

I nodded. Seeing the concern in his eyes, I understood about him and Grandma. About his comment about needing a drink to make it through the weekend

with her. He was worried, too. He didn't want to face
her death any more than I did. I held my pinkie out to
him and smiled. "All right. I swear it. I will keep the
details from Grandma. I promise."

He linked his pinkie finger with mine and shook like
he had when I was little and we were keeping secrets
from Mom. Then he gave me a one-armed hug. I loved
my dad. I linked arms with him as we walked to the
field house and made our way through the carnival atmosphere of the open party, to the back and the special
invitation-only VIP pre-gaming party.

Dad spotted Grandma first. She was already seated
and watching the party like a grand dame, jealously
guarding a table and saving seats for us. We had to go
through a receiving line with the university president,
Dr. Lawrence, and some of the regents before we could
get to her.

I'd met Dr. Lawrence before at one of the president's honor roll receptions I'd attended. The last re-
gent in the reception line, a gorgeous blond, was one of
our star alums, Amber Ranklin. I'd seen her at the
house before, though I doubted she would recognize
me. She wore a white gold sorority lavaliere necklace
with the Double Deltsie letters and a big-ass diamond
around her neck. I was wearing my Dad's Weekend
Double Deltsie sweatshirt.

Her eyes lit up when she spotted it. "A fellow sister!"
She hugged me instead of shaking my hand. While I
made small talk with her, I spotted Dakota and Al come
in and join the back of the line. I felt Dakota watching

me, trying to catch my eye. I ignored him. He deserved
it.

Dad and I finally made our way through the line and
joined Grandma. I kissed her cheek. "Sorry we kept you
waiting!"

She smiled at me. "Laughing and talking with a re-
gent like you're old friends, I'm impressed!"

I laughed at her pleased grandma look. Like I was
some kind of VIP myself. "Don't be. She's an alum sorority sister."

"Mom, how are you holding up?" Dad took a chair
next to her.

"Don't worry about me." Grandma shook her head.
"This old woman can take a lot."

"Morgan, get your grandmother something to
drink." Dad had a way of ordering me around like I was
still a child.

Like I wasn't just about to offer. "What would you
like, Grandma? I'll bring you something to drink and
then go back to get you a plate of food." I wanted to
show her I was thoughtful, too.

"Iced tea would be lovely."

I patted her hand and turned around, coming face to
face with Dakota and Al. I put a hand to my chest, startled.

"Hey." Dakota's eyes sparkled.

My heart raced at the nearness of him. I caught a
whiff of his cologne and silently cursed my reaction to
him.

"Are you going to introduce me to your dad and
grandma?"

"Eventually." I smiled at Al. "You're looking good for a guy who took second in an epic beer pong tourney last night."

"Flatterer. You mean I don't look hung over. Winners don't have to drink as much as losers," Al said.

Dakota stepped between me and Al. "Dad has a high tolerance."

"Too bad it doesn't run in the family." I smiled sweetly at Dakota to partially sheathe the barb. Before he could react, I turned around and pulled him forward to meet my family. "Dad. Grandma. This is my friend Dakota and his dad Al. We're joining them for dinner tonight. They were gracious enough to add us to their reservations. It's nearly impossible to get a table anywhere decent in this town on Dad's Weekend unless you book months in advance."

Grandma's eyes lit up at the mention of us having dinner with Dakota and his dad. It was like I'd just thrown down the gauntlet. I could almost see her train of thought. *Is there something going on between my granddaughter and this young man? How serious is it?* She was going to be watching us with a keen eye now.

"I was just going to get Grandma some tea." I took Dak's arm. "Come with." I led him to the beverage table. I leaned into him and went up on my toes to whisper a warning in his ear. "Grandma doesn't know our history."

He put his hands in the small of my back and pulled me closer. "What history?"

I was too aware of him. I cupped my hand around his ear and put a ton of breathiness in my voice. I was practically blowing in his ear with the force of my words. Teasing him. Tantalizing him on purpose. "The night you tried to kill me."

He leaned in to me and whispered, "Not that again."

"Whatever. She doesn't know about you and the accident. Or me ending up in the hospital." I explained the situation. "Dad made me promise not to tell her. You have to promise me, too."

He brushed a lock of hair out my face and tucked it behind my ear. He used my almost-blowing-in-the-ear trick, whispering directly in my ear so that I felt a tingle race through me. "I promise." He grinned down at me and stroked my cheek. "Let's get your grandma her tea."

As I poured Grandma's tea from a pitcher on the table, a guy came up to me.

"If it isn't the party ref. You're out of uniform."

I looked over to see Logan, from the Halloween party. "Hey, Viking! I almost didn't recognize you with a shirt on."

He laughed. "Yeah, no shoes, no shirt, no pre-game with Dr. Lawrence and company. Funny thing."

"Rules is rules. FYI, I don't ref official university functions." I winked at him. "The atmosphere's usually too dull."

Next to me, I felt Dakota stiffen and go territorial on me, clearing his throat to make his presence known.

"Logan, you remember Dakota," I said by way of re-introduction.

Logan nodded. "The other ref."

"Can I pour you something?" I held up the ice tea pitcher.

"No, I'm good. Just on my way back to my group."

I glanced in the direction he pointed and saw Amber among the group.

"I have to get back. Good to see you again, man. You too, Morgan."

"You two seemed friendly." Dakota took my arm.

"What can I say? I'm a popular girl." I brought Grandma her tea and went back to the buffet to get her a plate of air. With her restricted diet, there was practically nothing on the buffet of pulled pork sandwiches, baked beans, and fries that she could eat.

Dakota and Al took up residence at our table. There was an uneasy truce in the air between Dad, Al, and Dakota. I hoped Grandma didn't notice the tension. Truthfully, I thought she was too busy watching Dakota and me for any signs of a budding romance. And damn him, Dakota kept flirting with me. Sitting too close to me. Being too solicitous. Too courteous and polite to Grandma. Too charming, like he was trying to impress her and flirting with her, too. He quickly had her in smiles and laughter.

I wanted to scream at him not to lead her on. But he seemed determined to give both of us the wrong signals. Unlike Grandma's, my heart may have been in perfect, full-capacity working order. But it was just as delicate in its own way.

After the main course, Dad and Al excused themselves to hit the dessert table, which consisted mostly of trays of cookies. I stayed with Grandma. Cookies weren't on her heart diet.

I encouraged Dakota to go with them.

"We'll go together after they get back." He squeezed my hand and gave me that killer, heart-melting smile.

I would have been totally distracted by him if I hadn't been keeping a wary eye on Al and Dad. They'd been getting along so far. But they seemed to be engaged in a heated discussion by the cookies. Dad was gesturing at Al with the cookie tongs.

Next to them, a drunk guy was harassing a pretty girl. He bumped the table, rattling the dishes and coffeepot.

"You really think you're hot shit, don't you?" The guy raised his voice with every word.

"Stop it, Schwartz. Leave the past alone. Austin and I are good now. Keep your nose out of it." The girl tried to leave.

But Schwartz wouldn't let it drop. He grabbed her by the elbow. "You think you're so high and mighty. Regents' scholar. Dating a rich boy. You're nothing. Just a little cock tease.

"Austin said your mom was a much better lay than you. Hotter, too. He should have done your old lady again and forgotten about you." His voice had risen to a yell, an angry bellow.

The room went silent. Her face flamed. I was horrified for her. Logan was at the bar. He turned to stare at them, looking like he wanted to kill the Schwartz guy.

Logan got out of his chair and charged to the cookie table. Without saying a word, he slammed Schwartz with a right hook that sent him staggering back into the buffet table. Dishes rattled. Dad and Al jumped out of the way as Schwartz landed on his ass in the plate of cookies, crushing them to crumbs. The coffeepot at the end of the table tipped over, soaking the white tablecloth.

The girl screamed, "Stop! Stop it."

Schwartz let out a roar and hurled profanities at Logan as he struggled to his feet to fight back, knocking over more dishes. Sending the pitcher of cream next to the coffeepot tipping over.

The girl grabbed Logan's arm as he cocked it to swing again. "Logan, don't. No! Please."

Schwartz got his feet beneath him again. He slammed Logan with a fist to his left eye. Logan's head whipped back.

The girl screamed and wedged herself between them as Schwartz wound up again.

Dad and Al jumped into action like two superheroes. They grabbed Schwartz and restrained him before he could deliver his next punch. Several servers appeared at Logan's side, ready to hold him back.

Logan dropped his punching arm and waved them off as he wrapped his arm around the girl. "I'm done."

They backed off, hovering anxiously nearby, like they didn't quite believe him. I jumped out of my chair and ran to Dad's side.

Amber crossed the room, stopping at Logan's side. She put her hand on his shoulder and surveyed the damage. A tiny smile played at the corners of her mouth as she grabbed several pieces of ice from a bucket on the table, wrapped them in a napkin, and held them gently against his eye. "That eye could get nasty."

Double Deltsies to the rescue, I thought, proud of Dad and Amber.

President Lawrence, his face an angry red, broke through from the back of the crowd to see what the commotion was. Frowning slightly, and obviously trying to maintain his presidential composure, he turned his gaze to Amber in question just as a dad who must have been Logan's appeared at the front of the crowd, too.

"It's nothing." Amber gave a delicate shrug and laughed. "Too much pre-game exuberance. A little horseplay that got out of hand. A *boy* took a tumble." She spotted Logan's dad at the edge of the crowd. "I'm sure Harlan will make this good."

"Absolutely," the man named Harlan said. He was staring at Logan and the girl, still held tightly by the arm Logan had wrapped around her waist.

So this is the girl Logan was heartbroken over at the party, I thought.

The girl slid out of Logan's grip, turned, and ran out of the room. Logan stood staring after her, stunned.

"What are you waiting for, Viking?" I said to him. "If she's the one, go after her."

CHAPTER TWELVE

Morgan

I watched Logan run out after the girl, cheering him on. Cheering for true love. For a happy ending. Yeah, I'm a romantic. And I would like my own white knight. There are worse things.

Two security guards relieved Dad and Al of their restraining duties and hauled Schwartz out.

Dad rubbed his ribs gingerly.

I touched his arm. "You okay?"

He laughed like he was having the time of his life. His eyes were bright with fight and adrenaline. "I'm great. Fucking fantastic."

There's nothing like breaking up a good fight, with all the associated bragging rights, to bond two former-ly antagonistic dads. Logan taking a swing at Schwartz was the best thing that could have happened. For Dakota and me.

"Schwartz was a strong bastard. He put up a hell of a fight. Got me with an elbow." Dad rubbed his ribs as we walked through the field house. Super slowly, because that was the pace Grandma set.

Al rolled his shoulder. "Holding that boy back, I thought I was going to rip my shoulder out again. I dislocated it playing high school football. Hasn't been the same since."

"I could get you an instant icepack, Dad," Dakota said.

Was it just me who noticed how solicitous he was being? I resisted calling him a suck-up.

"I'll be fine." Al stretched. "Just need to work it out."

Dakota rolled his eyes.

I rolled mine back at him and whispered in his ear, "We're never going to hear the end of this. *The dads who saved the university tailgate party from disaster.* Should be front-page news, don't you think?"

He grabbed my hand and laced his fingers through mine. "Small price to pay for them to get along and forget how highly unsuitable I am for you."

Am for you? What the crap did that mean? I should have pulled my hand from his. We were giving everyone the wrong idea. Including my heart. But my hand felt good in his. Against all good reason, being near him made me happy and warm in the middle of a cold November day. I squeezed his hand and let myself enjoy the moment all the way to the stadium.

My family and Dak and his dad had seats in separate sections. I would have preferred to sit in the student section with my sorority sisters. And Dakota. But Dad had bought fifty-yard-line tickets in the alum section near the top of the stadium, close to the exit and concessions. For Grandma's comfort, so he said.

Inside the stadium, we came to a fork in the road. We started toward our seats in the alumni section to the right. Dak and Al had seats with his frat in the student section to the left. I tried to pull free of Dak's hand.

He held firm. "See you at halftime?"

"Maybe." Why was it so fun to tease him?

"I'm not letting go until I get a yes."

Was he trying to kill me with his flirting? Two could play that game. I caught him off guard with a kiss on the cheek, escaping his grip in the process. "Maybe."

I slipped into the crowd behind Dad, leaving Dakota to stare after us.

It was cold in the stands. The infamous campus wind blew incessantly. Dad pulled a packable down lap blanket from his pocket and tucked it around Grandma's legs. I went through the motions of standing for the national anthem, watching the coin toss, and yelling like a true fan during kickoff. But mostly I scanned the crowd across the stadium in a futile attempt to spot Dakota in the sea of school colors. I thought I was being totally stealthy.

Until Grandma called me out on it. "Looking for that handsome boy?"

"What?"

She chuckled. "Oh, child, you have it bad." She glanced at my father and then winked at me like a conspirator. "You don't have to sit here with us two old fogeys. I'll cover for you if you want to sneak into the student section and sit by the boy."

"And give up my time with you!" I shook my head and smiled, vowing to be less obvious. "Grandma!"

She laughed full out and reached over to squeeze my hand. "Oh, to be young!" She sounded way too wistful. "Enjoy every minute of it, kiddo."

We stood up. Sat down. Yelled, "Fight, fight, fight!" By halftime, Grandma was clearly flagging.

"You look tired, Mom." Dad was being particularly sensitive to her needs.

It worried me that he was worried about her.

"Let me take you home. I'm sure Morgan will understand." Dad gave me a look that warned me I'd better understand.

I saw the sly look in Grandma's eyes and panicked. Like she was going to cut me loose to spend the second half with Dakota. I needed my grandma. We hadn't even had a chance to chat, really. "Of course I will." I tried not to look as crestfallen as I felt at the thought of her leaving so soon.

Grandma studied me. I tried not to let her see, but she did anyway. "Stop treating me like spun glass, Rob! I hardly ever get out anymore. I never get the chance to spend time with my favorite granddaughter." She smiled at me. "I'm not going home a minute before I have to. I wouldn't turn up my nose at a little nap, though. Morgan can take me to the sorority and get me settled. I'll nap while you two come back for the second half and be fresh as a daisy for dinner."

I wouldn't come back to the game without her.

"I'll go with you two." Dad stood and offered Grandma his arm while I folded up her blanket and offered her my arm, too.

We flanked her and helped her up the stairs, one slow step at a time.

Dakota was waiting for us at the top of the stairs, his way down blocked by a stadium employee. His eyes lit up when he saw me. He broke into a grin that made my heart race. Alcohol goggles make some butt-ugly guys look good. Completely sober, Dakota looked better to me than any guy ever had.

His hair was tousled and windblown. He looked so totally adorable and hot. I steeled my heart against him. He was probably just toying with me again. Why did I feel like he was making a show of things? Setting me up? And yet when I looked in his eyes, he seemed totally genuine.

I gave him a slow up-and-down as we approached him. "They wouldn't let the riffraff in, I see."

He kept grinning. "You promised to spend halftime with me."

"Did not."

He stepped out of the way to let us pass.

"I promised to spend it with Grandma. She's tired. We're taking her back to the house to rest." I stared at him, trying to get a read on him. Trying to still my rapidly beating heart. "We'll see you at dinner."

"Did I mention we don't have to spend halftime at the stadium?" He turned to my dad and offered his arm to Grandma. "Let me. Morgan and I can get Mrs. Peterson to the house."

"That's very kind of you." Grandma tried to let go of Dad.

Dad pressed his hand over hers and held her firm. "We can manage."

"Dinner," I mouthed to Dakota.

One of his frat brothers spotted him and called out to him.

"Go!" I gave him a shove. "I'll see you later."

Just outside the gate, a motorized cart waited for us. Grandma spoke as we loaded her in. "You were a little rough on the boy, Rob."

He shrugged. "Was I?"

"I wouldn't have minded being escorted by a handsome young man." She winked at me. "It's clear he's in love with our little Morgs."

"Stay out of my girl's love life, Mom." Dad went all alpha dog on us. "If she doesn't want that boy, she doesn't."

It sounded more like he didn't want me with Dakota.

"My Morgan can have her choice of any young man on campus." He looked fierce, even as he beamed with pride.

"I didn't say she couldn't," Grandma said. "She takes after me, after all. I'm not blind to the looks the young men give her as she walks by. But I like Dakota. He's a considerate young man. If she wants him, she should go after him. Make sure he knows she wants him."

"Are you giving me love advice from Jane Austen?" We'd watched all the Jane Austen movies together, from the seventies versions to the most current versions. "You're sounding an awful lot like Charlotte Lucas in *Pride and Prejudice*, Grandma. When she was warning Lizzie that Jane should show Mr. Bingley more affection than she felt. Gush over him."

Grandma chuckled. "Am I? You know what I think about Jane Austen. She was a genius at observing people. Wisdom of the ages. Men haven't changed."

"Mom, the boy's a drunk. He has an MIP."

I couldn't believe what a traitor Dad was being. And after he'd warned me not to upset Grandma.

"He's not a drunk! No more than any frat guy on campus is. He parties like all the other guys." I came to his defense without thinking, sounding fiercer than I should have. My cheeks flamed. "I have an MIC, too. That doesn't make me a drunk, does it?" I told myself I wasn't defending Dak, just myself.

Dad looked about ready to explode. But he couldn't very well tell Grandma the full extent of what he had against Dakota.

"Anyone can make a mistake." Grandma gave Dad a pointed look as she gripped the rail of the cart. "I like him."

***

Dad returned for the second half of the game. I stayed with Grandma and did homework while she slept. And tried not to think about Dakota.

Grandma rallied after her nap. She was a tough one. We got ready for dinner together. She curled my hair, like she had when I was little, until it fell over my shoulders in waves. I loved the feeling of her fingers in my hair. So comforting I could have sat there all day.

"Let's give your dad a fit." She went to my closet. "Wear something sexy and provocative. Something that will curl the young Dakota's toes."

"Grandma!"

She grinned. "Believe it or not, I was a young sorority girl once. I know what men like." She went to my closet and started leafing through my dresses, sliding them along the bar as she inspected them. After rejecting half a dozen, she pulled one out. She held it up to me and grinned. "This one will do nicely." She grinned wickedly. "Let me live vicariously through you tonight."

I shook my head as she went to my dresser and looked through my lipsticks. "You know, Dakota and I are just friends."

She acted like she didn't hear me. She was going a little deaf. She picked up a tube and rolled out the lipstick. "Sexy vixen. Nice. We look good in this shade." She stared into the mirror and puckered her lips. "May I?"

"Help yourself."

She applied the lipstick and grabbed a tissue to blot it. "You can fool yourself, but you can't fool me, child. You like that boy. Now get dressed." She handed the lipstick tube to me. "And wear this."

Traffic in town was crazy. We had to hunt for parking at the Mexican restaurant where we were meeting Dak. The line curled out the front door and along the outside of the building. We got dirty looks as we bypassed the crowd and went to the hospitality desk at the front of the line to check in for our reservations. Dak and Al were already seated and waiting for us.

When Dak saw us coming, he jumped up and pulled a chair out for Grandma. His gaze bounced between us. "You two look gorgeous. Are you wearing the same shade of lipstick?"

Grandma grinned. If there had ever been any doubt, Dakota had just won her heart.

He sat next to me, so close our thighs brushed. He reached for a tortilla chip when I did. Our fingers touched as we reached for the salsa. I was sure it was purely intentional contact on his part. Like the way he rested his arm across the back of my chair. Or his fingers stroked my thigh as he adjusted his napkin in his lap. And damn it, I tingled at his touch. And wanted more. Much more.

He smelled good. He looked better. He was on his best behavior. If only all this flirting and feigned passion were real. I couldn't take him teasing me again and then refusing to even kiss me goodnight. What did he want? For me to beg him to hook up again?

Screw it. If anyone would beg, it would have to be him. I didn't want a hookup. I wanted a relationship.

I was startled to realize I wanted one with him. A *real* relationship. With love and caring and a certain level of commitment. One where everyone knew we were a couple. He'd had no problem having one with Alexis on the spur of the moment. But he was just teasing me for fun. The more he flirted, the more upset I became.

I excused myself to go to the restroom while we waited for our flan.

"I'll go with you." Grandma slid her chair back. She smiled at me.

Dad helped her up, giving us that "ladies never use the bathroom alone" look.

In the ladies' room, I felt a wave of nausea. I dashed into a stall and took deep breaths until it passed. The day had gone so well. I cursed Dakota. I cursed being reminded of the predicament I was probably in. When I came out, Grandma was leaning close to the mirror as she reapplied the lipstick she'd borrowed from me. She smiled at my reflection.

I took the sink next to her.

She studied me in the mirror.

I concentrated too hard on scrubbing my hands. The process really wasn't that interesting.

Grandma turned to stare at me. "There's something different between you and Dakota."

I'll say. But I didn't. Not out loud. My heart pounded with fear that she would find me out. I shrugged. "He's a good friend." And a total douchebag at the same time. It was easier to be angry at him than at myself.

"He wants to be more." She paused. "You clearly want that, too."

I froze and opened my mouth to deny it, silently cursing myself for being too obvious.

She rested her hand on my arm. "You and Dakota have a special chemistry that's very rare. He can't stop looking at you. He can't keep his hands off you. He's trying to impress your family for your sake."

I wanted to strangle Dakota for playing games with me, and leading my Grandma and her weak heart on, too.

Grandma held my gaze. "He could be the one."

I looked at her like she was really crazy now, and made a scoffing noise. "I don't think so." I couldn't tell her all the reasons why. "We've been out of sync since we met. He had a thing for me our freshman year. But that moment passed. Now we're just friends." But as much as I tried to deny it, deep in my heart I wanted more.

It must have shown on my face, because she nodded. "You can lie to yourself if you want. But it won't change things. Take it from me. I knew the minute your dad brought your mom home that she was the one. And your uncle and Millie—"

I scoffed again. "And look how well Mom and Dad turned out. They hate each other now."

"They made mistakes." Her voice was gentle. "I'm standing by my advice—if you want this boy, go after him. Better to have loved and lost."

I shook my head, vehemently. "You know I chased Dakota's best friend from high school for two years?" Grandma knew about my crush on Zach. "Look how that turned out." I almost blew things, forgetting for the moment that Grandma didn't know about Dakota running over Zach. "He's in love with my little."

"He wasn't the one."

"You never saw us together."

"That was my first clue." Her eyes sparkled. "Maybe he's right for your little. Lucky escape for you."

"I don't want to do the chasing. I want the guy to pursue me."

"Fair enough." Grandma squeezed my arm. "Isn't that what Dakota's been doing all night?"

Another wave of nausea washed over me.

"Are you feeling all right?" Her look was penetrating as well as kindly. "You haven't eaten much today. Been picking at your food and looked peaked from time to time."

I nodded too quickly.

Her eyes narrowed. "Is there something you should tell me? A reason you aren't going after Dakota? Another young man?"

I shook my head.

She still looked suspicious. "If you were in trouble, you could come to me." She glanced at my abdomen.

I resisted the urge to cover my stomach with my hands. "I would. I definitely would." I forced a smile. "Just having my period. You know how that goes." I wish I knew about the immediate discomfort of periods right now.

She kept studying me. "It's been a long time. But yes, I do." She didn't look like she believed me.

I took her arm. "The boys are waiting."

Through dessert, Dad cast worried looks Grandma's way. He spoke almost as soon as she took her last bite of flan. "It's a two-hour drive home, Mom. We should be going." He signaled the waiter for the check.

Al waved the waiter away. "Forget the check, Rob. This one's on me."

Crap, now even Al was trying to impress my dad and grandma.

Dakota covered my hand with his. "Stay. Dad and I will take you home later." Damn, he practically cooed the words.

My pulse raced. I felt tingles in all the right places. I was weak, but not that weak. And so tired, I was practically dead on my feet. I pulled my hand free and stood. I had my pride. "Thanks, but Dad can drop me off."

I turned to Al. "It was great meeting you. Thanks for dinner." I reached behind me, grabbed my coat and purse from the back of my chair, and slid the chair back to stand.

Dakota stood with me. "I'll call you later."

I wanted to tell him not to bother. But Grandma was watching us with so damned much hope sparkling in her eyes. *Let her live vicariously a little longer*, I told myself. *If she wants to believe in true love and the one, who am I to stop her?* I nodded and let him help me with my coat and gave him a hug.

As I walked away, I turned to look back at him. He was watching me with hunger in his eyes. What the hell was wrong with him? What was he up to?

CHAPTER THIRTEEN

Dakota

I watched Morgan walk away. There's nothing as emasculating as not having a car. Not being able to drive. Being stuck in a restaurant with your dad while the girl you want, and shouldn't, leaves you standing alone like a sucker. I clenched my fist as I watched Morgan disappear.

"I like her." Dad was still sitting, watching her walk away, too. He downed the last of his beer as the waiter delivered the check.

I turned to stare at my father. "Morgan? You like *her*?" I was irrationally angry. I shook my head as I took my seat. "She has a rep as the bitch of the Delta Delta Psi house." What was I saying? I was mad as hell at Morgan for toying with me. For embarrassing me in front of my old man.

Dad shrugged and laughed. "Maybe I like bitches. She's funny. She's hot—"

"Dad, please—"

"What?" He shot me a teasing look. "I'm not dead yet. And I have eyes." He grinned at me. "She has you wrapped around her little finger." He pulled his credit card out and slid it into the bill folder. "Hot girl like that, what's not to love?"

Plenty.

The waiter swooped in and picked up the bill.

The booze had loosened Dad's tongue. "Zach comes back tomorrow, doesn't he?"

Shit. Now Dad wants to talk? "Yeah."

"Huh."

"What does that mean?" I said.

"Nothing." He nodded toward the door. "I'd keep her away from him. You don't want to be second to Zach ever again."

I stared at him. Yeah, the old man had too much faith in me. I took a deep breath. "Too late. He's the one who pulled her out from behind my car." He had no idea how too late I was.

"And you're the guy who's helping her through the aftermath." He looked at me like he had total faith his son was a stud who could win the girl in the end. "You're a *Bradley*. We never give up. Kill her with friendship and understanding. Listen to her and sympathize. Girls love that sensitive shit."

Morgan

Sunday morning the dads packed up and left, taking their deep voices, fatherly disapproval, and pride with them. I slept late. When I got up, my stupid period still hadn't started. I'd given it fair warning. It was time to take matters into my own hands and force-start my period. Girls in the house did it all the time. You didn't want the curse to start in the middle of the spring formal. Or finals. Method number one—birth control pills—had already failed me. Number two, large quantities of ginger tea, required a trip to the grocery or health food store. I didn't have the time for that. Number three, high doses of vitamin C, consumed with tons of water.

I kept a bottle of vitamin C for cold and flu season. I filled a water bottle and swallowed several vitamin C tablets, trying not to gag them back up. Only as a last resort would I resort to method number four—sex. That was what had gotten me into this stress mess of possibly being pregnant in the first place.

I showered and dressed with care. Zach was coming back. I wanted to look good, but not so good it looked like I was trying too hard. I wanted to be just the right amount of casual Double Deltsie fineness. I did my hair and applied my makeup.

The house was bustling with activity when I finally finished and came downstairs, foraging for something to appease the queasiness upsetting my stomach and my nerves.

As I walked past the living room, Kelly was hanging crepe paper streamers. Victoria and Sarah were hanging a Welcome Home banner. A balloon bouquet waved in the entryway.

Zach comes back today. The thought had been assaulting me all morning.

My heart pounded, but not with lust or love. I hadn't seen him since before he'd left. I'd popped by to thank him for saving my life. Everything had been fresh and raw then. He'd looked so battered and broken. Not like Zach. I wondered, just for a second, if I was so superficial that the sight of him not looking robust and handsome had turned me off. Or the thought that he might not really be Zach when he fully recovered. Alexis had never wavered. Was I just a coward?

I'd been so angry with Dakota then. How things had changed.

Danielle, a sophomore, one of the girls who'd complained her period was late, sat on a sofa, blowing up balloons. She was laughing and happy, even as she complained about cramps. A complete contrast to how I felt.

The live-in frosh Katie sat next to her, stretching a balloon in preparation to blow it up. I overheard her tell Danielle how perky she looked.

"Yeah." Danielle nodded, grinning from ear to ear. "The minute my dad left, the curse started. Like it was just holding out so I didn't have to mess with it while he was here." She laughed. "All weekend I worried for nothing about the worst."

I was still worried. Petrified. Queen of denial. I took a swig of water from the bottle I carried.

Kelly spotted me. "Hey! Look who's up." She thrust a package of streamers and a thing of tape at me. "Get to work. Zach will be here in a couple of hours. We need every hand." She pointed across the room. "Start there. String them so they look pretty. We'll meet in the middle."

I was curling a streamer when Alexis walked in. Her hair and makeup were perfectly done. She wore her diamond Double Deltsie necklace.

Our eyes met. I smiled like we were old pals. Like I was an encouraging big. "You must be so excited!"

Distrust shone in her eyes. She looked like she thought I was up to something. Get a rep as a bitch and it follows you forever. And here I thought we'd been making progress.

She still didn't completely trust me. Not with her man on the horizon. I didn't really blame her. With Zach's return imminent, I wasn't sure I trusted myself. There was a part of me that worried I would fall back into my old pattern of wanting what I couldn't have. And part of me that worried I had a new obsession.

Dakota
Dad left just after one. "Don't forget what I said," he said as he tossed his suitcase in the trunk. "Don't lose that girl to Zach. Bradleys aren't number two."

Could have fooled me. I'd been number two to Zach's QB1 for as long as I could remember. Which reminded me—shit, Zach and Alexis were the only two who knew about Jordan. Alexis had already bitched to me about how I was hanging out with Morgan. And what was I thinking? What about Jordan?

Yeah. What about her? She'd been bitching at me lately about how I was ignoring her. How I wasn't as attentive as I used to be. She was getting clingy jealous. A complete turnoff that made me avoid her even more. She was right. I'd been distracted. By Morgan. Jordan and I had been through a lot together. She'd always been faithful to me. She deserved better.

I hadn't told Zach much about me hanging with Morgan. I was sure Alexis had filled him in with what she knew. What the hell had I been thinking when I'd told Morgan I would call? It put me in the douche position of breaking my word and avoiding her rather than calling.

She'd get the wrong idea and think I wasn't interested. That I'd led her on. When the opposite was true. I burned with desire for her. I'd had a wet dream about her last night and woken with a woody that wouldn't die. I didn't trust myself around her.

Zach, Alexis. Me, Jordan, Morgan. The whole thing was a complicated pile of shit.

The Double Deltsies had planned a welcome home party for Zach. Kelly, the house president, had texted me specifically to invite me. More like to command my presence. There was no way I could back out. I had to go to the sorority to welcome Zach back. Wouldn't miss it, in fact.

I got ready with Dad's warning echoing in my ears. I sure as hell wouldn't relish watching Morgan's eyes light up at the sight of Zach.

Who would have thought Morgan could still come between Zach and me? Everyone thought Alexis was the problem.

I grabbed my wallet and keys. I was on my way out as Cody and Brian came into the hall from the dining room, dressed like they were on their way out, too. We'd been in the same pledge class. We were tight.

Cody looked me up and down. "Don't you look fine."

Brian took a deep sniff of the air. "Is that your *I'm about to get laid* cologne I smell?" He cocked an eyebrow and slapped me on the back. "On Sunday afternoon? That's my boy! Who's the lucky lady?"

"I'm on my way to the Double Deltsie house." I slipped on my coat.

"Oh, that's right," Cody said. "The girls are throwing Zach a surprise party. Well, you could still get lucky, I suppose."

Brian let loose with a string of curses, "You're going to a party for the houseboy?" He shook his head.

"When Kelly calls, I jump," I said. "If I blow our relations with the Double Deltsies, I'm screwed. The guys will never forgive me. The fate of the collective house's sex lives rests on my shoulders."

"But the houseboy?" Brian said.

Cody shot him a warning look. "A man's got to do what a man has to do. They're friends."

"Dude, I don't get that," Brian said. "After what he did to you—"

I sidestepped them. "You don't have to get it." I gave Brian a look, warning him to drop it.

Brian and Cody followed me out.

"Drop us by The College Grind, would you, bro?" Cody said.

"I would, but I'm walking," I said. "Until late January."

Brian shook his head. "You can't go on foot to the party, dude. Unless you want to look like a wuss."

I stared at him, thinking about Zach pulling up in his ride in front of the house.

"Like anyone's going to catch you." Brian pulled the door open. "The cops have to have probable cause to stop you, don't they? Like, dude, do they have you memorized? Memorizing the face of every student with a suspended license around here is impossible." He slapped me on the back. "Live a little, buddy."

He was right. "Fuck it!" I pulled my keys out of my pocket.

Brian grinned. "That's the spirit."

Morgan

It was a cool, sunny November day. Kelly had put a sawhorse in a parking spot out front to save it for Zach.

Alexis came bouncing into the room. "He just texted. He's almost here!"

Kelly grabbed me. "Help me move the sawhorse."

Alexis went outside to sit on the steps and wait for him while Kelly and I cleared the parking spot. Something was up. Something everyone had been keeping from me and Alexis. Kelly pulled me back into the house, where everyone had gathered in the living room.

When I saw his car turn up the street, my heart pounded. Alexis ran to him, bouncing she was so excited, as she waited for him to park.

He jumped out of the car and pulled her into his arms. He looked whole again. Hot and handsome like his old self. I expected to feel the old familiar pang of jealousy. The old heart flutters. Nothing.

Zach kissed her. And kissed her.

Nothing. Nothing. Nothing but joy—I was over him.

Kelly stood at the window, peeking through the curtains. "Now! Come on."

She gathered us on the front steps of the house.

Zach pulled something out of his pocket and held it up for Alexis to see. He was saying something too low for me to hear.

My heart stopped. Was he proposing?

He opened a wooden jewelry box. I craned to get a look, but I was too far away. The breeze carried one word to us. "So?"

"Yes! Yes!" Alexis bounced on her toes.

"Is that an engagement ring?" Victoria whispered beside me.

Kelly shook her head. "Promise ring." She seemed to be in the know. "Isn't it sweet?"

"Not as good as being lavaliered or pinned." I realized too late how snide I sounded. And probably jealous. Which wasn't the case at all. I was happy for them. But a promise ring meant practically nothing. Being lavaliered or pinned was nearly the same as being engaged. It was all but. I was only trying to point out the distinction.

Zach took Alexis' hand and slid a slender ring on. She threw her arms around his neck and kissed him. As we swarmed around them, welcoming Zach back and congratulating them, I got a glimpse of a ring with a tiny diamond. Like microscopic. Nothing to be too excited about, other than sentiment. That wasn't even sour grapes on my part, just truth.

A familiar car pulled up. It took me a second to recognize it. I swore beneath my breath and cursed Dakota's stupidity in the strongest language I knew as he jumped out of his car. Despite my anger at his foolishness, my heart did backflips at the sight of him.

What the hell was Dakota thinking? If he were caught driving while his license was suspended, they'd revoke his continuance.

Looking completely laid back and cool, Dak joined the group and put his arm around Zach. "Welcome back, QB1!" He took Alexis's hand, holding it like a knight about to kiss it as he studied the ring. "Congrats, man. Both of you!" He kissed Alexis on the cheek. "It's gorgeous."

In that sparkling moment, I glared at Dak, so angry with him for risking everything to show off for Alexis that I wanted to kill him.

CHAPTER FOURTEEN

Dakota

Ever heard the expression, *Her eyes shot daggers?* As I admired Alexis' promise ring, Morgan was shooting them my way. I guessed she was pissed I hadn't called. Come on. Give a guy twenty-four hours. She had no idea I wasn't planning on calling.

I found myself in a cloud of perfume as the girls streamed in around us, everyone offering their congratulations and admiring the ring. Which was nothing spectacular.

Kelly let the admiration society go on for a while before shepherding us inside with the promise of food. "We have cake!"

Morgan avoided me. I watched her to see if she was watching Zach. Damn it, she made me insecure.

Inside the house, the girls handed out plastic champagne flutes and filled them with sparkling cider. Kelly made a toast, welcoming Zach back and offering him his job again anytime he wanted it. A couple of girls stood behind a table in the dining room, cutting cake.

I grabbed a piece of cake, finally cornering Morgan as she talked to Victoria in the actual corner of the room. She and Victoria were sorority twins. Alone, they were hard enough to handle. Together, they were undefeatable. I would have backed off from the fight if I hadn't been so desperate. Morgan ignored me until I cleared my throat.

She slowly looked at me, acknowledging my presence at her leisure. "Fancy seeing you here."

Victoria gave me a cold look. She was smart enough to sense the tension between Morgan me. But, shit, you would have to be dead not to feel it. I returned her look with one warning her to scram. Uncowed, she looked at Morgan for guidance.

Morgan nodded almost imperceptibly. Victoria shrugged and backed off. "Nice to see you, Dakota. I was just leaving." Her voice dripped acid.

Morgan was empty-handed.

I held up my plate. "Not drinking? Not eating? Allergic to cake?"

Her eyes were dark. "Allergic to calories."

I leaned in and whispered in her ear. "You look good to me."

She glared back at me. "You drove here!" The words exploded out of her. "What the hell were you thinking?"

Damn, she was hot when she was concerned about me. "So that's it. You're worried about me." I smiled, relieved. And smug. She was just pissed about the car.

"Worried?" She frowned. "You're crazy. I'm your sobriety buddy, that's all. It's my duty to keep you from doing dumbass things."

"I'm completely sober."

"And a completely idiotic douchebag." Her eyes snapped.

"It looks like you failed in your duties."

"Some people are irredeemable. You aren't driving home."

I laughed and took a step closer to her, invading her personal space until we were just inches apart. "How are you going to stop me? Drive me yourself?" I brushed her hair back over her shoulder. The feel of her silky hair made me pulse with desire for her. Much as I fought it, the chemistry between us was too strong. Everything from her snapping eyes to the way she stood up to me turned me on.

"Screw you."

I leaned into her and whispered in her ear, "That's exactly what I want to do to you."

She wrapped her arms around me and went up on her toes to whisper back to me. "Do you?"

The next thing I knew, her hands were in my pocket, relieving me of my keys. She had them and stepped away before I could stop her. She wasn't dumb enough to dangle them in front of me and tease and taunt me with them.

I reached for them as she spun away from me. I grabbed her arm. "Damn it, Morgan. Give them back."

Before I could grab her hand, she slid the keys in her ample cleavage. "Are you man enough to come get them?" Her eyes dared me.

I scowled. She had me and she knew it. If I reached down her blouse in the public area of the house in front of her sorority sisters, I'd be in bigger trouble than just an MIP. My eyes lingered on her chest. "That has to be uncomfortable."

Her gaze held mine. "I've had worse between my breasts." She laughed like it was a joke.

There was a commotion near the exit. Zach and Alexis were making their exit.

"They didn't stay long." Morgan's tone was dry and amused.

I watched her watch the happy couple walk away, looking for any sign she still wanted Zach. A tiny smile played at the corner of her mouth. What the hell did that mean?

She grabbed my hand and started pulling me toward the door. "Party's over. I'm taking you home."

I squeezed her hand, feeling tight and wound up and horny as hell. "I like the sound of that."

I expected her to roll her eyes. Instead, she just smiled. "If you're very good I might even give you your keys back."

My mouth went dry. "I'm not leaving without my car."

One of the houseboys, Seth, walked by just then. Morgan grabbed him. "I have a favor, Seth. Drive us to

Dak's frat? It will take you less than five." She shot me a look. "We'll take his car. Silly boy, he forgot and accidentally drove it over." She shot me a look. "At least I hope it was accidental."

Seth ignored me and put his arm around Morgan. "What kind of trouble are you up to, my pet?"

She laughed and snuggled into him like they were old friends of the too-cozy sort.

My blood pressure went through the roof. So jealous I wanted to punch Seth out and tell him to get his hands off her.

"Just doing my duty as the dumbass' friend. Friends with suspended licenses don't let other friends with suspended licenses drive."

I scowled at her, but the promise of sex kept me in line. One quick screw and she'd be out of my system for good. After that, she could go to hell.

"Very admirable. Philanthropy project?" he teased.

"No, but I should get credit for saving his ass." She pulled the keys out of her bra and handed them to Seth.

She took my arm. "Let's go."

"You don't have to come," Seth said to her. "I can take him myself. Should I put on a chauffeur's cap?"

She grinned at him. "Don't be silly. I'm coming with you." She glanced at me. "He can't be trusted." She took Seth's arm.

I was forced to follow them out. To make matters worse, and to make a point, she climbed into the front passenger seat and laughed and joked with Seth, ignoring me during the short drive.

Five minutes later, Seth parked my car in the president's spot behind the frat and handed my keys back to me. "Nice ride."

Morgan hugged him and whispered her undying thanks.

Seth addressed her, but shot me a warning look. "Call me if you need me to come get you."

"I'll be fine." She winked. "He's not as dangerous as he looks."

Morgan

I didn't know what possessed me. Seriously. All this talk about not using sex to bring on my period, about not hooking up again, and suddenly it seemed like the perfect solution to my problem. But it had to be with Dak.

Jealousy is a wicked, cruel beast. I'd seen him looking at Alexis and gone completely green. I had to convince myself I was more attractive than Alexis. That he could want me for me. I would *make* him want me for me.

And bring this damn period on. No more pregnancy scare. No more fears about what I would do. About being irrevocably linked to him forever. Dak out of my system. Good for all.

I took his hand. "What are you waiting for?"

"Is that a come-on?" His eyes were round and dark. He was already turned on.

I glanced at the bulge in his pants. "Keep talking and I'll lose the mood."

He took my hand and led me to his room. Neither of us spoke as he locked the door.

I kicked off my shoes and shed my coat. He did the same and took a step into me.

I wanted him. Wanted him so badly. He put his hand at the back of my head and pulled me into a kiss. I opened my mouth to him and reveled in the taste of him as I ran my tongue over his lips until he shivered.

He grew tired of my teasing and pulled me hard against him, holding my lips to his with bruising passion as he ground his boner against me. Kissing wasn't supposed to be part of the equation. Kissing was too personal. Kissing him, I wanted more from him than just sex. I broke free and unzipped his jeans.

I let him pull my blouse off over my head and helped him shed his shirt. He tossed it onto the pile my clothes were making on the floor.

"Shit, you're beautiful." He kissed the tops of my breasts.

I was too impatient for a slow seduction. I needed things fast and hard. Impersonal. I unfastened the front hook of my bra and slid it off over my arms, standing before him and giving him a good look.

His eyes became even darker and rounder. I watched the gentle rhythm of his chest rising and falling, running my fingers over his chest. I sucked his nipples until he gasped and unzipped my jeans. I pulled back and shimmied out of them, letting him watch my breasts bounce. Bouncing them for his sake.

"Get out of those boxers." I tried to distance myself from the emotions that could break me.

He stepped out of them and kicked them aside. "Get out of those thong panties."

"Why? Too much of an impediment for a big guy like you?" I liked taunting him.

He grabbed me around the waist and pulled me into his big, hard boner, sliding a finger beneath the waistband of the panties and inside of me. "You're already wet."

"I've been wet since the car." I squeezed his finger.

"Fuck." His breathing was shallow. He pulled his finger out and my panties down.

I kicked them aside.

He pulled me into him and took a step back toward his bed. I read his intention—he wanted me on top.

"No." I shook my head.

"No? Now?" He looked incredulous.

Whatever Dak was, he wasn't a rapist. No meant no. I knew I could trust him that way. "Save the story about how much pain you'll be in if we don't finish." I gave him a seductive smile. "I'm not saying no to sex. I'm saying no to that way of having sex." I grabbed a pillow from the bed and tossed it on the floor. "We do this my way."

I ran my fingers along his jaw line, wanting him. Wanting his love. If I couldn't have that, I was going to give him something to remember. His body would always want mine.

I ran my fingers down his body as I bent to suck his dick. Guys didn't need blowjobs, but they sure made them happy. I grabbed his butt and licked his dick like a big, pulsing ice cream cone. I sucked and licked until he moaned. I teased him to the edge. "Don't you dare come. I'm going to let you have me like no guy ever has."

I pulled away, stood, and turned my back to him as I went down on all four on the floor.

"What—"

"Run with me." I put my head on the pillow. "Come closer. Back up behind me and hold still. Let me do the work for now. Your turn is coming." I laughed at the double meaning as I went up in a partial headstand and walked my legs up until they were around his waist.

"We're having a naked wheelbarrow race?" His voice was ragged. "Should I grab your ankles?"

"No." I bit my lip and swallowed hard, concentrating, squeezing him between my legs. I rested my arms next to my head on the pillow and positioned myself over his dick. "Grab my hips and hang on."

"Naked hot yoga?" He grabbed my hips.

"Stop talking." I rubbed his dick between my legs, positioning him as I curled my legs against his chest, my head still on the floor on the pillow. This was an impersonal position, but erotic. Which was exactly what I wanted. No eye contact. No face-to-face. Just sex. This position was supposed to hit my G-spot and give me the climax of my life.

His hands were hot on my hips. I was totally wet for him. I took a deep breath and slid him inside me.

He swore beneath his breath.

I gently moved my hips. "What are you waiting for, QB? Fuck my brains out."

He didn't need any more encouragement. He pounded into me so deeply my G-spot went wild. I rode him, upside down with my head on the pillow, letting him ram into me again and again.

Sex in this position shouldn't have been easy. Our rhythm should have been off and taken time to find. But it wasn't. Our timing was perfect. We moved like we belonged together. Almost like we were one. As the blood rushed to my head, every part of me tingled.

Wave after wave of pleasure built with each thrust. The rush was a total high. My arms went shaky. My head pounded into the pillow. Just when I thought I couldn't take another thrust without climaxing, the biggest orgasm of my life crashed over me. I moaned and called out his name. "Dak, Dak, Dak!"

"Morgan!"

I swear I felt him ejaculate into me.

I rested my head on the pillow, my arms shaking. My heart breaking. My resolve leaving. My body sated in a way it never had been.

He pulled out. I slid my legs down him and rested on the floor, curled over my legs, arms outstretched, trying to catch my breath and my sense of reason.

"Wow!" He sounded stunned.

I thought he would leave me there. I pictured him flopping back on the bed behind him. Instead, he scooped me into his arms and carried me to the bed.

He set me down gently, like a true lover, and lay down beside me, cradling me in his arms. "I have never had such an earth-shaking orgasm before. That was...indescribable."

I felt myself breaking. I couldn't look at him.

He brushed my hair back out of my eyes. "Is that a bruise on your forehead?"

"Is it?" My voice was shaky, like the rest of me.

"Could be a floor burn." He kissed it gently. "How will we ever explain this?"

How could we explain anything? I tried not to look at him. He was being too tender. Too lover-like. Part of me wanted him to put on his pants and act like a hookup, impatient for me to go. Part of me was begging him to love me.

He looked me in the eye. "I love you." His voice was husky. He looked almost as surprised by what he'd said as I was.

I covered my face with my hands and started to cry. "It's too much."

He pulled me against his chest and held me tight, with his hands cradling my head. "I'm overwhelmed, too. It will be all right."

It would. Once my period started.

I love you. That was what all guys said after hot sex. It was only code for *thank you*. I knew that. But I hoped...

Hope was a terrible bitch.

CHAPTER FIFTEEN

Dakota

I held Morgan until she stopped crying. What the fuck had I said to upset her? I love you? Yeah, said after mind-blowing sex, it sounded like total BS. But I meant it. I was as surprised as she was. In that moment, anyway, I meant it. Would it last? The thought scared the shit out of me. Morgan was the one girl who could break my heart. I'd already let her get too close.

I stroked her hair and held her. I was ready to go again. And it was blatantly obvious. Holding a naked girl as hot as Morgan, I would have to have been dead not to get another boner. I couldn't get the sight of her hips and her toned back out of my mind. Or the way she felt when I entered her. Or the way she'd rocked me to my core. But I also felt tender and protective of her.

She stopped crying. I brushed her lips with a gentle kiss. She gave me a sad smile and disentangled herself from me.

She glanced at my dick and away again just as quickly as she sat up. "I have to go."

I grabbed her arm as she slid off the bed. "Stay."

She shook her head, shook off my arm, and stood up to look around for her clothes.

"Finding your panties—ten points." My dick still hadn't realized it wasn't getting a second shot at her.

She made a distracted noise as she put her bra on, totally missing my humor.

I slid off the bed and grabbed my boxers and jeans. "I'll walk you home."

She'd found her jeans and was slipping into them. She shook her head. "No, that's okay. I'll be fine."

"Drive you, then?" I teased. I wanted her to stay.

"Don't you dare!" She pointed her finger at me, and her voice was fierce, like she didn't see I was kidding. Her eyes were moist again. "That's what got us into this in the first place. I broke my no-hookup rule...never mind."

I grabbed her hand and kissed her finger with the lightest of kisses, trying to ignore the barb about hooking up. I sure as hell didn't see it that way. But I knew she was right. I wasn't ready for a relationship with her. "I'd get behind the wheel again if it would get me laid like that again."

"Don't press your luck." She slid her blouse on and bent to pick up a shoe.

I grabbed my socks and sat to put them on as she slid her second shoe on and grabbed her coat.

"See you around." She blew me a kiss and raced out the door before I could stop her.

I thought about going after her, but what was I going to say? So I let her go, wondering if I'd just had a pity fuck. Wondering if she'd been imagining I was Zach. Wondering if I was ever going to get over that.

You had your one fuck, buddy, I told myself. *She's out of your system now.*

But I lied. I couldn't stop thinking about her. She was in my blood now. I couldn't get her out. I was a weak guy. But I'd be damned if I texted or called her. She clearly didn't want me.

Morgan

Dakota didn't call or text or send me a smoke signal. Not like I thought he would. That was the way of hookups. I knew that. I had been a convenient lay to forget Alexis. Just like the time before. Nothing more.

But my heart broke all the same. Somewhere along the way, I had been falling in love with him.

Of course, I'd used him, too. But it, and all the vitamin C, hadn't worked. I felt better, though. Except for being desperately period-less, I felt normal. All those male hormones in Dak's cum had apparently cured me. The nausea disappeared. I had energy again.

By Tuesday morning I had convinced myself I wasn't pregnant. I'd imagined it. If my period didn't start by Thanksgiving, I would see my doctor. I mean, if I was preggo, wouldn't I still feel crappy? I wasn't far enough in to feel better.

I needed to think. I needed coffee and the buzz of disinterested people around me. I needed to get out of the house and study where my brain could fly. I went to The College Grind, ordered a pumpkin-spice latte, and found a table as far out of the draft of the door as I could. Which is to say, a cold breeze blew in every time the door opened. There was no safe spot.

I hung my coat on the back of my chair and took out my laptop. I was quickly in the zone, deep into working on a paper. In that mode, I shut the rest of the world out. Someone could call my name and I wouldn't hear it. I ignored the cold blasts that clutched their way to my small corner of the coffee shop.

I was reaching mindlessly for another sip of my latte when the worst cramp of my life hit out of nowhere. I gasped and doubled over in mortal pain, clutching my abdomen.

Breathe, breathe, breathe!

I felt the surge of warm blood soaking my panties and leggings. It happened so quickly I didn't have time to react.

In the next instant, I was sitting in a pool of warm blood, mortified. I had soaked through the panty liner I was wearing. The pain was so bad I could barely move.

"Morgan?" Dakota stood over me.

Crap. My heart stopped again. How was it possible to be horrified and overjoyed at the same time? I needed him in the worst way. I repeated the *breathe* mantra as my face flamed. I forced myself to look up at him.

His face that was pale with worry.

I opened my mouth, with no idea what I was going to say, just as another cramp hit and took away my voice. I moaned and, tears welling in my eyes, grabbed my purse. Blood, my blood, dripped off the chair. I swayed, dizzy and nauseous.

"Go!" Dakota took my arm and helped me up with incredible gentleness. "I'll take care of this." He took his coat off and wrapped it around my waist as I stood. So gentlemanly, like we could cover what was happening.

I ran to the bathroom, which was mercifully empty. I had never been so embarrassed and so thrilled at the same time. I slid into one of the two stalls and pulled a tampon out of my purse. I managed to get to the toilet just as another cramp hit. I looked between my legs into the red water. There were clots, big ones.

No, I thought. *No, I can't be. This is just a bad period.* I'd had bad ones before.

I grabbed my phone and looked up what to do for miscarriages and menstrual clots. My hands shook as I typed and prayed. The screen swam before my eyes. Before eight weeks—I counted back, less than eight— the fetus should spontaneously abort without medical intervention or the need for medical attention. Seek medical help if the clots got too large or there was hemorrhaging.

I'm fine, I told myself. But I was shaking and scared as I cleaned up. How was I going to get home? How could I walk out of the bathroom with the butt of my leggings stained with blood and my legs shaking? I put my head in my hands and brushed back a tear.

The door to the ladies' room slammed open.

"Morgan! Morgan, are you all right?" Dak!

His footsteps had never sounded so good. They stopped just outside my stall until his Toms peeked beneath the door. If they had been nervous and twitchy, I think I would have lost it. But his feet were firmly planted, like a knight to the rescue.

I blushed to my toes. This wasn't exactly the kind of throne I'd hoped to be sitting on when my knight in shining armor arrived. Or the most romantic damsel-in-distress situation. I forced myself to reply, but I broke up and my voice cracked, betraying me. I wasn't brave at all. "I'm...I'm fine."

He swore beneath his breath. "Shit, Morgs. Don't lie. You sound crappy."

"Bad choice of words." I grabbed a square of toilet paper and dabbed at my eyes. "I *am* on the toilet."

"Shit!" His voice was tender.

"Watch it!"

I pictured him smiling. His Toms inched closer. The stall door rattled. His fingers appeared over the edge. "Need any help in there?"

"No! Are you crazy? What are you going to do? Rush in here and wipe my ass?"

His fingers were white. He shook the stall door like he was ready to pry it off. "I'm serious. Look, I have change. Want me to buy you a tampon and toss it over the stall?"

I panicked. "Don't peek over the stall! No one sees me sitting on the john."

"Shy?" He lowered his voice to a whisper. "I've seen everything you own."

"Modest. I have to preserve some mystery."

"There are two kinds of girls—those who let you see them pee and those who don't."

"Profound. You should put that on a T-shirt."

"Maybe I will."

"Damn, now you know my secret—anyone sees me pee and I lose my superpowers." I smiled through my tears.

"Seriously," he said. "Need a tampon?"

"Thanks, I have my own." I smiled through my tears.

"Okay. I'll wait for you here."

I didn't have the courage to send him away. I nearly slumped in relief—he wasn't going to leave me alone.

The door to the bathroom opened. I heard a girl gasp.

"We'll just be a minute," Dakota said to her, then mumbled something I couldn't hear.

Footsteps receded as I flushed the toilet and pulled up my soaked leggings. I was still blushing when I came out and handed Dakota his coat. "I should wash that—"

"Don't worry about it."

My legs were shaky. I was trembling as I walked to the sink and washed my hands. I couldn't look at Dakota. My face flamed.

He cleared his throat, like he was nervous and embarrassed, too. And uncertain what to do or say. "Everything's cleaned up out there."

I still couldn't look directly at him. Out of the corner of my eye, I saw he was wearing both his backpack and mine. I nodded. "Thank you."

He gently caught my arm. "This, what happened, seems extreme." He paused. "I'm taking you to student health."

"No!" I panicked. I didn't need to go. If I went, they'd be able to tell for sure whether I was miscarrying or not. And I didn't want to know. "I have heavy periods." Would my face ever stop flaming? TMI. "I'm fine."

"You keep saying that." He took a deep breath. "I'm not convinced."

I reached for a paper towel. "I was caught by surprise." Not a total lie. "I'm usually more prepared." It had never happened like this.

"I'm taking you home. No arguing."

I nodded, meek and pleased. I needed him.

He was holding my coat. He held it for me while I slipped into it.

I stared at the door, trembling at the thought of walking out in public.

He put his arm around my shoulder. Why did it feel so damn good?

"Screw them, Morgs. People understand. This shit happens." He squeezed my shoulders. "Put your arms around my neck. I'll carry you out."

I could have argued, but I had neither the mental nor physical strength to. I put my arms around him and bent at the knees so he could pick me up.

He carried me out of the ladies' room and through The College Grind, out the door and into the freezing day and biting wind.

"You can't carry me all the way home," I said.

"Watch me," he said.

I rested my head against his shoulder.

Dakota

I didn't even notice Morgan's weight as I carried her to the Delta Delta Psi house. She cuddled into me and felt too damn good in my arms. Shit, I was worried about her. She looked pale and in pain.

I carried her up the steps to the house and kicked open the front door with my foot, startling a couple of girls who were sitting in the living room. I ignored them and headed for the stairs.

One of them rushed at me, trying to block my way. "You can't go up there."

I glared at her. "The hell I can't. Morgan's not feeling well. I'm not setting her down until she's in her bed. She needs someone to sit with her. Is Victoria around?"

The girl took one look at Morgan's pale face and backed off. "I'll find her. Or someone."

I brushed past her and up the stairs with our two backpacks bouncing against my back. I'd never been upstairs in the Delta Delta Psi house. "Your room or the sleeping porch?"

"My room. I have a bed."

"Which way?"

"Third floor." She gave me directions.

"Guy on the floor!" I yelled as I carried her through the fire door onto the floor.

The class day was in full swing. The sorority was nearly empty. No half-dressed girls in sight. I caught glimpses of rooms through open doors as I carried Morgan to the end of the hall. Blow dryers, makeup, clothes strewn around. Zach had described it to me. He hadn't exaggerated about the girlie mess.

Morgan's door was closed, but unlocked. I managed the knob and pushed the door open with my foot again. Her room was bright and smelled like her perfume. Her bed was covered with girlie pillows.

I set her on a chair, dumped the backpacks, swept the pillows off the bed, and opened it for her. I held out my hand to help her into it.

She bit her lip and shook her head. "I need to get out of these clothes first."

"I'm not leaving until there's someone here to sit with you. I won't look." I turned my back.

I heard her rustling in a drawer behind me. "Modesty's a funny thing, isn't it? You've seen everything I own, but this embarrasses me."

"It shouldn't."

I heard the bedsprings creak.

"I'm decent," she said.

When I turned around, she was sitting in bed with her pillow propped up behind her, wearing a white cami that showed her dark nipples. I wondered if she was just trying to torment me. I grabbed a few of her decorative pillows from the floor and put them behind her, making her comfortable.

The girl from the living room stuck her head in the room. "Victoria's on her way back from class. She'll be here as soon as she can." The girl hesitated. "I can sit with Morgan until then."

She looked like a scared frosh.

"Thanks," I said. "I'll sit with her until Victoria gets here."

The girl looked like she wanted to argue. I gave her a hard, unyielding stare. She nodded and cast a worried glance at Morgan. "Give me a shout if you need anything."

"You really don't need to stay," Morgan said to me after the frosh had left. "Vicki will be here in no time."

I didn't move. I had a sick suspicion. I needed to know. "This isn't an ordinary period. You aren't...?" I couldn't make myself say the words.

She shook her head and looked into her lap. "I don't know." She bit her lip. "I'm late. Does it matter? It's over now."

"Was there anyone else?" I had to know.

She met my eye and shook her head.

I held her gaze. "Would you have told me?"

"I don't know." Her voice was soft. "I really don't."

Victoria charged in before either of us could say more. She was red from running, and out of breath. She glanced at me and then at Morgan. "I came as soon as I could. I'll take over now."

CHAPTER SIXTEEN

Morgan

I was sure I'd lost Dakota there, in that moment when neither of us could voice our true fears. Hookup guys don't hang around in general. Hit them with a pregnancy scare and they're long-gone history.

So I was surprised when he called me later that night to see how I was doing. And when he texted me the next day to check up on me again. But there was a strain now, a polite distance. He didn't mention getting together again. And our sobriety buddy companionship seemed like a thing of the past. And then communications simply ceased. I shouldn't have been surprised.

I recovered quickly. By Saturday, I was back to my old self. I was sitting in the living room on Saturday evening, trying to look politely bored and done with the party scene, like it was beneath me, when Zach strolled in to pick up Alexis.

I set down the magazine I'd been mindlessly leafing through. "Well, if it isn't my savior."

He turned my direction and smiled. "Savior? That's a little over the top."

"You did save my life." I felt another huge sigh of relief that all I felt when I looked at him was friendship and gratitude.

He shrugged.

"If you say it's no big deal, I'll have to smack you." I gave him my sly smile, wondering if he could see the difference in me. The lack of desperation. The lack of longing for him. "I suppose you're here for Alexis."

"Yeah. She texted. She's running behind." He came into the living room and took the chair next to the sofa where I was sitting.

"If you say that's typical female behavior, I'll totally forget you saved me and have to kill you."

He laughed.

"How's apartment life?" I asked.

"Almost a week in—epic." He leaned forward like he was about to tell me a secret. "Just between you and me?"

I nodded.

"I'm trying to talk Seth into moving in with me at semester."

"Miss the old roomie, huh?"

"Yeah. He kind of grew on me. And I could use someone to take out the garbage."

I laughed. "Then what will *we* do about the garbage if you steal our new favorite houseboy?" It felt good to be joking around with him again.

"You'll survive." Secret over, he sprawled back in his chair. "How are you feeling? Alexis said you were sick earlier in the week."

It seemed to me that the question was more than innocent. That he and Alexis suspected something. I felt a blush creep up my cheeks. "Better, thanks."

"Good to hear." He studied me, looking too nonchalant and casual. "I hear you and Dakota are tight now."

My cheeks went into full flame mode with the implication. Gossip ran high in the house, and either Dak or Alexis could have filled him in. There was no use denying it. I kept my tone casual and light. "Misery loves miserable company. Odd bedfellows and all that crap. Dak has probably told you. We're keeping an eye on each other. Sobriety buddies, we're calling it. Just until our birthdays and we move past that MIC/MIP mess."

"Just buddies?" He didn't look like he believed me.

"Yeah, of course."

His eyes narrowed. He knew. Of course he knew.

I deflected any further questions by going on the offensive. "How are things with your parents? Who are you spending Thanksgiving with?"

He swore beneath his breath. "Both of them. I get two Thanksgivings this year to make up for all their shitty behavior for my entire childhood. The newness of my near-death episode hasn't worn off yet. When it does, I'm sure it will be back to business as usual. And I can go back to living my own life without being smothered." He paused. "Alexis and I are giving Dak a ride home for the break."

He was testing me again.

"Are you? Good to know he isn't getting behind the wheel of a car again. I guess I can cross checking up on his ride home situation off my sobriety pal checklist." I smiled, trying not to show I was hurt by Dak's sudden lack of attention. "Keep an eye on him over break, will you? Make sure he doesn't do anything stupid."

"Talk about giving a guy an impossible task!" Zach smiled and shifted in his chair. "How about you?"

"Victoria's giving me a ride." I sighed. "It's going to be a hellish week. Torn between two Thanksgivings. Half the day with Dad, half with bitter Mom. Who will make a huge dinner and expect me to gorge myself as a form of torture. So I won't be able to eat a bite of my stepmom's cooking. And to cap off the week, a baby shower for my stepmom and soon-to-be baby sister."

He winced. "Family drama."

"Yeah, welcome to the asylum." I shook my head. "A word of advice—pace yourself with the eating."

He grinned and patted his stomach. "No problem there. I'm a bottomless pit." He studied me, looking like there was something more he wanted to say. "Morgan, you've always been a little like a sister to me."

Which was true. But then, so were most girls in the house. Zach was always trying to brother people to make up for accidentally killing his little sister when he wasn't much more than a baby himself. But we had a special bond because I had an older brother who died before I was born. I was the replacement child. I should have seen that Zach had been brothering me before, and nothing more. But having a crush on a guy kills good judgment and common sense.

I smiled encouragingly and tried not to get emotional. I was glad he still felt that way after all that had happened.

"Take this as brotherly advice." He hesitated, holding my gaze. "For your own good, don't lose your heart to Dakota. He's my best friend. I know him better than anyone. He's a good guy. But he's capable of being an epic douchebag, too."

I started to stutter a lame response just as Alexis came down the stairs and spotted us.

Her gaze bounced between us. Although she smiled, her eyes grew narrow and suspicious. "There you are!"

Zach stood. She ran to him and threw herself into his arms. It was clear she was making a statement.

The truth was—I looked on dispassionately. I wasn't in love with Zach. But why had he warned me about Dakota? And was I that obvious?

Dakota

I sailed into Thanksgiving break feeling like the world's biggest jerk for avoiding Morgan. I needed time to process. I needed time to figure out what the hell I wanted and what I was doing. I needed to figure out my feelings for Jordan.

My first night back for break, Jordan insisted on partying with a group of her friends from high school. Four of her girlfriends shared a rented house in Ballard. The night was dark and stormy. Rainy. Typical for Seattle in November. The weather restricted the bounds of the party to the house, which rocked with music.

Jordan drove, which pissed her off. Her car was old, parking was hard to find, and gas was expensive. When I slipped her a twenty to cover it, she took it gladly, but scowled at me to show her displeasure with my situation. That it had all been over a fake show of hurt and anger over Alexis peeved her. She hadn't forgiven me for that.

As we got out of the car and walked toward the party house, she hung on my arm like she owned me, possessive in a clingy way I hadn't noticed before.

She cooed in my ear, "Be good and you'll get laid later." She stroked my cheek. "I've missed you, baby."

I wasn't turned on. I didn't reply or rush to assure her I'd missed her, too. I'd never been good at lying to her. I was saved from responding when the door to the house opened and Marsha, her high school best friend, waved to us.

"You're here! Let the party begin." Marsha hugged me and pulled us into the house as I held Jordan's hand. "Dakota! Long time no see. Come on in and get yourself a drink. Coats in the first bedroom to the right. Keg's in the kitchen. Hard stuff's on the table. There are a ton of new people here, Dak. A good crowd. You'll like them.

"Jordan, introduce him around." She whispered something into Jordan's ear while slyly looking at me. The two of them had a good laugh at whatever she said.

Jordan pulled me up the stairs, introducing me to person after person. I felt like I was on display, the trophy boyfriend. The rich boy.

In the kitchen, I poured Jordan a beer and grabbed a cola for myself.

"Are you serious?" She stared at my beverage as I handed her a beer. "Is there anything in that?"

"What do you think?" I said.

She grabbed a bottle of cheap rum from the table and poured a healthy dose into my cup so quickly I didn't have time to pull it away. Then she grinned. "There! All better."

I glared at her.

The party was a bore. Over half the people worked together. I was on the outside of their inside jokes. Jordan chugged beer after beer and hung on my arm, chiding me for being a stick-in-the-mud when I dumped my drink down the sink untouched.

"Righteous prick." She glared at me and pouted. Then begged me to get her another beer.

As the night wore on and people got drunker, they laughed at the stupidest, most inane things. Jordan thought they were hilarious, and drank more.

After a couple of hours, I couldn't take it anymore. I grabbed her arm and pulled her away from the group she was hanging with. "Let's ditch this place."

"Good idea." She slurred her words.

Shit. She was plastered.

She grabbed my arm, as much for balance as seduction, and pulled me to the bedroom where the coats were stored. We were alone in the room. She shut the

door and threw her arms around me, grabbing my
crotch in the process. "I've missed you. Let's do it.
Here. Now. I want you so bad."

"Not when you're like this." I held her at arm's
length. "You're drunk."

"What? Now you've become a romantic?" She fumbled with the zipper to my jeans.

I caught her hand, staring her down.

She burped and turned green. "Let go!"

I was no dummy. I dropped her hand and watched
her rush to the connected bathroom. A second later, I
heard her puking. We'd been here. Done this before.
But we usually got hammered together. The world was
a different place when you were the only sober one at
the party.

I'd been resisting the urge to drink all night, but I
was tired. And tired of fighting it. Tired of being odd
man out and feeling misplaced. A downer. A wet blanket. Me, the life of Tau Psi. My rep would soon be in
serious tatters. My mouth went dry.

Ah, shit.

I had to talk to Morgan before I pounded down a
beer or six. I pulled my cell phone out and called her
before I thought too much about it or how calling her
complicated things. "Hey, sobriety bud. I'm at a party
and my ride is puking in the bathroom, totally shit-
faced. What do I do?"

"Call a cab," she said without missing a beat.

The sound of her voice made my heart race. Fuck, I
wanted her. I needed her. I'd been furious with her
about the pregnancy scare she hadn't shared with me.

Scared. Relieved. You name it. Now I just missed the hell out of her.

"Now why didn't I think of that?" I said.

"Party fog. It messes with the mind." She paused. "You aren't drunk, too?"

"I'm insulted. Do I sound drunk?"

"Not a good test, Dak. You can be a surprisingly erudite drunk."

Her laugh made me smile.

"I'll take that as a compliment. It's taken great restraint to avoid drinking. I'm surrounded by saboteurs. That's why I need you." Why had I said that?

She laughed. "Need me, do you?"

Shit, she had to pick up on that slip of the tongue.

"What do you want me to do?" she said. "Jump on my white public transit steed and rescue you? Where are you, anyway?"

"Ballard."

She paused again, like she was thinking. "Too far."

"Where are you?"

"Dad's. In Puyallup."

"Ah," I said. "Far away."

"Far, far away. Locked in a tower under the watchful gaze of my evil stepmom." She sighed. "There will be absolutely no fun here. And no temptation to drink. She's warned me she's put a sensor on the liquor cabinet. If I so much as open the door, the security company will send her a message. And she'll know who the culprit is. Apparently, I'm the only one without the code to disarm the alert."

"Wicked. And shows no sense of trust."

"Yeah. And she's totally naïve. If I wanted to drink..." She laughed again. "Call a cab, Dak. Text me when you're home safely." She hung up just as Jordan staggered to the bathroom door and braced herself against it.

She was trying to be seductive, but she was wobbly on her feet. She summoned me with a crook of her finger.

I sighed and went to her. As I put my arm around her to support her, she breathed puke breath in my face. I looked away. "I'm calling a cab and taking you home."

"I'm not leaving without my car."

"You can get it tomorrow." I pulled her toward the bed to look for our coats.

She punched me in the shoulder and swore. "I'm not leaving. What's wrong with you? I'm not going home in a cab." She glared at me.

"I'm going."

"Fine." She glared at me. "You're going alone."

"You can't drive home."

She shook loose from me, swearing. "I'll spend the night here."

"Have it your way." I grabbed my coat and turned to leave.

She caught my arm. "Dakota Bradley—walk out on me and we're through!"

I was used to her threats and the way she used them to manipulate me. This time, she'd unwittingly given me the out I'd been looking for.

I shook her off and stormed out.

CHAPTER SEVENTEEN

Morgan

My phone rang an hour later. Like *rang*. With the ringtone I'd stupidly set for Dak. Like he was someone special. As if he thought I was someone special beyond a sobriety buddy of convenience and sometimes hookup. No more hookups. I repeated it again to myself. *No. More. Hookups. With. Dak. Period.*

My heart was doing that odd fluttery thing it did with anything regarding Dak. I let the phone ring until the last second and picked it up against my better judgment. "Home?"

"Safe and sound." He sounded seductively happy. Light and free.

"Caught a cab or took your chances?" I had to know.

"Took a taxi. Not easy to get in Seattle. Left the ride at the party." Okay, he sounded almost euphoric.

It made no sense, but then I guess it didn't have to. The joy in his voice was contagious. "Your ride, how is he getting home?"

"Spending the night at the party house."

Was that relief in his voice?

"You hope," I said. "Did you take his keys?"

"No. Should have thought of that. Don't worry...they'll be fine." He paused. "Morgan, I'm sorry." His voice was low and genuine. So true and emotional, my resolve cracked and my eyes watered.

I tried to brush it off. "About what?"

"You know what. About being a douche and not calling after—"

The phone shook in my hands. I bit my lip and blinked back tears. Crap, the whole thing made me so emotional. It was like I was almost grieving. Which was stupid. A pregnancy would have made my life beyond complicated. But I wasn't the hard-hearted bitch some of my sorority sisters made me out to be. "Let's not talk about it. Ever."

"Let me just say one more thing and I promise I won't mention it again."

I took a deep breath and nodded. As if he could see me. We weren't Facetiming. I cleared my throat and made some lame noise that passed for permission.

"You could tell me. I'm not the kind of guy who would leave you in a lurch. I'd feel better knowing you trust me and that we can work things through together. You can tell me anything." He cleared his throat. "That's all."

I pictured him with that sweet, apologetic look on his face. The look that made me want to take his face in my hands and kiss him softly and sweetly. The look that made me want to cry. I couldn't speak.

"Morgs? Still there?"

My voice caught. "Yeah."

"Everything okay?"

"Perfect."

"We started off on the wrong foot."

"You mean by being enemies?" I laughed and brushed aside a tear.

"Enemies to frenemies to friends to...something more. I've missed you these last days. I didn't realize how much until I came home and couldn't get you out of my mind."

Crap! He was determined to make me cry.

"Let me make it up to you. Let's start over. Go on a real first date. Are you busy tomorrow?"

I laughed through my tears. "It's past midnight. By tomorrow, do you really mean today or Monday?"

He laughed back. "Either. I have to see you. As soon as possible."

Could a heart break because of too much joy? I took a deep breath. "I have family plans tomorrow. Monday?"

"Excellent! Monday it is. That will give me a chance to plan it."

I smiled. "Where should I meet you?"

"Meet me? I'm picking you up like a real gentleman." He laughed again. "I'll need an address."

"On Monday I'll be at Mom's in Kirkland."

"Even better. I'm in Bellevue. It will save me the long drive to Puyallup. I'll text you the details tomorrow. I'm thinking afternoon into evening. We'll make a day of it."

"I'm thinking that's perfect."

"Goodnight, Morgs."

"Goodnight, Sweat Prints." I didn't know why I said it.

"Did you just call me Sweet Prince?"

"No, I called you Sweat Prints. You have to earn the Sweet Prince title. Make the date good."

He laughed again. "Goodnight...Sweat Print Cents."

I laughed as the line went dead. Then I fell back on my pillow, smiling.

Dakota

Fallout. I should have known there would be fallout. There always was after a breakup with Jordan. This time, I was serious. It was over.

There's only one way to move on. You have to make a hard, cold-turkey break. Sever all communications. Otherwise, it's too easy to get sucked back in out of pity. To find myself apologizing for shit I hadn't done. For wanting someone else. What could I say to Jordan, anyway? That we'd changed and grown apart? That she didn't understand how serious the charges I faced were? That she was trying to ruin me?

I ignored her pleading texts. Deleted her *I'm sorry* voicemails. Ignored her rants and begging.

Zach called. "We need to talk."

"So talk."

"In person. About Jordan."

"You heard."

"Oh, yeah. I heard." He sounded nervous, which was odd for easygoing Zach. "Coffee? In an hour?"

"Usual place?" I said.

"See you there."

Zach and I arrived at the same time and walked in together, making small talk. The coffee place smelled of pumpkin-spice lattes and caramel-apple cider. The pastry case was filled with cranberry scones and their delicious seasonal cranberry cake. We ordered. I got cake with my latte. We waited for our order to come up and found a table.

Jazz music played in the background. In another few days it would be the house blend of Christmas jazz and arrangements. Already the fall mugs were on sale. Outside it was raining. Even that couldn't dampen my spirits. I was grinning like a damn idiot. Wondering why I had hung on to Jordan so long. Why I'd nearly fucked everything up for her.

Zach studied me. "You look happy."

"That obvious?"

"Not if you're blind and deaf." He grinned, but he still looked nervous. "You're that happy to be rid of Jordan?" His eyes narrowed. He spoke before I could answer. "Does Morgan have anything to do with this? You can't fuck with her, QB2."

I glared back at him, on the defensive. "What's that supposed to mean? You're suddenly her defender? After what she did to you and Alexis?" Where the hell was he going with this? And who was he to call me out?

"Morgan has been going through some serious shit this year. She finally seems to be coming out of it. People have the wrong idea about her and me. We're friends, in a weird way. You aren't using her for cover again, are you? Like you used Alexis? But without Morgan's knowledge?"

I squeezed my cup, threatening to crush it as I stared at Zach. "What the hell are you getting at?"

"What are your intentions with Morgan?"

"What are you, her dad now? I just broke up with Jordan, didn't I?"

"Is it going to stick this time?"

I scowled at him. But why should he believe me?

He grinned at me. What the hell? "You really like Morgan."

"Shut the fuck up. Of course I like her." I leaned across the table and hissed at QB1. "She doesn't need to know about Jordan."

"Dangerous game, buddy." He took a sip of his coffee. "Jordan is pissed. She called me and tried to cry on my shoulder. She also threatened me." His grin was wry. "Blackmailed, more like."

I cocked an eyebrow. "What? How? What does she have on you?"

"You're not getting back together with her."

"Is that a command or a question?"

"Both."

"Jordan and I are done."

"I've heard that before." His expression became serious as he studied me. Finally, he looked like he believed me. "I have something to tell you that should seal the deal. But first, you have to promise not to punch me after I tell you."

I shook my head and grinned at him. "What are you getting at, man? Are you a chickenshit now?"

He was serious. "We've barely reestablished our friendship. I don't want to lose it, buddy."

My heart pounded. My mind raced with shitty, disgusting possibilities. "Whatever it is, it can't be worse than what I'm imagining. Give it to me straight. I promise not to throw a punch. Or my coffee." I forced a grin.

"I slept with Jordan."

My mouth fell open. "What the fuck? When? What about Alexis?" I reflexively rose out of my seat, ready to break my promise and beat him senseless.

He stood too, ready to defend himself, as curious bystanders went quiet around us and the manager looked like he was about to come over or call security. "Sit down," he whispered in a hiss. "It was ages ago. The summer after high school."

I fell back into my chair, stunned, doing the math. "Wait a minute—Jordan and I were together then..."

He nodded. "Yeah. I'm sorry. I'm not proud of it, buddy. I was out for revenge."

My mouth went dry as the implications set in. "She screwed you behind my back? Why?"

Zach looked away. Which was telling. All this time I'd been hanging on to Jordan, thinking she was the one girl who'd wanted me above Zach. It had all been a lie.

I saw red. My stomach burned with rage and betrayal. And relief.

"You okay?" Zach fell back into that defensive posture again as his forehead creased with concern.

"I'm glad she's not here, is all I can say." I swallowed hard. "I wouldn't be accountable for what I might do."

"And us?" Zach stared at me with sympathy and remorse in his eyes. "I'm sorry, dude. I wish I could take it back."

"Shit," I said. "I was trying to hurt you, too. Bygones." I stood.

He stood. We took a step toward each other and slapped each other on the back.

"I won't forgive her." I realized I was playing with a double standard. I'd been with Morgan, after all. Maybe there wasn't any defense. But she'd gone a step further and slept with my best friend. That was unforgivable.

Morgan

Dakota texted me and told me to get ready for a day in Seattle. He'd pick me up around two. I felt like a nervous high schooler as I tried on outfit after outfit, finally settling on a cute fall dress, tights, and thigh-high boots, with my black coat that tied around the waist and flared into a skirt.

Mom insisted on meeting him. She was already upset that Dad had met him first. And approved of him. I hoped she wouldn't be perverse and dislike him just to be contrary. She and Dad used to be in lockstep about everything. Now they rarely agreed on anything.

I'd been wondering how Dakota planned to pick me up. I half expected to go on a double date. Instead, he showed up with a limo and driver. He was smart enough to come to the door. He charmed Mom like she was a pliable snake. Until she'd coiled her approval all around him and was singing his praises as he escorted me to the car.

He was dressed casually in jeans, but he looked so hot I couldn't take my eyes off him.

The driver held the door open for me.

"Where are we going?" I asked Dak as I slid in.

"You'll see." He slid in next to me and grabbed my hand. "You look beautiful today, Morgs. Breathtaking."

I laughed as I leaned into him to whisper in his ear. I caught a whiff of his cologne and the fresh mint of his breath. I ran my fingers along the back of his neck and watched him shudder with pleasure. "Be still my heart. You don't have to shamelessly flatter me."

"What if I want to? What if it's how I see you and I want you to know?" His eyes were shining and completely serious.

I had no answer, except the wild beating of my heart.

His smile was dazzling. "I'm trying to prove I'm more than a hookup. I can be something more serious." He brushed my lips with a kiss.

More serious. I liked the sound of that. "Where are we going?" I asked again as we pulled out of the driveway.

"On the quintessential Seattle date."

"The Wheel!" I clapped and laughed. Since its completion while we were in high school, no relationship was legit without a ride on the giant Ferris wheel downtown on the waterfront.

He grinned. "And Sylvester the mummified man. I'll buy you all the cheap touristy curios you want."

"All?"

"Absolutely everything you can carry."

"I can carry?" I bumped him playfully with my shoulder. "You won't be my packhorse?"

"Absolutely not." But he was grinning.

"The market?"

He nodded. "We'll watch them toss fish."

"Beecher's mac and cheese?" My stomach almost rumbled at the thought of it.

"If you want. But I have dinner planned for later."

"We're hitting all the touristy stuff downtown?" I squeezed his hand.

"Yeah."

The morning had been foggy. Marine air. Onshore flow. That was what we called it in Seattle. In the late fall, it sometimes didn't burn off until late in the daylight hours, if at all. It was lifting as the driver pulled to a stop in front of the Wheel. Dak gave instructions to the driver, took my hand, and helped me out.

He bought our tickets and we stood in line to be loaded. We shared a gondola with a couple from British

Columbia who were down celebrating an American Thanksgiving. The view over the sound to the Olympic Mountains was stunning. Even better was the possessive feel of Dak's arm around me as we watched the ferries coming and going. When our gondola stopped at the very top, he tipped my face toward his and kissed me, sweetly, deeply, full of passion. The tenderness of it rocked my world.

"How long have you been dating?" the woman from BC asked us.

Dak slung his arm over my shoulders. "This is our first date." He looked so casual and handsome.

"Your first date!" Her eyes went wide. "I would never have guessed. You seem so comfortable with each other." She smiled widely. "You two have something special. I see a long future together ahead for you." She wagged her finger at us to make her point. "I know special when I see it. I know the one. I've never been wrong. Didn't I tell you, Roy, that my brother would marry Connie? And that was after the first time I saw them together."

Roy looked apologetic, but his wife would not be stopped.

"Big things!" she said. "You'll be married inside two years or I miss my guess."

"The good news for her is, she'll never know whether you are or aren't. Her record will remain intact." Roy winked at us.

His wife gave him a playful shove.

"We've been friends for a while," I said.

"Friends first, that always works best," the woman said.

After the Wheel, we went to Ye Olde Curiosity Shop, then up the hill to Pike Place Market, which was crowded with shoppers already preparing for Thanksgiving. We stood in line at Beecher's and bought a cup of mac and cheese to share. The market was always crowded. There was no place nearby to sit.

I grabbed Dak's hand and pulled him along. "I know where there are always tables."

"Where? In the market? You're crazy. This place is always packed."

"Shows how little you know. Of course in the market!" I pulled him past the shops and restaurants and down the stairs at the far end of the market to the floor below. Sure enough, there were half a dozen available tables, just like always.

"See!" I pointed. "Most people don't come down here. They don't even know these tables exist."

"An in-depth knowledge of the market. I'm impressed." He held a chair out for me.

I sat and held a finger to my lips. "Shhhh. Don't spread the word about these tables. They're our little secret." I laughed. I couldn't believe I was so happy. With Dakota Bradley.

He handed me a plastic fork. We dove into our mac and cheese together. It was gooey, cheesy, and rich. Perfect.

"Having fun?" he asked.

I grinned at him. "What do you think?" I rubbed my foot over his.

"I wish we were at school." He wiggled his eyebrows.

"No more hookups," I said.

"I wasn't talking about a hookup." He held my gaze. "I was talking about something more."

I looked down, embarrassed and afraid I would give my deep longing away.

Our plastic forks clicked and our fingers brushed as we both dove in for another bite of food.

He cleared his throat. "How are things at home? How was the family thing yesterday?"

"Horrible!" I rolled my eyes and twisted my mouth to one side. I took a deep breath. "At dinner last night, my dad and stepmom made a big announcement. You know how I thought I was going to have a little sister who would be daddy's new princess?" Dak had teased me about that before.

He nodded.

"Turns out, the princess is going to be a prince. They showed the new ultrasound pictures, featuring his little dick. Just to prove the point. He's a cute little guy. He was sucking his thumb. You could even tell he looks a lot like Dad." I couldn't keep the fear out of my voice.

"That's great!" He saw my face and stopped. "What's wrong?"

I forced myself to smile. "Besides the fact that I have to return all the girl stuff I bought for the shower and get boy things?"

"Small detail." He reached across and squeezed my hand.

I swallowed hard. "Dad's always wanted another boy. I was supposed to be the replacement for my older brother who died. Now this little guy will be."

Dak looked sympathetic. "Being the replacement isn't all it's cracked up to be. Think unrealistic expectations. Your dad loves you." He grinned. "I could tell by the way he looked like he wanted to kill me when we first met."

I laughed.

"Cheer up. It will be okay," he said.

"What about you?" I asked. "You survived a bad party. What else have you been up to?"

He shrugged, watching me closely. "Zach and I hung out yesterday."

I realized he was looking for my reaction, trying to see how I felt about Zach. "That's nice. I'm glad he's doing well." I bit my lip and screwed up my courage. "It's crazy how things change after a crush dies. I used to think Zach was the hottest guy on campus."

Dakota's face became a mask.

I laughed. "And now I think you are."

His eyes lit up. He smiled and pulled me into a kiss. "Tell me again how hot I am."

I shook my head and grinned. "You're impossible."

We finished our mac and cheese and went back into the main part of the market. We watched the guys at the fish counter toss and wrap fish. Explored the vegetable, fruit, and flower stalls. Dak bought me the largest bouquet of fresh fall flowers he could find. Then made me carry them.

It was getting dark by the time we left the market, even though it was only a little after five. We walked up the hill to the shopping district. Holiday dresses graced every department store window.

I saw the most gorgeous powder-blue one in the window of one of my favorite stores. I stopped to admire it, and sighed.

"What's wrong?" Dak gave me a worried look.

"That dress would be perfect for the winter semi-formal the week after we get back."

"So buy it," he said. "Let's go in. You can try it on for me." He gave me a wolfish smile.

I shook my head. "What's the point? I'm on social probation, remember?"

He frowned. "We could still go in and see if they have your size."

"No," I said. "That would only depress me. Ugh. It's going to be excruciating watching all the excitement of getting ready while I sit on the sidelines."

"I don't want my girl depressed. Let's go." He squeezed my hand and led me to Westlake.

We browsed the mall. Then he called the limo and we drove back to the waterfront and had dinner at a restaurant on the pier looking out on the sparkling night waters of Puget Sound. The meal was phenomenal. For dessert, we had their famous flaming volcano cake.

After dinner, Dak called the limo again. I thought he would take us home.

"I have one more surprise," Dak said.

The limo dropped us off at the Wheel again.

Dak took my hand. "We saw it during the day. I thought we should see it at night."

We went to the ticket window.

"I want the VIP package." He pulled out his wallet.

"What!" I said. "No, we don't need that."

He looked at me. "We do."

The clerk smiled at us. "You're in luck. It's available. What T-shirt sizes do you need?"

"We get a T-shirt?" I grinned.

"This isn't the frat. But we have to have a T-shirt to commemorate the occasion."

We gave the clerk our sizes. He handed us two T-shirts and vouchers for a champagne toast at a nearby restaurant. "You have to be twenty-one for those," he said.

Dak didn't reply. I hooked my shirt over my purse.

"Not going to wear it?" he asked.

"It clashes with my dress."

He slid his arm around my waist and pulled me close.

The VIP gondola had leather seats. And we didn't have to share it with anyone else. As part of the package, we were taken to the front of the line and loaded first.

I snuggled into him in the gondola. The stars sparkled above. The city sparkled below.

"It's breathtaking," I whispered, in awe.

"You're breathtaking." Dak tucked a strand of hair behind my ear. "I've never felt this way about anyone. I'm falling in love with you."

My pulse raced. He looked at me expectantly. I slid my arms around his neck. "I'm falling in love with you, too."

He kissed me, tenderly at first, and then with skilled yearning. He kissed my breath away. I slid into his lap.

"You are so damn beautiful." He stroked my cheek. "As soon as we turn twenty-one, I'm taking you back here and we'll have that champagne toast."

The thought of us still being together at our birthdays made my pulse race. Hookup guys didn't talk long term, as in months ahead.

"We're supposed to each be having a huge bash, trying to outdo each other," I said. "I've been dreaming of my birthday run. I've planned it down to my outfit and the banner I'm going to wear."

"You'll come to the Tau Psi house." His eyes danced.

"First stop." I smiled seductively at him.

"Make it your last. I'll be waiting for you with a big-ass bottle of your favorite alcoholic beverage. And then I'll show you my room." He winked.

I laughed. A frat guy "showing you his room" was, of course, code for having sex there. "At midnight, we'll ring in your birthday with a bottle of your favorite."

"What? You're trying to horn in on my birthday celebration now?" He ran his fingers through my hair.

"No. Yours will be completely separate. I'm actually sharing and giving you a fighting chance at an epic birthday. Mine's on Saturday and yours is on Sunday. So I have the party advantage. Sunday everyone will just be hung over.

"If we celebrate together—my birthday until midnight on Saturday, and then yours until dawn—yours can be awesome, too."

"Sounds good to me. Two parties together will be twice as legendary."

We stared out at the view, cuddled in each other's arms.

The ride ended all too soon. And so did the evening. I would have stayed out all night, but Mom would be worried and furious.

Dakota took me home and walked me to the door. Just as he kissed me goodnight, his phone rang.

I pulled away. "Are you going to get that?"

He shook his head. "No. Nothing's more important at this moment than you."

CHAPTER EIGHTEEN

Morgan

Thanksgiving vacation went by in a rush. It flew by so quickly, there was no time to see Dak again. Though we talked every day. I was back at school before I knew it. Facing the few weeks before finals and the holiday season without drink didn't seem so bad with Dakota by my side.

I flew back into his arms the minute I got back into town. From that minute forward, we were together every second we could find. We fell into the steady rhythm of a committed relationship. But I steadfastly refused to sleep with him. It was like I was testing him—how badly did he want me? How hard would he try to prove he was serious? That I was no hookup?

If you had told me at the start of the semester that I would fall in love with Dakota Bradley and be his girl, I would have laughed in your face. Now I laughed with joy every time I thought about it.

"When we sleep together again," I told him, "I want it to be special."

"When will that be?" His voice was husky with want.

"When the time's right." I was trying to be enigmatic.

Though the longer it went, the more I wanted him. No sex. No drinking. How long could I hold out?

Although I was on social probation, I was allowed to help decorate the house for Christmas. But while the rest of the house was getting ready for the winter semiformal, I tried not to think about it. The dance was being held at a local hotel. So at least it wasn't in my face at the house. Dakota, who could be so totally sweet, told me he was taking me to dinner that night. I should dress up and look hot. I knew what he had on his mind.

On Saturday, as the rest of the girls got ready for their dates to the semiformal a package was delivered for me.

Kayla delivered it to my room and handed it to me. "What a gorgeous package! Look at this beautiful blue bow. It's not your birthday yet, right?"

The package was pretty, silver with a blue ribbon. Wintery. Sparkly.

"No. Not until late January."

"Early Christmas, then."

"Maybe." I frowned. It looked like a clothing box.

"Open it!" She plunked onto my bed.

I sat beside her, slid off the ribbon, pulled off the lid, and folded back white tissue paper.

I gasped. "The blue dress." I breathed the words.

A card sat in the middle of the dress.

Kayla peered over my shoulder and gently fingered the delicate fabric of the dress. "Wow! Stunning. What's the special occasion? The dance?"

I shook my head. Kayla knew as well as I did that I was on social probation. Everyone either knew or guessed. But she was too polite to come out and say it. Instead she simply sounded politely puzzled.

"I'm not going."

My name was written on the card in Dak's handwriting. I didn't even care that Kayla was there. I slit the envelope open and pulled the card out.

Wear this tonight. I love you! Dak

Kayla hugged me. "I'm happy for you, Morgan. I really am. You and Dakota make a cute couple. Keep this up and you'll be lavaliered by the end of the year."

Lavaliered. Being lavaliered was tantamount to being engaged. It was a big deal. Lately, I'd begun to dream about it.

After Kayla left, I pulled the dress out of the box and held it up. A pair of see-through lace thong panties, silver, rested on the tissue beneath the dress. Yes, Dak was definitely trying to seduce me.

***

Dakota picked me up at eight. He was wearing a suit and blue tie that matched my dress. The matching tie was the thing that the girl usually picked out. I was happily surprised he'd thought of it. And he was carrying a corsage for me.

I wore the dress, and the panties, and left my hair down so that it flowed over my shoulders in long waves. I'd spritzed on the perfume that turned him on. I wore a pair of silver sandals that were totally impractical in the frigid December night. And not appropriate for walking anywhere on the uneven hills of campus and town.

He pulled me into a passionate kiss and held me possessively around the small of my back with the corsage box still in his hand. "You look good enough to eat."

I wiped my lipstick off his face with my thumb. "My lipstick looks good on you."

He grinned and pulled away, opening the corsage box and helping me slip the corsage over my wrist.

The pink rose looked good against my pale, nearly winter skin. I inhaled deeply. It smelled like a commercial rose, light on scent, but like every dance I'd ever attended. "What's this for?"

He just grinned.

Guys were showing up to pick up their dates. We blended right in.

"You're a man of mystery tonight. Where are we going and how are we getting there?" I smiled up at him. "Do I need my bus pass?"

He took my arm and led me toward the door. "The car and driver awaits."

"Driver? In this small town?"

He wrapped my shawl around me and led me outside. "Pledges have their uses."

He helped me in the car. I recognized our pledge driver and smiled at him. He drove us to a small hotel in town that housed a popular Italian restaurant. Dak had booked us a private table in the corner. We sat next to each other and flirted through dinner.

The restaurant had a small dance floor that was outside the bar.

"Want to dance?" Dak asked me after dinner.

The music was old-fashioned and cheesy, but when I was in Dak's arms, it didn't matter. I didn't care. The room melted away and it was just the two of us.

I whispered in his ear, "This is so sweet. Much better than the winter semiformal."

"That's what I was going for." He stroked my hair.

"I wish it didn't have to end."

"It doesn't. Not tonight. Not if you don't want it to."

I looked up into his eyes and raised an eyebrow. "What are you saying?"

"I booked us a room here. If you want it." He looked nervous. "I think it's time."

The low huskiness of his tone sent shivers of anticipation down my spine. "Me too."

He smiled and ran his hand down my arm. "Good. I was hoping you'd say that."

I put my mouth to his ear. I wanted him in the worst way. "Do we need to check in?"

"Checked in this afternoon."

I kissed him lightly, wanting so much more. "Confident move."

"No, just damn optimistic." He pulled a room key from his pocket and took my hand. "Whenever you're tired of dancing, say the word."

"I'm tired now." I smiled seductively at him. "Of dancing."

He mumbled something beneath his breath, took my hand, and pulled me back to the table to collect our coats and my purse. The hotel was small, only three floors. Our room was on the third floor. We took the stairs.

He unlocked the door and held it open for me. The room was softly lit with flickering electric candles. A single red rose sat in a vase on the table near the bed. And the bed was turned down, with chocolates on the pillows.

"It's not much." He was grinning. "But it is the best this town has to offer." He swept me off my feet and carried me across the threshold like it was our honeymoon, kicking the door closed with his foot. I wrapped my arms around him as he carried me to the bed. He was breathing hard with anticipation as he set me down.

"Lock the door," I said as I leaned down to unfasten the buckles on my sandals.

He grabbed my hand. "Don't get undressed without me." He locked the door, put the chain on, shrugged out of his jacket, and put it over the back of the chair by the desk.

He came to me and kneeled before me.

"What are you doing?" I felt breathless with anticipation.

"Undressing you." He ran his hand up my bare leg, beneath my skirt to the edge of my panties, teasing the pulsing between my legs by stopping just short of touching me.

He unbuckled one shoe and gently pulled it off. Then the next.

"Take off your shirt," I said as he stood.

He unbuttoned it like a male stripper, while I went hot all over at the sight of his rippled abs and defined chest. I'd seen him before, but not like this. Not with the light of love shining with the lust in his eyes.

The air crackled with desire. Whoever said you can't feel chemistry pulsing in the air was wrong. I felt it, a tangible thing I wanted to reach out and grab.

He grabbed my hands. "Stand up." He pulled me to my feet and slid the straps of my dress off my shoulders. "Spin around."

I obeyed, feeling my breath catch as he unzipped me, stroking my back with a light touch designed to turn me on. My dress fell off.

I turned around to face him, seeing my reflection in the mirrored closet doors opposite the bed. Looking at the fine lines of his sculpted, muscled back. I reached out for him, wanting to lick him and suck his nipples. Wanting to coil around him.

"Patience." He pulled me close and kissed my neck as he unfastened my bra.

I reached for his pants.

He grabbed my hands and held me at arm's length. "You are so gorgeous." He sounded almost reverent.

The look in his eyes was a mixture of love, adoration, and passion.

I'd never made love to him face to face sober. The last time we'd had sex, it had been just that. This felt like the first time as he pulled my bra off and bent to kiss my breasts.

I gasped with the pleasure of the feel of his hot tongue on my nipples. I longed for him to lick me all over. I wanted him in me. "Take off your pants."

He grinned and stripped off his pants and his underwear in one move. His dick was hard and ready and aiming for me as he laid me gently on my back on the bed.

"You're naked." I kissed him lightly as I stroked his dick. "I'm still wearing my panties."

"As a barrier to entry, those panties are useless." He flashed me a rogue's grin. "Why do you think I gave them to you?" He slid one finger beneath them.

I moaned at his touch, wet and ready for him.

He kissed my neck and then my breasts as he made little circles of pleasure with his fingers between my legs.

I clutched his hair and brought his face up so I could look at him. "Dakota Bradley, stop teasing me."

"I'm seducing you slowly."

"I've had enough seduction. Take me. Now." I wrapped my legs around his naked waist and positioned myself beneath.

He moved his mouth to within inches of mine. "Any way you want it."

I was still clutching handfuls of his hair. "I want it now."

He covered my mouth with his and plunged into me with his tongue and his dick at the same time. Dak could kiss. Oh, how he could kiss. His tongue caressed my mouth in the most intimate way.

I arched beneath him, rocking with him. Our rhythm had always been perfect, like we knew instinctively how to move together. Like we belonged together, I realized with a shock.

He broke the kiss and turned. I realized he was looking in the mirror, and followed his gaze.

"Seeing what a stud you are?" I asked him.

He looked down at me. "Watching your beautiful body moving with mine."

I cupped his face. "I like watching, too."

He smiled. "I love you, Morgan. I love you."

My breath caught. I thought my heart would break with joy. No guy had ever said he loved me in the middle of the act. They said it after, like it was a thank-you or something. The way Dak said it, I knew he wanted me to know he did. *He loved me.* The knowledge was both erotic and fulfilling. The pleasure grew between my legs in a way that only Dakota made me feel.

I was a tightly wound spring, waiting for him. Wanting to come together. "I love you, too."

He thrust deeper and deeper and deeper.

I gasped and so did he.

"Dak!" The pleasure was so intense, my eyes rolled back and I sighed.

"Morgan!"

I felt him come, felt his pleasure and release. When he collapsed on top of me, we were both hot and flushed.

"Wow!" I ran my fingers through his hair.

"Is that all you can say?" He kissed the tip of my nose.

"I'm lucky I can speak at all."

He laughed and braced himself, holding his full weight off me. "I meant it. I love you."

"I know." I kissed the tip of his nose. "And I love you. Desperately."

"Love shouldn't be desperate, Morgs. We belong together."

CHAPTER NINETEEN

Dakota

I'd fully intended to impress Morgan with my dashing, romantic nature. I wanted sex. I wanted her love. I wanted everything. So, yeah. I went full out. But I meant every word I told her. Was it deceptive? I wasn't always the most romantic guy.

Maybe it was. One thing I knew, when you wanted something, you went after it full force with everything you had. No half-assed attempts. No lack of confidence. No weakness. I'd let Zach win her before with his gentle, brotherly attention. This time I wasn't leaving her in any doubt where I stood.

She kept telling me that private winter semiformal I gave her was the most romantic thing she'd ever heard

of. She was going to write an article about it and send
it in to that sorority gossip site she was always reading.

If it got published, my fellow men were going to
hate me forever for that move. I would be right up
there with that article on why guys don't need blowjobs. Shit, didn't we have enough pressure when we
finally decided to lavalier a girl or propose? You had to
upstage every viral proposal any other guy had ever
done. I'd just raised the bar on dates.

I thought about her all the time. All. The. Time. She
was like a drug in my blood. More addictive than alcohol. I barely kept my head through finals.

I bought her a necklace for Christmas, a snowflake
pendant studded with tiny diamonds. To remind her of
that winter dance I'd given her. And because I wanted
to see it sparkling around her neck while she wore that,
and only that, while I made love to her.

We made love almost every night. It was only *almost*
because there were a few nights she insisted on actually
studying alone, or hanging with her sorority sisters and
sleeping in her own bed at her house. She claimed she'd
really bonded with most of them during her social probation pariah phase. She was tired of being the witch of
the house. Now that she was happy, she actually liked
most of her sorority sisters. The rest of the nights she
spent with me at the frat.

I dreaded Christmas break. I was going to be horny
as hell without her. And lonely. Morgan had replaced
Zach and my frat buddies as the best friend I had. Or
had ever had.

As the Grinch found out, though, hard as you try, you can't keep Christmas from coming. So it came all the same, on the heels of finals.

I couldn't stay away from her. If only I could drive, damn it. I took the bus. I rode the light rail. I bummed rides off friends. I even conned Zach and Alexis into double dating so he could do the driving.

"Morgan and Alexis are big and little," I said to Zach. "Alexis could learn a lot from Morgan. We're best friends again. We'll be hanging out. They need to get along."

Zach nodded. "They're working on it."

"What do you think about Morgan and me?" I asked Zach.

He shrugged. "Do you need my blessing?"

"Just asking your opinion."

He grinned. "I think you're good together."

It was damned refreshing to be out with a girl my friends and family approved of. Mom invited her over for dinner several times in the days before Christmas. She couldn't stop raving about Morgan. Even the Pomsky Mom had carted home from the frat loved Morgan. She brought the dog a sweater. The dog let her dress him in the silly thing and cart him around in her arms like he belonged there. For a while, I was almost jealous of the dog.

The other challenge was making sure Morgan didn't run into Jordan. Shit, like I needed that to happen.

The day before I left for school, Jordan cornered me as I stepped out of Starbucks.

"Dakota!"

"Shit, Jordan! You startled me." I was carrying a hot cup of coffee. I nearly dropped it when she appeared from nowhere around a corner. "Were you lying in wait for me?"

"You've been avoiding me."

Her eyes were sad. I felt like a douche. I shrugged.

"I've seen you around with a girl. A sorority bitch, by the looks of her. Is that who you threw me over for?"

"What's the point of talking about it?" I tried to step around her. "We're through. Let's leave it at that and part as friends."

"Friends?" She nearly snorted the word. "Is that what we are?" She grabbed my arm. "Friends answer texts and take each other's calls."

"Jordan, don't."

"Don't what?"

"Don't be desperate. You have your new life. New friends. I don't fit into it any more than you fit into mine."

"Is that what you think?" She looked genuinely stunned. "That you don't fit in my life?"

"It was pretty clear I didn't at that party."

"I *said* I was sorry." Her grip tightened. "We don't have to go to any more of my friends' parties. We've been together forever. We belong together."

"Is that why you slept with Zach? While we were still together. Because we belong together so much?" I shook her off and walked away.

"Who told you?" she screamed after me. "Zach?" She let loose a stream of threats and foul language. "I'll get you back, Dak. We belong together. Our breakups never last. This one won't, either!"

I kept walking.

Morgan

The new semester started off the second week in January with bitter, biting temperatures in the single digits and a chill factor below zero. My baby brother had been born the day after Christmas. He was a cute little thing. I hated to leave him, but I was glad to be back at school.

Seth moved out to live with Zach in his new apartment. Two new houseboys—babes, really—took their places. They were all awkward angles and gawking expressions, like they'd never seen so many hot chicks in all their lives. It was annoying. And sweet, in almost geeky way.

Breaking in new houseboys was the pits. It wasn't the same around the house without Zach and Seth. Paul and Dillon had their hands full bringing the new guys up to speed.

Fortunately, I was so busy I barely had time to notice. I was too happy. Dakota had made all the difference. Our birthdays were just a few weeks away. We were planning to have a party at the frat. With plenty of booze. Dak had already recruited a couple of seniors in his frat to buy it for us a few days ahead.

I had ordered a cake from the best bakery in town. In university colors. One half had the Tau Psi letters and *Happy Birthday, Dakota* on it. The other half had the Delta Delta Psi letters, *Happy Birthday, Morgan,*

and flowers and bows and candy pearls. Two champagne glasses clinking met in the middle. I'd ordered
us matching monogrammed champagne flutes. And
we'd made a date for the Monday after to pick up our
driver's licenses.

I'd gotten Dakota a jacket and sweater he was going
to look so hot in. And as a special surprise, Dad had
used his connections to get Dakota on as an alpha test-
er of the next big video game. It was the game everyone
was going to want. They'd already spent several hundred million on its development. I could hardly wait to
see his face when he found out.

Dakota had been hinting since Christmas that he
had something special planned for my birthday. Something that involved jewelry. Since he'd given me a
necklace for Christmas, and it was too soon to get engaged, I had fantasies of him lavaliering me. The Tau
Psis both lavaliered and pinned. The order of a serious
Greek relationship here went lavaliering, pinning, and
finally engagement.

Two of the seniors in my house were pinned. Three
were lavaliered. Two of them had been lavaliered at
least twice. Lavaliering was a huge deal. The guy gave
you a necklace with his house letters. It meant he valued you as much or more as his house and his fraternity
brothers. Pinning was even more serious. He gave you
either his own pin with his letters, or a special girlie
version made just for pinning. Both pinning and
lavaliering involved a special ceremony.

Both were public declarations of the guy's love before his house and hers. Very big stuff. Yes, it was ear-

ly. Most of the time the couple had been dating a year or more. But we were already halfway through our junior year. And it was important to show everyone that he was over Alexis and I was over Zach. And we were serious about each other. No one took this kind of thing lightly.

Although we'd only been a couple a few months, we were each other's complete support. And we'd known each other from almost the first minute of our freshman year. Plus, how many people had the bond of almost running over the other one? I teased him about that.

A huge snowstorm hit on the first Thursday of class. We didn't get blizzards in the Pacific Northwest, but this was a complete whiteout, with blowing winds and the chill factor below zero.

I met Dakota for coffee at The College Grind, ducking in to get out of the wind before facing the icy hills of Greek Row. I wore my white coat with the fake fur collar, white boots with more faux fur trim, and white mittens.

He was waiting for me at a table, with his hands wrapped around a steaming cup of coffee and one waiting for me. He jumped up and kissed me, his lips hot with the promise of more body heat as he warmed my frigid blue lips.

"You look like the Snow Queen." He pulled my gloves from my icy hands, tossed them on the table, and rubbed my bare hands between his to warm them.

"Frozen, like I have a chip of ice in my heart?"

"No. Fucking beautiful."

I laughed. My phone buzzed in my pocket. I pulled it out. "I'm amazed this thing still works in this cold. Good to know my smart phone is rated for below-zero temps." I glanced at the screen and couldn't help frowning. "It's Dad. I'd better get it."

Dak nodded as we both sat.

"Hey, Dad!" I tried to keep the tremble of fear out of my voice. My father didn't call just to chat. "What's up?"

There was a pause. "Sweetie..."

My heart stood still. He'd only spoken a single word. But I knew. Bad news.

"Grandma?" I could barely speak.

"I'm sorry." His voice broke with emotion. "She's had a major heart attack, honey. She has the best doctors. Don't get your hopes up. It's not looking good. Her heart is too weak. They don't expect..."

It was like if he didn't say the words, it wouldn't be real. But we both knew it was.

He took a deep breath. "They don't expect her to make it through the night. I'm trying to catch a flight out of Seattle to fly to see her. Nothing's flying into eastern Washington right now. I'll keep trying."

"Is anyone with her?" My heart pounded in my ears. Grandma lived about ninety miles away from the university. The rest of the family lived on the west side of the state, about three hundred miles away.

Dad paused a beat. "No. Your aunt left two days ago. Before any of this happened. No one expected...she was doing so well."

"She can't die alone!" I grabbed a napkin from the table and dabbed at my eyes and nose, trying to pretend the cold had made me a mess. I pictured Grandma alone in her room with no one there who loved her. She'd always been there for me.

"Don't get any ideas, Morgan. Stay where you are." Dad's voice was firm and worried. "I've seen the news. It's almost a blizzard over there. There's no bus service. The airport in that one-horse town is closed. So are half the roads."

"But Dad—"

"Stay put, honey. If anything happened to you... You're my baby. Stay safe and warm. I'll keep you posted." He hung up before I could argue.

I stared at Dakota and tried not to cry as I grabbed my gloves. "I have to go." I was going no matter what Dad had said.

Dakota swore and pulled his coat off the back of his chair. "Not alone."

"What?" I stared at him with wide eyes.

"I overheard your conversation. Sorry. Your grandma, right? You have to go see her. You'll never forgive yourself if you don't. I'm taking you."

"But you can't drive. If they catch you, they'll revoke your deferral and put you in jail."

"Put the sobriety buddy shit aside, Morgan." He stared me down. "You're planning on driving, aren't you? You're in the same shitty situation I am."

"She's my grandma. I love her more than almost anyone in the world." Meaning him. "It's worth the risk to me. But I can't let you take the chance."

"Like hell will I let you go alone. You're too upset to drive, especially in this crap. My car's got snow tires and all-wheel drive. No arguments. I'm taking you." He took my arm. "Let's go."

There's a time to argue. And a time to give in. As much as it scared me, I needed him. I felt safer with him.

We bundled up and slipped and slid our way through the blowing snow to the frat. He tossed a sleeping bag into the backseat along with some bottles of water.

"I have an emergency kit with flares, hand warmers, and space blankets." He grabbed his ice scraper and brush and began clearing the car.

Like I cared or had even thought about that. *Hurry, hurry, hurry!* That was all that ran through my mind, over and over again in a continuous loop of fear.

He jumped in and started the car to get it warming up. By the time he'd finished dusting off the entire car, snow was already accumulating again on the roof.

We jumped in and buckled up. Greek Row sat at the top of the hill with the university. The roads out of it toward the edge of town and the freeway were all treacherously steep. Fortunately, the snow was light, and very cold. It wasn't slick, but visibility was practically nil.

We drove in silence toward the highway out of town, Dak concentrating on the road. Several of the roads down from Greek Row were already closed. We had to turn around twice. When we finally reached the highway, it was closed, too.

"I know a back way. It runs parallel to the highway, through a bunch of tiny towns. I was routed through it once when there was a fatality blocking the highway."

Fatality. That was not what I needed to hear.

He carefully swung the car around. "It will take longer, but I doubt they've closed it yet."

He crawled through town. He was right. It was still open. The truckers had thought of it, too. We got behind a semi. Dak stayed close on its tail. Even still, its lights were barely visible in the ever-darkening storm.

"I hope to hell it doesn't jackknife." His gaze was fierce.

I squinted, but couldn't see the road. "This is insane."

He nodded. Up ahead, we caught a glimpse now and then of a car or truck ahead of the one we were following.

"I hope the lead car, wherever it is, can see where it's going." I bit my lip. "And that we're not driving across wheat fields instead of roads."

His gaze didn't leave the road. "I hope so, too." He handed me his phone. "Put some music on, will you?"

I plugged it in. "What do you want—smooth and calming? Or loud and screaming?" He liked screamo and hard rock.

He named a band. I brought it up. We rode without speaking, listening to his music as the miles inched along. I put my hand on his arm. His muscles were taut and tense.

The truck ahead of us slowed as we crawled up a hill. Dak downshifted, cursing beneath his breath as the car fishtailed. "Black ice? What the hell? It should be too damn cold for that. Why hasn't it dried up? If that truck stops, we'll never get going again."

I said a silent prayer. The truck kept inching forward. We reached the top of the hill and picked up speed.

I let out a sigh of relief. "There's no one else I'd rather be stuck in a snowstorm with. Just so you know."

It broke the tension just enough. He actually grinned. "It would be fun staying warm with you."

The two-hour drive stretched into three. We finally merged back with the highway, but we hadn't reached the divided road. Everything was white. I had no idea how far away we were.

I just wanted to be there. This couldn't all be for nothing. If Grandma died before we reached her...

Dak snapped off the music. "We'll make it in time, Morgs. Keep believing that."

It was like he'd read my mind. "Yes," I said, like he was right. Because I had to believe. "Let's think of something happy." Suddenly, I was Little Miss Sunshine. Because if I thought of anything sad, or scary, I was going to lose it.

"Like what?"

"Like our birthdays."

"Our birthdays?" He grinned again.

"Yeah. What do you have planned for me?"

"Like I'm going to tell you. What do you have planned for me?"

"Something that will show you how much I love you." I covered his hand, which rested on the gearshift, with mine.

"That's exactly what I have planned for you." He paused.

"How much do you love me?" I said.

"I'm driving through a snowstorm for you."

I smiled. "I know that. But am I more important to you than your frat brothers?"

He smiled as he studied the road. "You're more important to me than anyone else. Now stop prying." He paused, and then casually said, "Do you like pink roses?"

A pink rose on the table at dinner in the sorority was a sign that a girl was going to be lavaliered.

"Love them. What are you implying?"

"Nothing. I'm not implying anything. Just that, maybe, a birthday run won't be the most important thing on your mind that day."

The truck in front of us geared down and pulled toward the right. That was when I saw the flash of police lights.

"Shit!" Dak geared down and swore beneath his breath. "The cops are pulling everyone over."

CHAPTER TWENTY

Morgan

My heart beat so hard, it threatened to pound right out of my chest as Dak pulled to a stop.

"What are we going to do?" I whispered. "If they ask to see your license—"

Dak rolled down his window.

A cop stuck his head in. "We're closing the road. Where are you headed?"

"To the hospital." Dak's voice was confident. Polite. Totally respectful. "This is going to sound like a smartass excuse, sir. But it's the absolute truth. We're on our way to see her dying grandma." He nodded toward me.

I teared up. It wasn't faked.

Dak winced and gave me an apologetic look before returning his attention to the cop. "We got a call this morning that she might not last through the night. We're trying to make it before it's too late. You can check with them if you like." He sounded completely sincere.

I let out a gasp of pain and sorrow, sniffed, and dabbed at my eyes. "Please." I held my breath.

The cop looked thoughtful for a moment as he studied us. "All right. Take it slow." He pulled his head back out of the window and waved us on.

I let out a sigh of relief and started shaking.

Dak grabbed my hand. His touch steadied me. "It's all right. I love you. We're at the divided highway. We're almost there."

I nodded.

The drive should have taken another half-hour. It took an hour and a half before Dak pulled into the hospital parking garage. We jumped out of the car. He took my hand and beeped the car locked.

"You okay?" He squeezed my hand.

I nodded, but I was a mess.

We found the cardiac wing and asked for my grandma. I nearly collapsed into Dak's arms when they said she was in ICU.

"She's not dead," I whispered to myself as much as Dak. "We made it in time." I clutched his arm. He was my hero.

I had to show ID to prove I was indeed family. All I had was my student ID. Thankfully, no one asked any questions about why I didn't have my license with me.

They refused to let Dak into the room with me with the excuse that only family, and only one person at a time, was allowed. I would have pushed it, but I was sure they'd ask for his ID. We didn't need more questions. And he wasn't family.

Dak squeezed my hand again and gave me a light kiss on the lips. "I'll be right here, waiting." He left "as long as it takes" unsaid.

I nodded and followed the nurse alone toward Grandma's room, looking back over my shoulder just before we turned a corner out of sight. The sight of him gave me courage. I couldn't believe we'd made it.

Inside, Grandma's room sounded like the machinery of hospitals and a fight for life. The rhythmic pumping of a respirator. The beeps of a heart monitor. The electronic pulse of a half-dozen machines. The drip of an IV. She was behind a curtain that slid on metal rings.

The nurse held the curtain aside for me without looking, and disappeared to give me privacy as I stepped behind the curtain.

My grandmother was hooked to every possible machine. The beating of her heart looked weak even to my eyes as it pulsed on the monitor. She gasped and struggled for each breath as a machine breathed for her.

Her blankets and sheets had slipped back. Her hospital gown was open in the front, revealing flat, old, sagging breasts. Exposing her in a way that would have petrified her. That upset me.

I took a quick step to her bed and gently pulled her gown together and pulled her sheet up to make her modest again, to preserve her dignity. I didn't speak or give myself away for a minute. She didn't stir or acknowledge me. She wasn't conscious. But I didn't take a chance.

I took a step back, hoping to make it seem like I'd been a nurse doing my duty. I took a deep breath and tried my approach again, sitting in the chair next to the bed and taking her cool hand.

"It's me." I clasped her hand gently between mine. My hand was cold, but warmer than hers. Her veins stood out in her pale hands, blue, like they were gasping for oxygen and life, too. "Morgan." I bit my lip. "I'm so glad you hung on and waited for me." Tears welled in my eyes.

"I came through a snowstorm like the one I was born in. Remember the stories you told about flying through a rare Seattle snowstorm to come to the hospital to see me be born?" And now I was coming to see her die. Snowstorms. Bookends on life.

I kept those thoughts to myself.

"I love you, Grandma. You've always been my rock. I'm trying to be like you. I promise I'll keep on trying and make you proud. And tell my baby brother all about you and what a wonderful grandma you are."

She didn't stir. Tears filled my eyes. I had no idea if she heard me.

It's hard to talk to a person who doesn't respond. I babbled about nothing and everything. About how Dad was trying to get here.

"Dakota brought me," I said. "Remember him? My partner in crime. I didn't tell you, Grandma. It's time I came clean. He almost ran over me with his car. But now I love him." I told her the story. The whole story from Zach to Dak. About how my license, and Dak's, was suspended. "For just a few more days now."

And how we fell in love after being thrown together in ADIS.

I leaned in close and whispered in her ear so only she could hear, "You were right about him."

The beat of her heart grew stronger onscreen. Her breathing became easier. I smiled through my tears. "He's my hero. He loves me so much he drove me here through that horrible storm, risking everything because he knows how much I love you."

Her heartbeat continued to grow stronger.

"You're never wrong about love, Grandma. You told me that yourself. And you're right. I think I'm going to grow old with him. Like you did with Grandpa. We'll have our own epic love story. I'll tell my grandchildren about it. Like you did to me. So they can believe in true love, too."

I leaned forward and kissed her on her forehead. Her hand squeezed mine so softly, like the pressure of a butterfly landing on a flower. But real. I smiled and squeezed back just as her hand went limp and her heartbeat flat-lined. I screamed for help and begged her not to go. To come back.

A nurse came into the room and put her hand on my shoulder as I sat crying. "I'm sorry."

I nodded through my tears, holding my grandma's limp hand, patting it like she could feel it.

"Do you want a few minutes?"

It took me a second to realize the nurse was speaking to me.

I shook my head. "No, she's gone."

The nurse took my arm and helped me up. "Your boyfriend's waiting for you." She led me to the waiting room.

Dak took one look at me and knew the truth. I nodded and flew into Dak's arms and buried my head in his chest. He held me while I sobbed and soaked the front of his shirt with my tears. He held me while I shook with the despair of losing her.

"Give her time," the nurse said.

He stroked my hair, making reassuring noises. Finally, he spoke. "Your dad will want to know."

I realized I was being selfish. I nodded.

"Do you want me to call him?"

I shook my head. "No. It's my responsibility."

Dak handed me a tissue. I pulled my phone out of my pocket. "Dad, it's me, Morgan. She's gone. Grandma's gone."

"What? But how do *you* know?" He sounded stunned and in shock.

"I was with her." I was shaking. "You knew I would be." I took a deep breath. "She wasn't alone. Dak drove me. You should thank him. She wasn't alone." I began to cry again.

Dakota

The storm raged all night. The roads around the city were all closed. There was no place to go. No hotels nearby. We slept on a hard sofa in the lobby, Morgan in my arms, our coats rolled like pillows. A kind nurse threw a hospital blanket over us. We were part of a small army of stranded visitors. As I held her, my conviction grew—she was the woman for me. Lavaliering her for her birthday was what I wanted. I could see myself eventually marrying her. I loved her more than anything.

When we woke in the morning, the storm had finally cleared. The skies were blue. And the plows were out. We went to the bathrooms and freshened up. I took Morgan to the cafeteria for breakfast. Her dad texted. He'd finally gotten a flight out. He was coming to town to make arrangements.

He met us in the cafeteria just as we were finishing. Morgan threw herself in his arms. He held her like she was his baby. Like they needed each other. Then he thanked me.

"You shouldn't have done it." He slapped me on the back. "But I'm glad you did."

Morgan needed to be with her dad. I felt like a fifth wheel. I had to get back to school. I offered to wait and take her back with me when she was ready. She decided to stay with her dad and help him. He promised to send her back on the bus. She promised to call.

"You're really driving back." She looked worried. "You shouldn't. What if you're caught?"

"Why would I be caught?" I grinned at her.

"You won't speed?"

I sighed. "Not even five over."

"You'll drive carefully?"

"Cross my heart." I made the motion.

"What if you slide into a ditch?"

I shook my head. "You worry too much."

"Only about you." She kissed me. "Seriously. Drive safely." She leaned in and whispered in my ear. "I told Grandma she was right—you're the one."

It seemed almost disrespectful, but I couldn't help smiling.

As I drove out of town and saw the piles of drifted snow, I realized we'd been lucky. It would have been easy to have driven off the road and been stranded. I wondered if I'd been heroic. Or foolish. Only a girl like Morgan could have made me risk everything for her.

I thought about the lavalier necklace with my Tau Psi letters in the jewelry box in my room at the frat. This was going to be the best birthday ever.

CHAPTER TWENTY-ONE

Morgan

Grandma's funeral was a week later. Just two days before my birthday. She'd left a gift for me. I brought it back with Dak and me on the bus. I'd been clinging to Dak's hand like it was a lifeline. "I'm glad you came with me."

He looked so handsome in his suit it made me want to cry with joy in the face of my sorrow. He was my guy. I could barely believe it.

He squeezed my hand. "Glad to."

I gave him a shaky, emotional smile.

It was just after eight in the evening when Victoria picked us up at the bus station. She dropped Dak off at the frat.

He gave me a quick kiss. "I'll change and come right over. See you in a few."

Dakota

A couple of my frat bros were lounging in the living room playing video games when I came in.

"Dak, there you are, buddy," Brett said. "A girl was here looking for you. She seemed upset and desperate to find you."

I frowned and my mouth went dry. "Who the hell would be desperate to find me?"

"That's what we were wondering." Brett went in for the kill in his game and blew something up. "She wanted to stick around until you got back. We told her you were at a funeral with Morgan and should be back around now. We thought you'd go directly to the sorority house. That's what we told her. She took off."

I made a fist. "Did she leave a name?"

Kirk looked up from his game momentarily and shrugged. "Maybe. I don't remember. Didn't recognize her."

I didn't know what made me ask. I already knew. "What did she look like?"

"Besides pissed?" Brett laughed.

My heart stopped.

"Dark hair. Average height." He paused and looked up like he was thinking. "Kirk, here, has the memory capacity of a pea. She said her name was Jordan. Or something like that."

Shit. I swore beneath my breath. "She just left? How long ago?"

Brett glanced at me. "I don't know. I lose track when we're playing. A few minutes, maybe."

Or way too long. I raced out the door.

Morgan

I was emotionally fatigued and weak with relief as I walked into the house, carrying the gift from my grandma, which looked suspiciously like a jewelry box. I was tempted to open it. And yet I wanted to savor it. I knew she'd left me things in her will. But this was the last true gift she would ever give me. I had an idea what it was. I would wear it forever.

A dark-haired girl sat on the sofa in the living room, apart from the clusters of my sisters who were sitting around studying and chatting. She stood when Vicki and I walked in. It might have been my imagination, but she glared at me. Her eyes were hard and her icy persona filled the room and killed the conversations going on around her.

"Morgan Peterson?" She stared directly at me like I was the girl who'd killed her dog or something. Hatred glittered in her eyes. She looked like a jealous girl-friend. Which made absolutely no sense. I hadn't even hooked up with anyone but Dak in ages.

I'd done a lot of crappy things in my life. Like trying to chase Alexis away from Zach. But even she didn't stare at me with such sparkling malice. Like she was in the right, and justified in whatever she was about to say.

I frowned, trying to place her. I came up with noth-ing. "Yes?"

Victoria came up beside me, ready to intervene, as the girl took a step toward me.

The last murmurs in the room fell into stone-cold silence. A group of people, including Sarah, Katie, Kayla, Kelly, Alexis, and Zach, came around the corner from the study room.

The girl got in my face. "I came to warn you to stay the hell away from my boyfriend." Her face contorted with rage.

"You must be confusing me with someone else." I stared back at her with pity. "I don't have your boyfriend, whoever he is."

"Damn right you don't have him."

She must be drunk or high, I thought.

The door to the sorority flew open, bringing with it a gust of cold air. Dakota stood in the door, his cheeks pink from the cold. Even still, I thought he paled when he saw the girl.

Another group of my sisters heard the commotion and came down from upstairs. They froze on the steps.

The girl pointed to Dakota. "Dakota has been mine since high school." She smiled at him. "Tell her, baby. We're off. We're on again. But we always get on again."

"Jordan—" Dakota took a step toward her.

I felt sick, dizzy with fear as I realized he knew her. And was afraid of what she was saying.

"You're just his cover girlfriend." She spat the words out and laughed like it was all a joke. Like I was a joke.

My sisters let out a collective gasp.

"So he could be with me," Jordan said. "His parents don't approve of him dating a girl like me. A working-class girl. They want a blond sorority bitch with family connections like you for him. Or a girl like Alexis." She turned and grinned evilly at Alexis. "Tell her, Alexis. Tell her how you pretended to be Dak's girlfriend so you could sneak around with Zach and Dak could be with me."

All around me, my sisters were wide-eyed with shock.

Everything moved in slow motion. I looked at Alexis and saw the truth written on her face.

Jordan wasn't lying. The truth felt like a sucker punch to my gut. Everything made sense now—their crazy friendship, the way Zach and Dak had remained friends after his "betrayal." Everything.

"Jordan, stop!" Dak came toward her.

Jordan took a step back from him.

He pleaded with me. "Don't listen to her. It's over between her and me."

"He was dating me. And playing you, making you think you were something special." She put me between her and Dak. "I'm not mean. Just trying to save you time and heartbreak. He always comes back to me. We've been together over four years. Tell her, Zach. You know as well as Dakota. We've all been buds since high school. I'm his girlfriend back home."

The room spun. Dak took a step toward me. Victoria caught my arm to steady me.

"No!" I shook my head and fought back tears. "Stay away from me!"

Dakota reached for me. Victoria stepped between us. I ran for the stairs. My sorority sisters on the stairs broke rank and let me pass, forming a wall behind me.

Dakota ran after me. "Morgan! Morgan! Come back. I can explain."

He tried to push his way through, but the girls held him back.

"You need to leave, Dakota," I heard Kelly say. "And take her with you."

I didn't hear any more. I ran to my room, shut the door, and threw myself on the bed in a gale of sobs. I'd just lost two of the people I loved most.

I let Victoria, Kayla, and Kelly in. Vics was my twin, after all.

"He's gone," Victoria said.

Kayla sat beside me on the bed and leaned her head against my back, circling me in a hug. "Alexis would like to talk to you. When you're ready. Everyone's stunned." She hugged me tighter. Kayla's gift was her compassion. "We're your sisters. We're all on your side."

I let out a sob.

"You should see Alexis," Victoria said. "It would help to hear the whole story." She paused. "You and Dakota were so good together."

"I know he loves you." Kelly sounded fierce.

How could she be so sure?

"There has to be an explanation."

"Such bad timing. She just got back from her grandma's funeral. She needs time to recover from the shock. Time to think. Get her a glass of water, will you, Vics?"

Dakota

After Kelly asked me to leave, I grabbed Jordan and dragged her out of the house and down the street. "What the fuck were you thinking in there? Why are you here?"

"Isn't it obvious? I want you back. I came for your birthday. Now that you'll finally be twenty-one, too, we'll celebrate like we always planned."

I cursed to myself. I'd forgotten about those long-ago plans. Generally when you broke up, you assumed they were off. "That was a long time ago."

"Last summer."

"We broke up since then."

She shrugged. "Breaking up never sticks with us."

"It does this time." I sighed. I had to make her see. "I'm in love with Morgan."

Morgan

I didn't answer Dakota's calls or his texts. I put my status back to *single* on all my social media and cried myself to sleep. I woke up the next morning a lonely, headachy twenty-one-year-old. The best birthday ever had morphed into a nightmare.

There would be no birthday call from Grandma. No joint birthday with Dakota. Crap! What was I going to do about the cake? I texted Kayla and asked her to pick it up and dispose of it. It was already paid for.

The jewelry box from Grandma sat on my nightstand, where Kayla had carefully set it last night.

"Happy birthday!" I said to myself, with little enthusiasm and my eyes full of tears. Then I pulled the pink ribbon off the box and lifted the lid. A black velvet ring box was inside. I pulled it out and opened it. My birthstone—a deep red round-cut garnet that had to be several carats and was surrounded by tiny diamonds—sparkled back at me. It was set in 14K yellow gold.

I pulled it from the box and slid it on my finger. It fit perfectly. This was the gift Grandma gave all her granddaughters on their twenty-first. My heart ached with missing her.

Alexis tapped on my door. "May I come in?"

I could have sent her away. But I decided to give myself the gift of truth and hear her out. "Sure."

"We need to talk."

I didn't want to hear what she probably had to say, but I nodded anyway.

"I feel horrible about all this. Like it's partly my fault." She looked miserable. She took a deep breath. "Dakota might not be the most honest guy around."

I snorted.

"But he loves you. That much is true. Don't listen to Jordan. She's desperate. She sees how much he loves you, too. She's scared and lashing out to try to stop him from leaving her for real. But she can't."

I crossed my arms. "How much is true?"

She sighed heavily and plopped into my desk chair. "I was Dak's cover girlfriend. I was seeing Zach secretly a long time before we were found out. Jordan and

Dak have been off-again on-again. But you were *never* his cover girlfriend."

"But he was seeing her while he was seeing me." My voice shook.

"Maybe. But not the way you're thinking. The situation isn't black and white. He was seeing her while you two were becoming closer. Until he could be sure."

I snorted. "Of what?"

"That you were over Zach and falling for him."

I shook my head. "You're telling me she was his fallback plan? That he always has to have a girl?"

"They were together a long time." She bit her lip. "He broke up with her once for you."

I stared at her, not believing her. I made a derisive sound. "Yeah? When?"

She answered without hesitation. "His freshman year. He was dating her when he came to college and met and fell for you the first time. He broke it off with her. Then you threw him over. It's not a good excuse, but I think he just had to be sure of you before he broke it off with her a second time.

"The point is—he did break it off. He chose you over her. That has to count for something."

Did it? My heart was begging her to be right.

***

For my birthday, I wanted to cower in my room alone. I managed to stay there in my sweats until nearly dinner. When Victoria dropped by to pry me out.

"It's your Saturday birthday! How often does that happen?" Her voice was full of that peppy verve that you use on depressed people to bring them back among the living and joyful. It never works, but people keep trying it anyway.

"Every seven years," I replied, deadpan.

"Longer than that if you get caught on leap year." She took my arm. "And only once if it's your twenty-first! Do you know how lucky a Saturday twenty-first birthday is?"

Not lucky enough, I thought. Or maybe I was looking at it wrong. Maybe this "lucky" birthday had prevented me from something worse.

"It's the new semester and you're officially twenty-one and have upheld your end of the bargain. As chair of the standards board, I pronounce you officially off social probation." She amped up the pep. Which wasn't really like the cynical Victoria I knew. "You can drink your heart out!"

"Fine. Bring me a bottle."

She shook her finger at me. "Not so fast, alky. You're not drinking alone on this momentous occasion. And we, your sorority sisters, aren't going to let you ruin this milestone birthday. You're going on your birthday run and it's going to be awesome! Now shower and get ready." She grabbed my arm and pulled me off the bed.

When I came back from the shower, my room was decorated with streamers and balloons. Someone had laid out the party dress I'd planned to wear before all this happened. And Kayla was waiting to do my hair and makeup. She was the queen of the birthday makeover.

She gave me the special treatment. Getting rid of puffy, crying red eyes and circles was no easy feat. When she was finished, I looked almost good enough to pass muster as an official Double Deltsie birthday girl.

I got dressed and hesitated at the top of the stairs. All my sisters were gathered at the bottom, waiting for me. They let out a cheer when they saw me, and sang "Happy Birthday" to me as they threw confetti at me.

In the dining room, Kelly presented me with my official birthday run banner the girls had made for me—a large poster board heart decorated with glitter, a glittery number twenty-one, and sparkly stickers, hung on a sash. A marker hung on a string on it. Half the house was dressed up and ready to go on my run with me. The sight brought tears to my eyes again.

The idea of the run was simple. You went from frat to frat, knocked on the door, and asked for your birthday drink. The guys gave you your drink and wrote you a message on the birthday sign you wore. Some were sweet. Some were lewd. It was all in good fun.

"First we eat!" Victoria said. "So we don't drink on empty stomachs."

I was touched by their support, and did my best to get into the spirit. "What? Me, Morgan Peterson drink on an empty stomach? Unheard of!"

Yes, I was known for going out on an empty stomach.

The night was cold, but it wasn't raining or snowing. I wore a cute, flared dress coat over my party dress. It was too cold to rely purely on an alcohol blanket.

We went to Zeta Nu first. When we arrived, the guys were waiting for us on the front porch like someone had texted them we were coming.

"If it isn't the birthday girl!" one of the guys called out.

They catcalled and serenaded me as me and my sisters came up the steps. Their president waited for me with a shot of tequila.

The guys chanted as their pres handed me a lime wedge and a saltshaker. "Drink, drink, drink, drink!"

I licked my hand provocatively, salted it, and slammed the tequila. It burned all the way down. The frat pres grabbed me and kissed me on the lips. "Happy birthday, baby!"

We went from frat to frat to frat and repeated the same scene until I was buzzed and unsteady on my feet. Months of sobriety out the window. But even the alcohol didn't numb the pain. I wanted to be with Dakota.

Dakota

At the stroke of midnight, the guys in the house who were already twenty-one were taking me on a bar run. I sat in my room, playing video games, waiting for the witching hour. The jewelry box I had planned to give Morgan sat on my desk. I didn't know why I left it there. Out of false hope, I guess. Just before midnight, when her birthday was finally nearly over, I admitted defeat, grabbed it, and tossed it in a drawer. She wasn't going to answer my calls or see me. She'd shut me out.

I didn't want to think it. I certainly didn't want to admit it. But it felt like we were as over as Jordan and I were.

Just as I slammed the drawer shut, like closing a chapter on my life, there was a knock on my door.

I grabbed my coat. "You guys are early—" I swung the door open.

One of our pledges stood in the hall, holding a bakery box. "This came for you. Special delivery." He handed it to me and walked off.

There was no card, nothing. I was thinking it was a birthday cake from my parents. I carried it to my desk and opened it without fear. A half of a half sheet cake, its edge neatly cut in down the middle to reveal white cake and raspberry filling, sat in the box.

Happy 21st Birthday, Dakota!

It was decorated with the Tau Psi letters and the university colors. One frosting champagne glass was tilted, like it should have been clinking a matching one in a toast on the missing half of the cake.

I picked up the cake, ready to throw it across the room.

My buddy Brett walked in with a group of my frat brothers. "Cake! Awesome!" He peered into the box. "Dude! Did you eat half a cake yourself?"

I set the cake back down on the desk. "Half the cake was hers."

"Sorry, man." Brett slapped me on the back as another one of the guys swiped a blob of frosting on his fingers.

"Delicious! You going to share? Never drink on an empty stomach."

I grabbed the cake box. "To the kitchen. For forks. Let's polish this thing off before we go."

The clock struck midnight as we reached the kitchen. The guys sang "Happy Birthday" and made short work of the cake. And the milk the cook had left in the fridge. No one seemed to notice that I didn't have a bite. When there were nothing but crumbs left, we grabbed our coats and headed out to the first bar, the one that was on the edge of Greek Row.

We'd just reached the sidewalk when a group of Double Deltsies turned the corner and came up the street on the opposite side. My heart lurched. Morgan was in front, laughing, stumbling in incredibly sexy shoes, and wearing her birthday run sign.

She was so damned beautiful. I swore beneath my breath, remembering everything I had planned for our joint birthdays. One day off sobriety and she was already drunk.

She glanced at me and looked away like she hadn't seen me. I knew she had. Damn it. As president of the house, I should have been giving her the birthday drink. I'd had it planned—all the guys would be waiting to sing her happy birthday. She'd show off the lavalier I'd given her. The guys would welcome her like a sister. We'd party into the wee hours.

I recognized Alexis, Kelly, Kayla, Victoria, and most of the others. It was obvious they had no intention of coming to the house for a birthday drink.

"Fucking stuck-up Double Deltsies!" Brett slapped me on the back. "We don't need them."

Maybe not. But I sure as hell wanted Morgan. I missed her. She'd left a hole in my heart in a way my breakups with Jordan never had.

CHAPTER TWENTY-TWO

Morgan
Victoria drove me to the courthouse on Monday to retrieve my driver's license. Dakota and I had planned to go together. Now I crossed my fingers I didn't run into him. And at the same time, prayed desperately that I did.

I hadn't found a way to get him out of my mind, especially since I'd seen him heading out for his birthday bar run. And looked the other way. Because my heart was breaking and I couldn't stand it. Because I'd been drunk, which made me more emotional than usual. And I was tired of crying, especially on my birthday, when all my sisters were trying to cheer me up.

Victoria understood my mood in almost the same way a biological twin would. She was hellbent on distracting me from my depressed, weepy thoughts. "Now that you're off social probation, have you thought about who you're going to invite to the crush event week after next?"

I shook my head and frowned. "No idea. Probably no one. I'm not crushing on anyone right now." Despite everything, I only wanted Dakota. Hearts could be traitorous like that.

She shook her head back at me and tsked. "Shame on you, party girl Morgs. You can't let the house down. We're counting on you to bring in some hot guys and liven things up."

We held the crush every year a few weeks before Valentine's Day. The idea of it was simple. We held a big dance party. Each girl invited three or four guys they thought were hot and might be interested in. Crushes. So the party would end up guy intensive and heavy with possibilities for everyone. Lots of choices. All the girls in demand for every dance.

And yes, there was always drama. You didn't have to stick with your own crushes. You could hit on or get hit on by anyone's. Poaching was totally allowed. Which led to some hard feelings at times when someone's special crush hooked up with a different girl. But the point was to up everyone's odds of finding a Valentine before the fact. And you just had to live with the risk of your crush finding someone else. Wasn't that the way it was, anyway?

We walked into the lobby of the courthouse and went to the reception desk. The lady there directed us to a window on the second floor, where we stood in line and claimed my license.

I'd just stuffed my license in its rightful place in my purse as we came down the stairs and headed for the exit. Dakota strode in through the lobby doors, blocking our way out. He froze when he saw us. There was no way to avoid him. We had to walk past him.

My heart seized up so hard it hurt, a tightly wound knot of emotions.

He looked as surprised to see me as I was to see him. Though, really, of course we would both be here today. But at the same time? What were the odds of that?

"Morgan?" He looked at me like he couldn't decide if I was a clone or something. Maybe a mirage.

He looked hot and hopeful. Eager and tentative in a way that cracked the ice I felt toward him. His eyes lit up at the sight of me.

I would have had to have a heart of solid stone not to be touched. "Dakota."

"Picked up your license already?" His tone was too casual, like he was trying too hard to be calm and collected.

My hands shook. I grabbed the strap of my purse to hide the trembling of my nerves, and nodded, feeling guilty.

His Adam's apple bobbed as he leaned in and whispered to me. "We made it."

It was like an inside joke between us. There had been so many times we almost screwed up. If not for him... Well, it had never been a foregone conclusion. I thought of him driving through the snow for me and getting stopped at the roadblock. Of the huge risk he'd taken for me. Now that I was calmer, and faced with the real him instead of the humiliation of standing in front of my sisters at the house while a girl called my boyfriend a cheater, I saw things more clearly. I smiled shakily back at him. Wanting. Hoping. Afraid.

"I guess this negates our sobriety buddy deal," he said. "Our vows were until we turned twenty-one."

My throat closed up. I nodded. "Yeah. You don't need me anymore." Why was my heart breaking again? Why was my pulse racing like I'd been too proud and too hasty? Like I should have trusted him instead of that screaming bitch Jordan?

"I'll always need you." His voice was soft. His eyes pleaded with me to understand.

Victoria and Brett had backed off and faded into the background. My heart was cracking. I felt about ready to shatter.

Dakota's breath was warm in my ear. "You were never my cover girlfriend." He kissed my cheek. "Happy birthday, Morgan."

I got a whiff of his cologne, which brought back so many memories of being in his arms. I wanted to throw myself in them now and hold him close.

He stepped back and stuffed his hands in his pockets. "They finally scheduled the victims' panel I'm supposed to attend. It's this Friday. There's probably still time to get on it if you want to." His smile was sad and seductive at the same time. "I deserve everything you can throw at me. Figuratively, of course. I don't think actually throwing physical items is allowed."

How could he keep breaking my heart like this?

"I'll text you the details." He pulled his phone out and began typing. "There."

My phone buzzed in my pocket.

"Now you have plenty of time to think up all the ways you want to berate me for ruining your life and trying to kill you."

"No." I put my hand on his arm. "Why would I lie? You didn't ruin my life. I think you saved me from myself. If you hadn't nearly run over me, I would have continued wanting the wrong things in life. The wrong guy." My words startled me as much as they appeared to surprise him.

But they were true. I cleared my throat. I was on the edge of losing the little composure I was clinging to so desperately. "You pick up your license at the window on the second floor." I nodded to Victoria. "Let's go."

Dakota stepped out of my way.

"Good luck," I said as we walked past him.

Dakota

Stupid little things gave me hope. Like Morgan telling me I'd saved her life. Like not showing up on the victims' panel. Like getting an invitation to the Double Deltsie crush the day after I saw her at the courthouse.

The invitation was pinned to my door while I was out. As was tradition, it was anonymous. You weren't supposed to know which girl in the house was crushing on you. Which was why it was done the old-fashioned way, on paper.

It was no use grilling the guys to see if anyone had seen it being delivered. The girl doing the crushing wouldn't have been the one who came to the house to deliver it. A sister of hers would have done it. The whole thing was top secret.

My heart beat out of control. I was hoping this was Morgan's way of making up. Hoping she was crushing. I was being a stupid fool in love. I got the lavalier out of the drawer in my desk and opened the box.

The gold letters sparkled in the light of my lamp. Shit. A plan formed in my mind. A bold, outrageous plan. I could end up looking like such a fool. Be humiliated before the entire Double Deltsie house. But nothing ventured, nothing gained.

I texted Kelly that I needed to see her about house business.

Morgan

The Wednesday of our annual crush, a pink rose in a bud vase appeared on the table in the entryway. The table where all flower deliveries were made. There was no card with the flower, and no explanation.

Speculation, however, ran high. A pink rose in a bud vase meant one of several things—a lavaliering or a pinning. Or even an engagement. Optimism thrummed in the air as half a dozen girls who had serious boyfriends in frats hoped they were going to be the lucky one.

Lavaliering and pinning requirements and ceremonies varied by sorority. Some required foreknowledge by the girl who was going to be the subject of the ceremony. In the Double Deltsie house, the guy could ask for a surprise ceremony.

Attendance at dinner that night was pretty much mandatory. We were instructed to dress up for the occasion, which was normal for dress dinner night, anyway. Whoever the girl was, she was spectacularly lucky. Her guy was a romantic to the core. It was clear he meant to be the best crush of the evening and make it into a lavaliering or pinning celebration.

The thing about pinning and lavaliering was that sometimes the girl knew for sure and was expecting it. Sometimes she knew it was going to happen, but not when. And sometimes it was a total surprise. Though usually the guy had to be pretty sure of a girl's desire before he went out with such a public declaration. You don't declare a girl is more important than your frat brothers just to have her publicly diss you by turning you down.

We were all excited and supremely curious as we dressed for dinner and did our makeup with special care. Whoever the lucky girl was, she was, remarkably, keeping things under wraps. Or she was simply in the dark. If I had to bet, that was what I would put my money on.

When we filed in for dinner, the tables were set for a formal dinner. The rose sat in the middle of the head table where the sorority officers were seated, along with a candle.

The house was filled with nervous anticipation as we nibbled our way through dinner.

When the dishes were cleared, Kelly called for order. "I have an announcement to make." She pointed to the pink rose in the bud vase before her. "As you can all see, tonight one of us is going to make one of our Greek brothers very happy. We hope."

We laughed, full of nerves and excitement.

"Lavaliering, pinning, and engagement ceremonies are special and solemn occasions. We respect our letters, as do our Greek brothers. To make a public declaration that you are putting a girl above your letters and your fraternity brothers is a serious statement to make." She stood up. "Would everyone please form a circle around the room for our ceremony."

While we formed a circle around the dining room, Kelly explained the ceremony for the new girls among us. "Our house tradition is to pass a candle around from girl to girl while I read a letter from the guy to the sister being honored tonight. Once around the room means we're having a lavaliering ceremony. Twice means a pinning. And three times means a proposal of marriage."

Sarah, one of our freshmen, was next to me. She was practically bouncing with pleasure at the thought of her first ceremony.

"The candle will stop at the girl who is being so honored tonight. The other part of the tradition is that the guy has written the girl a love letter for the house president to read to the house while the candle is passed. The letter is full of clues, and expresses his deepest feelings for her. The hope is that the girl will realize who she is by the time the candle stops at her."

Kelly picked up a match. "This is a surprise for the girl being honored tonight. It's doubly special because she invited her crush here, and tonight he shows his passionate commitment to her."

That took me out. Not that I expected to be lavaliered, pinned, or engaged. But I was supposed to have been the next girl in the house to be lavaliered. On my birthday. I tried to push my disappointment aside and be happy for my sister, whoever she was.

The ceremony started with Kelly reading a statement about the meaning of our house letters and his.

He's a Tau Psi. My heart stopped beating for a second. The guy was a Tau Psi. Like Dakota.

Who here was seriously dating a Tau Psi? Everyone was looking around, trying to guess. Three girls were involved with Tau Psis. One was just a freshman, which pretty much ruled her out. This was a ceremony that usually didn't happen until you were at least a junior. The faces of the two other girls lit up.

I breathed deeply, trying to be as happy for my sister, whoever she was, as the house had been supportive of me during the humiliation with Dakota.

Kelly lit the candle, and, holding her hand around the flame so it wouldn't go out, passed it to the girl to her right.

I looked around the circle and realized I was only about six girls from the end. Were any of the girls to my right the one?

Kelly picked up a folded piece of paper, opened it, and began to read as the candle slowly, and with much solemnity, made its way around the circle.

"'Some relationships start with fireworks and a bang,'" she said. "'Ours started with fireworks, all right. I was crushing on her while she was crushing on a former friend of mine.'"

My pulse raced, even though it was silly. So the first part of the story sounded familiar. This kind of thing happened all the time at college.

"'We slid from there into enemies. She wanted him. I wanted her so badly I became bitter and discouraged.'"

Eyes were tearing up around me. This guy was baring his soul.

"'I waited for over two years. It took me nearly running her over and being sentenced to attend the same session of Alcohol and Drug Information School for us to come together again and become frenemies. From frenemies, we became secret sobriety buddies, to best friends, to falling in love.'"

The candle reached me. Beside me, Victoria nudged me to accept it. I'd been entranced by the letter. I was shaking so badly, as I reached for it, I was afraid I would put the flame out. Or drip wax all over myself. Or start crying. This was my story. Mine and Dakota's. But that couldn't be. I hadn't invited him here. He wouldn't be so bold.

Kelly paused as I took the candle from Victoria and the flame flickered in my trembling hands.

When I tried to pass it to Sarah, she shook her head. "It's not for me."

Dakota stepped into the dining room from where he'd been hiding in the hall. He carried another rose and a black velvet jewelry box. "Baby, I love you. You were never my cover girlfriend. You were always the real thing for me. The *only* thing.

"You mean more to me than my frat and my fraternity brothers. More to me than anything. I couldn't bear to lose you." He walked up to me until he was standing directly in front of me. He opened the box. A gold necklace with his Tau Psi letters sparkled in the light of the candle I held. "When you invited me to the crush, it gave me hope. Would you do me the honor of wearing my letters?" The look in his eyes was sincere and so hopeful it made me want to cry.

I'm not a fool. I recognize deception when I see it. There was none there. Just love for me, and hope, shining in his eyes, like I held his heart in my hand.

I knew what I wanted. And it wasn't to crush it. Tears of happiness welled in my eyes. I nodded. "Yes. Yes. *Yes!*"

Beside me, Vics took the candle from me and the rose from Dak. Dakota pulled the necklace from the box, handed the box to Victoria, and held the necklace out to put it on me. "May I?"

I turned my back to him and lifted my hair so he could fasten the necklace. When it was on, I spun around, threw my arms around his neck, and kissed him as my sisters cheered and laughed and dabbed their eyes.

I forced myself to pull away and look into his eyes. I had to tell him. "I love you."

He grinned and pulled me to him.

I rested my head against his chest, hearing his heart beat for me.

Victoria was standing next to me, still holding the rose, the candle, and the jewelry box, and beaming like she was lit from the inside.

"You?" I mouthed to her.

She winked.

I owed her.

I tipped my face to Dakota for another kiss. I was his. And he was mine. And that was all that mattered.

STINGER

Morgan

I wore Dak's letters constantly. To class. At the house. To parties. I found myself fingering the necklace all the time and smiling at what it stood for. I loved that guy with all my heart, and wanted absolutely everyone to know. This Double Deltsie was off the market. Seeing how vulnerable Dak had made himself and how he risked everything for me in front of my house made me realize how much he loved me, too.

So. Maybe people and conventional wisdom were wrong. Hookups *could* lead to true love. And jealous exes could be terrible bitches. But in the end, love wins.

Since the night of the crush, I owed Victoria every-thing for going behind my back and inviting Dakota to the crush. That was what sisters were for, right? Especially sorority twins.

Social probation, which had seemed like the worst thing that could have happened to me, had given me a genuine relationship with the girls in my house. I was no longer the feared bitch of the house. They were truly now my family of sisters for life. Social probation had given me even more—the love of my life.

I had a lavalier necklace with my Double Deltsie letters that my mom gave me my freshman year. There was some debate in Greek circles whether it was appropriate to wear both necklaces together or at the same time. The general rule was that they should never be on the same chain. The rest was a gray area. So I sometimes wore both necklaces. But I never put the two pendants on the same chain. Even still, they belonged together.

I was rushing to The College Grind on a clear February morning a few days before Valentine's Day when I spotted Seth across the street. I'd barely seen him since he'd moved out with Zach. I waved to him. "Seth! Seth!"

He didn't hear me and kept walking. Guys, they never heard when you called.

I shook my head and dashed across the street to catch him. My breath was coming in large white puffs in the cold air as I caught up to him and tapped him on the shoulder from behind. "Hey, Seth! Are you stuck up now that you've left us to live with Zach? Have you forgotten your Double Deltsie roots?"

He stopped and turned to face me. He frowned, puzzled. "You're the second person to call me Seth today. I must look like a Seth?"

I realized my mistake—this guy was Seth's doppelganger. But on closer inspection, about ten years older.

"Ohmygosh!" I laughed. "Sorry! Not like a generic Seth. You look so much like my friend Seth it's uncanny."

His smile was just as dazzling as Seth's. He even had the same dimple in his right cheek. "I've been mistaken for him at least a dozen times since I arrived on campus. But not by such a gorgeous girl."

I felt myself blush. I was intrigued. "Are you new here? A transfer student?"

His laugh was contagious and charming, flirty—like Seth's. "New, yes. Student, no." He extended his hand for me to shake. "Dr. Ian Foster."

I was stunned. On campus, being a doctor usually meant only one thing. "You're a professor?"

He looked way too young and hot.

He laughed again. "I get that a lot." He paused. "And you are?"

I smiled back at him. "Morgan Peterson."

I have to introduce him to Seth, I thought.

Gina Robinson is the award-winning author of the contemporary new adult romances *Rushed, Reckless Longing, Reckless Secrets,* and *Reckless Together* and the Agent Ex series of humorous romantic suspense novels. She's currently working on the next novel in the Rushed New Adult and College Romance Series.

Connect with Gina Online:

My Website: http://www.ginarobinson.com/
Twitter: @ginamrobinson
Facebook: www.facebook.com/GinaRobinsonAuthor